WORKING IT OUT

Alex George was born in 1970. After studying law at Oxford University, he qualified as a solicitor and has worked as a lawyer in Paris and London. He is also a semi-professional saxophone player and restaurant reviewer, and has recently co-written a book of bar reviews. *Working it Out* is his first novel.

T0317960

ALEX GEORGE

WORKING IT OUT

HarperCollins*Publishers*

HarperCollins*Publishers*
77-85 Fulham Palace Road,
Hammersmith, London w6 8jb

www.fireandwater.com

3 5 7 9 8 6 4 2

A catalogue record for this book
is available from the British Library
ISBN: 978-0-00651-332-2

THANKS, ACKNOWLEDGEMENTS AND CHEAP DISCLAIMER

My thanks go to Rachel Hore and Jennifer Parr at HarperCollins for all their help and guidance. A huge thank you to Maggie Hanbury for humouring me at that party in Frankfurt. Thanks also to everyone who has read bits and pieces of the book and provided help, support and encouragement, especially Lara Anabtawi and Deborah Silver.

Extra special thanks to Lisa Darnell for being a wonderful agent, astute critic and good friend, and most of all to my wife Christina, for a few choice plot twists I wish I could take the credit for, for laughing when she was supposed to, and for everything else.

Whilst first novels always contain certain auto-biographical elements, I should point out that the disastrous sex scene in Chapter Four is purely a figment of my imagination and is not based on any real events or people. Certainly not me, anyway.

For Christina

ONE

Johnathan Burlip zipped up and sighed. There was something reassuring about peeing in Chloe's bathroom. Watching the blue, Domestos-drenched water in the bowl ripple and then assume the hue of the flesh of a ripe avocado, he had reflected that some things in life never changed, immutable in their truth and simplicity. Two and two still made four, and when you mixed blue and yellow, you still got green. Such things were precious, to be grasped in times of crisis.

He looked around the terracotta and black bathroom with distaste as he pulled the duck that sat suspended in mid-flight on the end of the flushing-chain. Blue noisily replaced green, ready for the process to be repeated. Johnathan sat down on the loo he had just used, and wondered what to do. He desperately didn't want to go back downstairs. He traced a line through the brown Terylene shagpile with his foot, and considered possible excuses. An upset stomach, perhaps. Chloe's aggressive vegetarian dietary tactics always had an adverse effect on his digestive system. Results were spectacular, having a similar effect on the lavatorial plumbing to that of a jack-knifed lorry in the Dartford Tunnel on a Friday night. Nothing got through. No U-turn. No U-bend, for that matter.

Johnathan decided that nobody would be convinced. He

belched chickpea and got up. He opened the door and slouched towards the stairs, stopping outside the kitchen to consider a petunia, which he had given Chloe some months previously by way of apology for some deemed transgression, he forgot what. The plant looked how he felt. Thirsty. And wilting.

The door opened and Chloe's sister Harriet appeared. She looked at Johnathan balefully. Her eyes were smudged with cheek-bound mascara.

'How is she?' he asked.

Harriet considered. 'Like Eeyore with a period.'

'Oh dear,' said Johnathan.

He went into the kitchen. Chloe was slumped in a chair at the large table in the middle of the room, staring into a half-empty wine glass. She did not look up as he approached.

'Um,' said Johnathan.

Chloe did not move.

Johnathan waited, wondering what to do. He glanced over towards the sink. Troilus was lying on the floor, horribly inanimate. The pool of blood which surrounded his squashed head like a halo had started to expand with a ghoulish inevitability towards the fridge.

'I'll get a cloth,' he said. He went to the cleaning cupboard and began to pad kitchen roll around the edges of the growing puddle.

Once the tide of blood had been stemmed and the sodden roll disposed of, Johnathan stood up and waited for instructions. Her eyes still fixed firmly on her wine glass, Chloe finally said, 'Bury him by the mange-touts, and then leave. Don't come back.'

'Right,' said Johnathan, wondering what decomposing cat did for the nutritional qualities of vegetables. He rolled up his sleeves and picked up the dead animal, who responded with a last spirited gush of cloying blood, scoring a direct hit on Johnathan's trousers. Johnathan smiled grimly. He didn't care. Got you at last, you little bastard. He went outside to look for a spade.

Johnathan Burlip detested cats. He was very, very allergic to them. If there was a cat within two hundred yards, it would unerringly track him down and snuggle up to him, purring in unreciprocated affection. He had about ten seconds in which to whip out a handkerchief with which to stem the ensuing nasal catastrophe.

Troilus, unfortunately for him, had been particularly fond of Johnathan. He loved to coat Johnathan with his fur, huge quantities of which seemed to disengage automatically on contact. Johnathan's enmity towards cats in general developed a new focus of Troilus in particular. Over time, this had gradually developed into an unhealthy paranoia. He used to have nightmares in which Troilus could speak, dance and sing. One night he appeared as Mephistopheles and explained how Macavity wasn't that much of a mystery cat, he just had a good agent.

Johnathan kicked Troilus into the hole he had hurriedly dug. The chapatti pan had scored a direct hit on Troilus's cranium, causing instant departure for Cat Heaven. Johnathan had been drying the chapatti pan after dinner, while Troilus, as usual, had been sitting archly at his feet, particles of cat wafting from his fur up Johnathan's nostrils. Just as the chapatti pan was dry, the urge to wallop Troilus became overwhelming. Johnathan hadn't really thought through the consequences. He was suddenly overcome by tiredness and irritation, and after a brief internal dialogue, the essence of which was ah, fuck it, he had deftly played a forceful on-drive with uncharacteristic accuracy and panache, Troilus's head obligingly playing the part of the cricket ball. Wop. Out.

Johnathan covered the dead body with topsoil and enjoyed a brief jig of victory on his victim's grave to smooth out the surface. He trudged back towards the warm lights of the house. Chloe had vanished from the kitchen. Instead Harriet had returned downstairs and sat at the table, watching the steam rise on the last cup of decaf of the day.

She looked at him. 'She's gone to bed,' she said.

'Right,' said Johnathan awkwardly.

There was a pause.

'Prat,' remarked Harriet.

Johnathan shrugged. 'I'll let myself out,' he said.

'Bye,' said Harriet.

Johnathan nodded, and opened the front door.

On the cold Fulham street a few empty crisp packets tangoed listlessly between the parked Peugeot 205s. He turned up the collar on his coat and headed down the hill towards Parsons Green tube.

TWO

The telephone was ringing.

Slowly, very, very slowly, its insistent shrilling filtered through the syrupy mire of Johnathan Burlip's sleeping brain. As consciousness arrived, he became aware not only of the telephone but also of a brutish throbbing just behind his eyes. He groaned, rolled inelegantly out of his bed, and tottered out of the bedroom. Barely awake, he picked up the phone and said,

'Ugh.'

There was a pause. Then:

'Bastard.'

Johnathan blinked. He swayed slightly. The throbbing was spreading from his eyes backwards into his brain and upwards to his temples, where it sat, deeply malignant, radiating pain. The clock in the hall seemed to suggest that it was six o'clock in the morning. He waited.

'Bastardbastardbastard.'

Johnathan closed his eyes. It was Chloe.

'Hello Chloe,' he said.

'Oh no you don't. Oh no you bloody don't. Don't think for one minute that you're going to sweet-talk your way out of this one. No way. Not this time. End of story. You're history.'

'OK,' said Johnathan.

'Look,' said Chloe, 'don't even bother trying. It's a waste of time. It won't work. It's pitiful, actually. You're pathetic. You're just a drivelly, snivelling pathetic man. God. I can't believe this. At least have a bit of dignity.'

'OK,' said Johnathan.

'I mean, *Jesus*. You killed my cat. You're a murderer. I should report you to the police. The RSPCA. You are in serious trouble. Serious. You can just forget everything. How you can even *ask* me to contemplate having you back at this stage is beyond me.'

Johnathan woke up. He had asked no such thing, and nor was he going to. Best to make that clear right away. 'You're right,' he said quickly. 'I killed your cat. I killed Troilus. I am a murderer. I am vermin. You wouldn't want to see me again even if I was the last person on the planet.'

Chloe's tone softened. 'This self-hate is not good for you,' she said. 'You've always had low self-esteem. It's not going to get you anywhere. You need to look at yourself in a more positive light. You *do* have some good qualities.'

Johnathan started to hop up and down in agitation. This was not going according to plan. 'I killed Troilus,' he reminded her.

Chloe sighed. 'I know. I don't pretend to understand why. You were looking for a form of externalizing your emotions, you wanted to project your frustrations. You were caught up in the sub-luminous ego strata.'

Johnathan frowned. 'What?' he said.

'But you have a problem. You're angry about something. You should try and talk about it. You need professional help. It's nothing to be ashamed of. I go all the time. It's been enormously uplifting, just to be able to share my problems

6

with a sympathetic ear. Voicing my hopes and fears out loud helps them to crystallize within me. I come out more fulfilled, more rounded. More *me*.'

More fucking nutty, thought Johnathan blackly.

'Chloe,' he said after a few moments. 'It's over, isn't it?'

'God, don't say that. Don't *ever* say that. It's never *over*. Things are never that bad. Christ. Things are worse than I thought. You must snap out of it, Johnathan. Come back from the edge. Take a step back and see the *better you*.' Chloe's reedy voice rose a few pitches with excitement.

Johnathan sighed. 'No, not that. Us. You and me. We're over. Finished. Aren't we?'

'Oh,' said Chloe, the disappointment audible. 'I see.'

'I mean,' said Johnathan reasonably, 'I did kill your cat.'

Chloe thought about this. 'We all have our moments of madness. The insuperable super-ego plays its trump card.'

'But surely you must hate me now,' said Johnathan hopefully.

'Hate? What *is* hate, at the end of the day?'

'Listen,' said Johnathan quickly, keen not to get side-tracked. 'You're obviously still very upset. I understand that. You need some time alone. I'm sorry to have caused you so much grief. I understand if you'll never want to see me again,' he said.

'Sweetie,' cooed Chloe. 'You're being terribly hard on yourself –'

'But I must, I must,' cried Johnathan, and slammed the receiver down. He stood still for a few moments, dazed, wobbling slightly with queasiness and sleep. His mouth felt as if a herd of camels had surreptitiously crapped in it during the night.

7

He went into the kitchen and opened the fridge door, squinting against the anaemic glow of the electric fridge light, which felt as if it was burning holes in his retinas. There was no bottled water left. Of course there wasn't: he had drunk it all when he had arrived home last night, hoping to stave off the mother of all hangovers. The empty bottle lay on its side near the bin. Johnathan dispiritedly took a glass and filled it with warm, slightly opaque liquid from the tap.

Chloe was addicted to self-help manuals. She could speak meaningless psycho-babble fluently, in several different dialects. She could analyse your dreams, tell you how to give up smoking or lose weight by meditation, determine what was the right job for you, and offer potted highlights of all of the world's leading religions. Johnathan had had enough of her hectoring, if well-meaning, didacticism. All he wanted was to be left alone. It was extremely trying to have one's numerous weaknesses pointed out and dissected at every available opportunity.

One of these weaknesses, it transpired, was spinelessness. Johnathan had decided some months ago that he could not take any more of Chloe's banalities, but since then had done nothing until his contretemps with Troilus the previous evening. With anyone other than Chloe the best way to end matters would have been to explain gently that it was time to move on, sorry, and there are plenty more fish in the sea, and it's not *you*, it's *me*, and I just don't deserve you, and so on. Johnathan realized that this approach would not work with Chloe: she would somehow manage to twist his words back on themselves and he would in all probability find himself engaged. Instead he had attempted a more oblique approach. In the lowest, slyest way possible, he did everything he could to make

8

life for Chloe so unbearable that *she* would feel obliged to dump *him*.

One of the difficulties with this, however, was that he would find himself blinking in disbelief at Chloe's equanimity as she calmly accepted his most outrageous and offensive behaviour with a brief shrug. Chloe clung on to the relationship with the tenacity of a pit-bull terrier. An entire section of her library was dedicated to Resolving Your Differences, Making that Love Work for You!, Talking it Through, and so on. Johnathan realized that there was a long, long way to go before she had exhausted the remedies available on her bookshelf.

Chloe's refusal to accept the obvious was the principal reason for Troilus's fate the previous evening. It had been in many respects a political execution, Troilus no more than a hapless pawn in an altogether more complex game. Johnathan had finally had enough. He had never knowingly killed anything before, apart from the odd mosquito or bath-trapped spider, but couldn't find it in him to feel much remorse. Troilus was only a cat, after all.

Johnathan went back to the bedroom and retreated under the duvet. Eventually he drifted off into a restless sleep, merciful respite from his aching head. He had not been asleep for long, though, when the telephone erupted once more. Cursing, he walked out into the hall.

Johnathan regarded the telephone suspiciously. He looked at his watch. It was now eight-thirty. It had to be Chloe. The ringing seemed to be getting louder. It felt as if someone was jabbing a needle into his ear. Finally he picked up the receiver, bracing himself.

'OK you crazy bitch,' he said. 'I'm ready.'

There was a discreet cough. 'Hello *darling*.'

9

His mother.

'Oh. Hi,' he mumbled. 'Thought you were someone else.'

'We're just off out of the door for this festival in Cardiff, so I thought I'd give you a ring.'

'Right.'

'So how are you?' asked his mother breezily.

'Fine.'

There was a slight pause. 'You sound a bit put out, darling. Are you sure you're all right?'

'I'm fine.'

'I didn't wake you up, did I?'

'Well, yes, actually, you did,' said Johnathan as equably as he could.

'But it's such a beautiful day,' said his mother. 'How can you *bear* to spend it all in bed?'

'I wasn't going to spend it *all* in bed. I was just having a well-deserved lie in,' replied Johnathan, aware of the disapproval emanating silently down the line but too hungover to care.

'And what,' continued his mother, 'are you up to this weekend?'

'All the usual chores,' said Johnathan. 'Washing, ironing, that sort of thing. You know me. Glamour glamour glamour.'

'Oh. If you didn't have anything special planned you could have come with us. Too late now, though.'

'Oh well,' said Johnathan, brightening slightly.

'It should be absolutely fascinating,' continued his mother. 'They're putting on a lesbian *Macbeth*, in Welsh.'

'I see,' said Johnathan. There was a long pause.

'Anyway, darling, we must dash if we're going to miss the traffic. I'll give you a call early next week. Bye.'

'Bye.'

Johnathan thought about his parents on their way to their latest jaunt in Wales. To them, culture was a commodity which could be acquired and traded. His parents patronized (in both senses of the word) a stable of unknown artists, whose works hung throughout their cluttered North London home. They invested speculatively but without aesthetic discrimination in the hope that one day the painters would become hugely important and their paintings hugely valuable. Some of the paintings were all right, others were capable of inducing powerful migraines. One looked like an ink-blot test given to deranged children from dysfunctional families. Others looked as if they'd been painted by the children who did the ink-blot tests.

Johnathan's parents firmly believed that there was a direct correlation between culture and society: the higher the culture, the higher the society. Put another way, the more impenetrable the culture, the more impenetrable the posh accents. They liked to surround themselves with creative people. They knew artists, musicians and writers of varying pedigree, members of the Hampstead authordoxy. They knew a *lot* of women called Hermione. They were so highbrow their foreheads were permanently stuck to the ceiling.

Johnathan, however, was a solicitor, and was therefore a considerable disappointment to his parents. It was not something they could drop into conversation with any hope of carving further notches on the bedpost of artistic pretension. 'My son the solicitor,' didn't have quite the same ring about it as 'My son the bleak playwright', or 'My son the post-modern poet'.

Johnathan, though, suspected that he had an even greater

failing in his parents' eyes. He was straight. He liked girls. He was incontrovertibly heterosexual.

There wasn't anything specific he could put his finger on to justify his suspicion, but the cumulative circumstantial evidence seemed compelling. He had been encouraged with his dried flower collection from an early age. For his fourteenth birthday he had received a copy of Joe Orton's diaries, and was earnestly told that it represented a viable lifestyle choice. His parents always looked rather crestfallen when he introduced them to new girlfriends. Worst of all, though, they had added an 'h' to his name.

Johnathan's extra 'h' had been a source of irritation and inconvenience for as long as he could remember. Nobody except for his parents knew quite why it was there, squatting like an uninvited guest in the middle of his first name. Every credit card, chequebook, and bill missed out his 'h'. The only people who ever spelled his name correctly were the promotions department at Readers' Digest who regularly tried to entice him into entering the Biggest Prize Draw Ever. He had grown accustomed to watching people frown slightly as they looked at his business card, while they tried to work out what was wrong with it. Johnathan had become convinced that his parents had burdened him with the redundant consonant to show that their son was somehow different. Well, maybe he was, but not *that* different.

Sexually Johnathan had grown up in a drearily unspectacular way. He finally managed to lose the millstone of virginity during his first, parent-free, week at university in the traditionally messy and awkward way. He was leerily propositioned by an unattractive and very drunk biochemistry postgraduate in the college bar, and woke in her bed the next morning experiencing elation, disgust, and a splitting headache. After that Johnathan had failed to have proper sex with anyone else until he had left university.

Johnathan remembered that there was a bottle of aspirin in the bathroom. His hangover was clearly too sophisticated to be dealt with simply by way of sleep. Something chemical was required. He sloped off to the bathroom, took three pills, and went into the kitchen.

Johnathan switched on his espresso machine, which soon began to chugger and whoosh and gurgle in a way more soothing than any mother's heartbeat. He had never really stopped to consider his relationship with his coffee machine from a Freudian perspective. It was certainly closer than the one he enjoyed with his mother.

When the little yellow light on the machine clicked itself off, Johnathan flicked the switch and watched as the twin nozzles which hung beneath the matt black belly of the machine began to trickle thick, black liquid into the waiting cup. A few seconds later, the cup was full. Johnathan lifted it to his nose and breathed in deeply, relishing the espresso's aroma. He sighed a small sigh, and then tipped the contents of the cup down his throat in two quick movements, rather as if he was taking medicine. Johnathan shut his eyes for a few moments, and allowed his mind to go blank. Then he opened them again, and switched the coffee machine back on. Round two.

Some hours later, fully caffeined-up and a few chores to the good, Johnathan sat on his sofa watching a children's Saturday morning television show. His hangover had slowly cranked itself up to full throttle at around ten o'clock but since then had been winding down so that now it only hurt when he moved or thought. Watching children's television required him to do neither.

Johnathan's dog, Schroedinger, was asleep next to him on the sofa, his head resting peacefully in Johnathan's lap. Nobody knew exactly what unlikely communion had produced him. He looked like the result of a bizarre experiment where a Scottie had mated with a porcupine.

When first-time visitors to the flat met Schroedinger, the conversation always followed the same course with an inevitability which Johnathan had begun to resent.

Visitor: Ah, what's his name.

Johnathan (gloomily, for he knows what is to come): Schroedinger.

Visitor (frowning): You can't call a dog Schroedinger.

Johnathan: Why not?

Visitor: Well, you know, Schroedinger's Cat.

Johnathan (peevishly): Yes?

Visitor: So. It would be all right for a cat, but not for a dog.

Johnathan (testily): But the *cat* wasn't called Schroedinger. The cat *belonged* to Schroedinger. Sort of.

Visitor: Yes?

Johnathan: So, logically, a cat is the *last* creature you would call Schroedinger.

Visitor (uncertainly): Because.

Johnathan: Because cats don't own cats.

Visitor: Are you telling me that your *dog* owns a cat?

Johnathan: No of course not –

Visitor: Well then.

Johnathan: – all I'm saying is that, *logically*, it makes more sense to call a dog Schroedinger than a cat.

Visitor (unconvinced): But Schroedinger's Cat.

Johnathan: OK, take another example. Take a Rubik's cube.

Visitor (unsure where this is leading): OK.

Johnathan: Well, you obviously wouldn't call a Rubik's cube 'Rubik', would you, because we all know that's the name of the chap who invented it.

Visitor: ?

Johnathan: Look, if you're going to be picky, Schroedinger's Cat was dead anyway.

Visitor (cleverly): Ah, but that's the point. We don't know that.

It was on days like this that Johnathan was relieved that Schroedinger was, if anything, lazier than he was. He was not the sort of dog which insists on dragging its owner for a brisk tour around all the interesting piles of dog shit in the area within five minutes of its owner's first bleary-eyed appearance in the morning, and Johnathan loved him dearly for it. Schroedinger preferred to remain in the relative tranquillity of Johnathan's small garden, where he could relax and defecate at leisure.

Johnathan sat back and sighed. He stared up at the ceiling and considered the weekend that lay ahead. His fridge was presently home to a half-empty jar of mayonnaise and an onion. His entire week's washing lay crumpled at the foot of his bed.

He decided to slip out to do his weekend shop at the local store. Gently he pushed Schroedinger's head off his lap and stood up. Schroedinger wagged the stump where his tail should have been, and yawned at Johnathan's disappearing back.

When Johnathan returned home, having bought some fantastically expensive baked beans and a pre-sealed pack of bacon, his answer-phone was winking at him. Chloe, he thought. He put down his shopping and debated whether or not he was feeling sufficiently robust of spirit to listen to the message. Finally he pressed the little red button. The tape whizzed back and crackled into action. There was a beep.

'Hi, it's Topaz. Could you give me a ring as soon as you get in, if you're back today? You could just be a life saver. OK. Hope to hear from you later. Ciao.'

Johnathan's heart leaped, and then sank again. He knew at once what Topaz wanted. Someone must have turned down her dinner party invitation, and she was one short for the night. Few things were as important to Johnathan's friends as getting the boy-girl-boy-girl seating arrangements just so at their dinner parties. Absences were not tolerated kindly. Johnathan had, by accident rather than design, carved a niche amongst his circle of acquaintances as a last-minute social substitute *extraordinaire*. He rarely had any social engagements of his own and so was always available to turn up on short notice and make up numbers. Unfortunately he had proved himself so reliable in this capacity that people had stopped inviting him to dinner parties at all, just in case anybody dropped out. His social life therefore depended upon other people falling ill, breaking promises, or suffering unforeseen mishaps. When things went according to plan, Johnathan was redundant. When things went wrong, he was a hero. Johnathan knew how members of the medical profession felt.

Still, he told himself, it *was* Topaz. At least she was thinking of him, if only as a last resort.

Topaz was the sort of girl Johnathan had dreamed about meeting for years. Now that he had, he found himself awake in the middle of a nightmare. They had met some years previously at the birthday party of a mutual friend whom

16

Johnathan had known at university. It had been a fancy dress party. The theme had been 'The Empire'. Johnathan had, rather wittily he thought, gone as a mint imperial. He first met Topaz, who was dressed as Princess Leia from *Star Wars*, as he was coming out of the downstairs toilet. When she came out a few minutes later, Johnathan was still standing there, trying to reach a zip at the back of his costume. Topaz took pity on him, and helped. Fuelled by embarrassment and alcohol, Johnathan had misinterpreted this act of kindness as a clear indication that Topaz wished to go to bed with him, and later on the same evening he had clumsily propositioned her. Topaz, crushingly amused, had politely declined his offer. Instead she had kissed him lightly on the cheek and told him he was sweet. Despite the 'sweet' comment, they had remained friends.

She worked as a subeditor for a home furnishings and interior decorating magazine. She was independently wealthy, intelligent, and impossibly gorgeous. She was also not the slightest bit interested in Johnathan in a sexual context. Johnathan, on the other hand, was extremely interested in Topaz in a sexual context. She appeared to him in his dreams, usually either sitting naked in his kitchen slicing up cucumbers or emerging from the sea in a low-cut rubber wetsuit holding a large harpoon that had already shot its bolt. This unhealthy obsession had continued unabated throughout Johnathan's other recent relationships. If anything, it had become worse. Topaz was a useful means of distracting Johnathan from Chloe's relentless barrage of inanities, and he would frequently drift off into a lustful reverie while she jabbered on, which had on one occasion been awkward as he had been unable to explain why Chloe's discourse on parachutes, and their colours, had produced a rather obvious erection. Chloe had begun to suspect that he was actually *turned on* by that stuff.

Johnathan had by now resigned himself to the fact that he would never summon up enough courage to ask Topaz whether she might consider taking their relationship beyond the merely platonic. He thought that perhaps initially there had been a flicker of interest from her, but now, nothing. Things were strictly platonic. Indeed, things were *so* platonic that Topaz felt able to regale Johnathan with stories of her sexual adventures with such attention to detail that it made him weep; not with sympathy or jealousy, but from the pain of his erection straining against his trousers.

It was a difficult position. He didn't love her, or anything complicated like that. He was just desperate to go to bed with her. As he became more and more obsessed, her company became less and less bearable. Now, of course, with Chloe out of the way, there was no reason why he shouldn't just ask her, but he knew that he was too much of a coward. He decided that he would rather suffer the priapic indignities of being her principal sexual confessor than run the risk of scaring her off completely. *This* sort of agonising pain was better than *that* sort of agonising pain.

Why? Johnathan asked himself as he picked up the phone. Why do I do this?

THREE

Johnathan arrived at Topaz's house late, sweating a bit and clutching a plastic bag with a bottle of red wine in it.

Topaz opened the door. She wore a mustard yellow velvet trouser suit and no make-up. Her hair fell around her bare neck in dark ringlets. She looked fabulous, wonderful, perfect, an angel.

'Hello. You look nice,' said Johnathan.

Topaz nodded, the compliment expected. 'Thanks for coming at such short notice.' She leaned forward and made smacking noises with her mouth about four inches from both sides of Johnathan's head. 'Haven't seen you for *ages*. Come in.'

Johnathan proffered the bag. 'A little something.'

'Oh, how lovely. Thanks. You really shouldn't have,' said Topaz, examining the bottle. 'Terrific,' she said after a while, thrusting it back into the bag. 'Well, we can't stand here and chat all night. Come and join the party.'

She turned and walked slinkily down the corridor towards the kitchen. Johnathan shut the front door behind him and watched Topaz's buttocks rise and fall delectably as she moved. There was something about velvet, something excessively sensual, that made Johnathan's mind fuse with desire. He sighed, deeply, and followed the buttocks down the corridor.

Topaz's kitchen was large for London. It was about the same size as Johnathan's entire flat. Sitting around a chrome and glass table were six impossibly glamorous people. The scene looked like a Vogue promotional shoot.

'Everyone,' said Topaz. 'This is Johnathan Burlip.'

The impossibly glamorous people eyed Johnathan dispassionately from behind a veil of cigarette smoke.

'Johnathan,' said Topaz, 'this is Jonny, Mark, Gavin, Sibby, Kibby, and Libby.' The names came out in rapid staccato, as Topaz jabbed the air vaguely with a manicured fingertip. 'Drink?'

'Thanks.' Johnathan shifted uneasily from one foot to the other and plunged his hands into his pockets. One of the girls, Libby or Sibby, regarded him silently as a thin coil of smoke trickled out of her left nostril and spiralled gracefully upwards. She was dressed in what looked like a chiffon nightie. Her skin was almost white, apart from some dark, brutally applied make-up around her huge, doe-like eyes. She was unquestionably beautiful, if rather corpse-like. She was also tiny. Her waist was about the same size as Johnathan's wrist.

'Johnathan's a lawyer,' called Topaz from the other side of the kitchen. 'Aren't you?'

'Well, yes,' said Johnathan apologetically.

'What sort of law?' asked one of the men, who spoke with an accent that made Leslie Phillips sound like an East End barrow boy. He wore a thick roll-necked sweater and a fashionably tatty green corduroy jacket.

'Commercial stuff, generally,' said Johnathan. 'Buying and selling companies, that sort of thing.'

'Do you do any Legal Aid work?'

'Well, not really, no. We don't do any of that sort of stuff.'

'Oh. Why not?'

'Well,' said Johnathan as politely as he could, 'we just don't.'

'So you're one of life's takers, then, not one of its givers.'

Johnathan reeled. What was this? Bash a Lawyer Week? Before he could reply, Topaz appeared by his side, and handed him a glass of what appeared to be Listerine. 'There you go,' she cooed. 'Tell me what you think of that.' Johnathan eyed the green, viscous liquid suspiciously, and sniffed it. It *was* Listerine.

'It's Listerine,' he said.

Topaz laughed. 'No, silly, it's TAG 69. It's this amazing drink Libby found on her last assignment in Paris, wasn't it Libby?'

The girl in the nightie nodded.

'It's just like crème de menthe, only more so,' continued Topaz enthusiastically. 'We can't get enough of it now, can we?'

The girl in the nightie shook her head.

'Well, I'd better leave you to it,' breezed Topaz and swept off towards the stove with a regal wave. Johnathan took a hesitant sip of his drink, uncomfortably aware that Libby was staring at him with a disarming directness. The drink was intensely minty, very sweet, and clearly very alcoholic. OK, thought Johnathan, so it's worse than Listerine.

'What was your assignment in Paris for?' he asked Libby, ignoring the man in the corduroy jacket.

'I'm a model,' said Libby.

What for, Crematoria R Us? wondered Johnathan. 'Right,' he said. 'What sort of stuff do you model?'

'Clothes,' said Libby, lighting another Marlboro.

He changed tack. 'Did you enjoy Paris?'

'Yeah.' Puff puff. In contrast to the dazzling sparkle of Topaz's jade, Libby's eyes were a lifeless blue. They flickered dully when she spoke, weighed down by half a tube of mascara on her eyelashes.

'Did you get the chance to go to any of the museums? Paris is full of wonderful museums.' Please say yes, prayed Johnathan. The conversational options were rapidly dwindling.

'No,' said Libby.

'Oh,' said Johnathan, defeated.

'I don't go for museums much,' said Libby.

'Did you know that the French Government puts as much money into the Louvre as the British Government puts into all of the museums in England put together?' said the man in the corduroy jacket.

'Really,' said Johnathan. There was a pause. 'Well,' he continued affably, 'it is a pretty large museum.'

'I suppose the British Government has better things to spend taxpayers' money on,' said the man. 'Illicit payments, backhanders, jobs for the boys. Greasing the palms of corrupt officials, or bent lawyers.'

'Careful Gavin. Your nostrils are flaring,' said one of the other girls. 'It's not very attractive.'

'Neither is the sight of the rich getting richer, parasites feeding off the carcass of the nation while everyone else is suffering.'

'God, give it a break, will you?' said the same girl. 'Change the record. Any more of life's iniquities and I'll throw up.'

'Your trouble is,' said Gavin, 'that you've just given up fighting the status quo.'

'Wrong. I haven't given up. Because I haven't begun. Nor do I intend to. Politics bores me.'

'This is more than just politics, Kibby. This is about life.'

'Well, yes, I suppose you're right, if life, as you so dramatically put it, is about the sort of vapid banalities that you obsess about.'

Gavin sat back in his chair, too mortified to reply. Johnathan decided that he liked Kibby.

'What about you, er, Libby,' he said to the waif next to him. 'Are you interested in politics?'

Libby ground her cigarette in the ashtray. 'Not really,' she said. 'I don't go for politics much.'

'Shan't be long,' shouted Topaz cheerfully as she crashed around on the other side of the kitchen. 'What are you lot talking about? Can't hear from over here.'

'Gavin is presenting his blueprint to salvage the country from the clutches of the filthy capitalist pigs who are bleeding society dry,' said Kibby.

'Jolly good,' said Topaz. 'Best to get it out of the way now while I'm doing this.'

'Ha ha,' said Gavin.

There was an embarrassed silence as everyone examined their glass except for Kibby, who was looking directly at Gavin. He was studying the health warning on Libby's cigarette packet. Johnathan shot an admiring look at Kibby. She caught the movement, turned towards him, and winked at him. Immediately Johnathan looked away, blushing furiously.

'Right, everyone ready to eat?' demanded Topaz as she

23

sailed towards the table. 'We'll have to rearrange ourselves a little bit. Libby, why don't you go there, Gavin here, Sibby there, and Johnathan over there?' Topaz issued directions with the assurance of a born hostess. People obediently moved into their designated positions. Johnathan sat next to Kibby. Gavin huffily moved to the other end of the table. Wine glasses were filled. A large pepper grinder was plonked on the table. It was at least two feet high. Gavin lit the candles in the middle of the table with Libby's lighter as Topaz staggered over with an enormous orange dish.

'Here we are,' she said cheerfully. 'Only lasagne, but at least it'll be edible. Riddled with shredded tofu, as usual. Not so much as a whiff of cow.'

Oh hooray, thought Johnathan.

Topaz began doling out portions on to the elegant plates which blended seamlessly with the kitchen's colour scheme. The plates were passed around the table. As Johnathan handed Kibby hers she smiled. 'So Mr Lawyer,' she said. 'You buy and sell companies.'

Johnathan nodded. 'Afraid so.'

'Sounds interesting.'

'Well. It can be. Sometimes.'

'Do you have interesting clients?'

Johnathan considered. 'Not especially. They're all large corporations. Individuals couldn't ever afford the fees.'

'I see,' said Kibby, prodding her lasagne with her fork. 'No juicy divorces, stuff like that?'

'God no. The partners decided a long time ago that human misery wasn't nearly lucrative enough.'

'Well, human misery is what some of us specialize in.' Kibby nodded up the table towards Gavin. 'Welcome to the world of the insufferably self-righteous.'

Johnathan smiled. 'I'm used to it. It does rather come with the territory. Although I must say that your friend over there was less backward in coming forward than most.'

'Oh, you can always rely on Gavin to call a spade a spade. Or a bi-manual broad-bladed gardening implement. I'm sure "spade" is quite unacceptable nowadays.'

'I wish I could be so frank,' mused Johnathan.

'I'm not so sure,' said Kibby. 'People like Gavin regard frankness as a huge virtue. They see it as a means of avoiding accusations of hypocrisy. They believe that if they spend all their lives facing the truth head-on, and then confronting everyone else with it, the world is somehow going to be a better place.'

'And you don't think it will?'

'Why should it? Discretion has its merits. Apart from anything else, Gavin has a highly idiosyncratic idea of what constitutes truth. All it means is what he happens to think this week. Gavin just *cannot* shut up, and all that really illustrates is his unshakeable belief in his own convictions. And his inability to listen to anyone else's opinion without butting in halfway through.' Kibby sipped her wine. 'Believe me, Gavin talks an awful lot of self-justifying, narrow-minded bollocks.' At the other end of the table Gavin was leaning towards Topaz, talking urgently in a low voice. Topaz looked bored.

'What does he do?' asked Johnathan.

'Not much,' said Kibby. 'Doesn't need to. He's fantastically rich. His father owns an extremely successful detergent manufacturing business.'

'Very nice.'

Kibby leaned towards Johnathan, a small heap of lasagne balanced on her fork. 'What we tend not to mention is that Daddy's business has recently been castigated in the national press for committing some of the worst ecological industrial abuse in the country, despite repeated fines and warnings from the authorities. Daddy has taken the view that it is more economical to pay the fines than to change the manufacturing process and institute a clean-up operation to rectify the damage he's already caused.'

'But he can't do that,' said Johnathan.

'You can,' said Kibby, 'if you indulge in a little "greasing of the palms of corrupt officials".'

'Oh,' said Johnathan. He looked up the table at Gavin. 'Presumably he's turned his back on his father's business in disgust.'

'Not exactly. Gavin's dad wouldn't give him the sort of job that he felt he deserved. Gavin thought that three years of doing absolutely nothing at university qualified him for a position on the main board. When his father offered him a position as production supervisor in the Coventry factory, Gavin had a bit of a tantrum. Hence the railing against the evils of capitalism.'

'Sour grapes.'

'As sour as they come.'

'So has he severed paternal links in his pursuit of the life of the righteous?' asked Johnathan. He poured some more wine into Kibby's glass, and then his own. He noticed that the bottle he had brought was not on the table.

Kibby snorted. 'Of course not. The detergent business might be morally reprehensible and it might serve to perpetuate the interests of the rich over those of the under-privileged, but it comes in handy to pay for the flat in Chelsea and the insurance premiums on the Porsche.'

Johnathan's eyebrows shot up. Kibby burst out laughing. Her laugh was extraordinary. It was not remotely what

26

Johnathan had expected. He had imagined a light, crustless cucumber sandwich of a laugh. What he heard was more a pie and gravy with dollops of mash laugh. It wouldn't have been out of place in a working men's club in Macclesfield on cabaret night. It ripped through everyone else's conversations like a cyclone. It was wonderful.

'And you,' said Johnathan, after the cyclone had died away. 'Are you one of us or one of them?'

'Not sure,' said Kibby. 'Gavin would doubtless say I was one of you.'

'What do you do? The suspense is killing me.'

'I work for a film production company.'

'Sounds glamorous.'

'Ha. Not really. I make the trailers you see in the cinemas.'

'The trailers for the films?'

'Yup. I get presented with two hours of dross and have to cut it down to two minutes of interesting and exciting footage which is going to fool people into spending their hard-earned cash to go and see it.'

'Sounds quite a job,' said Johnathan sincerely. It sounded a lot more fun than drafting legal agreements. 'To capture the essence of a film in that amount of time must be a challenge. Presumably you really need to *understand* the film, get under its skin and live its, sort of, quiddity.'

'Not really,' said Kibby. 'You just take the best jokes and the most violent bits, and stick them together. And if there's any nudity, you put it all in. Tits sell.'

'Oh,' said Johnathan.

'Basically, it's incredibly rare that there's anything worth watching in a film which wasn't in the trailer. I get to act as a sort of crap filter, if you like. Of course on occasions the films are so awful that I have to stick crap in the trailers too. Would you mind reaching over and passing me that enormous phallic thing, please?'

Johnathan reached for the pepper grinder. 'What do you think, Libby,' he said, turning to his right. 'Do you like films?' Libby had been staring vacuously into space having demolished her walnut-sized portion of lasagne in a matter of seconds.

'I don't go for films much,' said Libby.

'Christ, what a monstrosity,' said Kibby, as she struggled to control the pepper grinder.

'That sort of thing makes men feel terribly inadequate,' said Johnathan lightly.

Kibby looked at him. 'Do you know why Topaz bought it?' she asked.

Johnathan shook his head.

'She uses it as a sort of litmus test for prospective boyfriends.'

Johnathan stopped eating. 'Go on.'

'Basically, if Topaz can't decide whether or not she's going sleep with someone, she invites him home and cooks for him. At the relevant moment, she plonks this thing down on the table in front of him. And if he makes a remark about the grinder resembling a large penis, she won't sleep with him.'

Johnathan swallowed.

'Topaz's theory is that if they make that sort of fatuous remark that means they're either hopelessly unoriginal or have very small dicks, or possibly both. Are you all right?'

Johnathan looked stricken. That was it. This was why. He even remembered the moment. He had thought he was being rather witty at the time. He stared blankly at his plate.

'Hey, you two,' called Topaz from the other end of the table. 'Stop canoödling, you flirts. Have some salad instead.'

A few hours later the party had moved to Topaz's sitting room, where people were drinking coffee. A smog of cigarette smoke hung over the room. The conversation had veered between a variety of obscure and unrelated topics. Kibby, Johnathan noticed, took little part in it, preferring instead to sit back and listen.

Kibby wasn't exactly pretty. Not in the same way as Topaz. (Not many people were as pretty as Topaz, and those who were didn't get invited to dinner.) She had big, unfeminine eyebrows, which Johnathan liked. She had laughter-lines stretching in tiny deltas away from the edges of her eyes. Her nose was a bit flat at the top. She had a large mouth. Overall, Johnathan thought, she was all right.

Gavin got up to go. He had not spoken another word to Johnathan since their opening exchange. He surveyed the room with a supercilious air. 'Lift, anyone?' Sibby and Libby stuck up their hands together, as if they were being worked by the same puppeteer. There was a general murmuring and shifting of bodies and suddenly everyone was standing, muttering their excuses and preparing to go in that odd way people do at the end of parties, as if they had just been waiting all along for someone else to mention leaving first.

'Right then,' said Topaz, 'let's form a leaving committee. Where did you put your coats?' She got up and strode purposefully out of the room. Everyone else dutifully followed.

Just as Johnathan was about to go out into the hall, Kibby grabbed his hand and pulled him back into the sitting room, which had emptied. She looked him in the eye without letting go of his hand.

'You're not gay, are you?' she said.

'Er, no,' said Johnathan.

'Sure?' said Kibby with a smile.

'Christ, yes, sorry, no, of course. No, absolutely not.'

'Do you fancy having sex tonight?'

'What?'

'With me.'

'What?' said Johnathan again.

'You know. Sex. Having it off. A bit of the other. Rumpy-pumpy. Bonking.'

Johnathan reeled. 'Well, I –'

'It's not a very difficult question,' said Kibby.

'No, no, it's not, not at all,' stammered Johnathan.

'Well then,' said Kibby coolly. 'What do you reckon?'

'Er, OK.'

'Your place or mine?'

FOUR

They sat in the back of the taxi in silence. Johnathan looked at his hands and wondered what on earth was going on. Twelve hours earlier he had been celebrating his new-found freedom from Chloe and now here he was exercising it in the most obvious way possible. Such things, he mused, usually only seemed to happen to other people.

Kibby regarded him, amused. 'You once made a remark about the pepper grinder to Topaz, didn't you?' she asked.

'I don't remember,' said Johnathan.

'Thought so,' said Kibby.

Johnathan changed the subject. 'We should be there in a few minutes.' He watched the deserted London streets pass by.

'Good. It's freezing in this cab.' There was a pause. 'Johnathan,' said Kibby.

'Yes?'

'We're only going to have sex together. That's all. I'm not expecting you to propose marriage in the morning.'

'I know.'

'I just wish you'd relax. You look terrified.'

'I *am* terrified.'

'Why? Look, if you prefer, we can just play Scrabble.'

'I haven't got Scrabble.'

'Monopoly?'

'No.'

'Oh well, looks like sex it is, then.'

There was another long pause.

'Don't worry,' said Kibby, moving over the back seat and linking her arm through his. 'If all else fails you must at least have a pack of cards.'

A few minutes later the taxi pulled up outside Johnathan's flat. It was very late. Johnathan's hands were trembling as he fumbled with the fare. The driver watched him with amusement. 'Can't wait to get going, can you mate?' he asked jovially. 'First time, is it?' Johnathan regarded him with loathing, and halved the tip.

Kibby was waiting patiently on the pavement. As the taxi pulled away, Johnathan smiled at her nervously. 'Right. Here we are.'

Kibby beamed at him. 'Can't wait. Have you got any coffee?'

To his surprise, Johnathan laughed. 'Tons of it. Come on.'

He unlocked the front door and led Kibby into the hall. He took her coat. Kibby looked around, shivering slightly. Johnathan saw that the answer-phone was winking at him. He ignored it. It was probably Chloe again. 'What's that?' asked Kibby, pointing at Schroedinger, who had just stumbled out of the kitchen, looking around blearily.

'That,' said Johnathan, 'is Schroedinger.'

Kibby laughed her laugh. Schroedinger's ears went back as his hair stood on end. 'Hello Schroedinger.' She bent down and picked him up. Schroedinger was too surprised to do anything. He had never been picked up before. Kibby wrinkled her nose up at him. 'How are you? Have you missed

Johnathan this evening? Do you mind that he's come home with a strange woman?' Schroedinger wagged his stump non-committally.

'How about that coffee?' said Johnathan.

'Lovely.' Kibby put Schroedinger down and walked into the sitting room.

'Be with you in a minute.' In the kitchen Johnathan set up the coffee machine in a daze. His brain was a whirr. What was Kibby doing here? Did she really want to have sex with him? If so, what was wrong with the normal channels, the usual procedure? There was a sort of etiquette, after all. You didn't just *ask*. He clumsily arranged the cups and saucers on the work surface.

'Sugar?' he asked a few moments later as he walked into the sitting room with two full cups.

'No thanks. I like it black and strong. Like my men.' Kibby took her cup. There was a pause. 'Johnathan, I'm *joking*.'

'Sorry, yes, of course you are,' said Johnathan, sitting down beside her on the sofa. Schroedinger sat by the door, eyeing them both suspiciously.

Kibby turned towards Johnathan. 'OK?' she asked.

'I think so.' He paused. 'There is one thing.'

Kibby looked at him appraisingly. 'You don't have any condoms.'

Johnathan felt sheepish. 'No.'

'Don't worry,' said Kibby breezily. 'I've got stacks. Never travel without them. Be prepared is my motto.' Kibby saluted and sipped her coffee. 'Now, there's an easy way and a hard way of doing this,' she continued in a matter-of-fact way. 'Either I wait for you to make a pass at me, in which case we'll probably be here until well into Sunday afternoon, or you let me make a bit of the running. Does that sound all right to you?'

Johnathan shrugged helplessly. 'Er, yes, fine.'

'Right.' Kibby placed her cup carefully down on the table in front of her. She moved Johnathan's cup to the far side of the table. 'Don't want to knock the coffee over in the excitement, do we?' she said.

'Suppose not,' said Johnathan, who had begun to sweat slightly.

'Right,' said Kibby again. She moved purposefully towards Johnathan, and took his hand in hers. She looked into his eyes for several seconds. 'You look like a startled rabbit caught in someone's headlights,' she declared.

'Oh, thanks very much.'

Kibby moved gently towards Johnathan. She smelled of lavender. She kissed him lightly on the mouth. Their lips scarcely brushed.

Kibby drew back for a moment and looked at him thoughtfully. 'Very good,' she said. 'It's nice to meet a man who knows how to kiss properly.' Johnathan looked down modestly. 'Of course, he needs to know how to kiss improperly, too,' she added, before moving towards Johnathan again, this time with more propulsion. Her arms went around the back of his neck.

Johnathan was expecting another gentle almost-kiss, and was startled when Kibby unceremoniously stuck her tongue down his throat. He took a moment to recover and then retaliated by sticking his own tongue down hers. There wasn't enough passing space, and their tongues began to shuttle feverishly from one mouth to the other. Kibby's tongue gradually began to overpower Johnathan's and soon established a clear territorial advantage. She started to work towards his tonsils. Johnathan, breathing rapidly through his nose, began to knead Kibby's shoulders while surreptitiously checking out her bra strap.

With a small moan Kibby pulled away from him. Her face broke into a wide grin.

'Isn't this fun?' she said, turning to the table to retrieve her coffee.

Johnathan nodded, his arm flapping helplessly towards his own cup, out of reach. Kibby turned back towards him, straddling him. She placed her hands on his chest.

'Sure you wouldn't rather have a game of whist?'

'Quite sure,' gasped Johnathan.

'Good.' Kibby put her arms around the back of Johnathan's neck and lowered herself on to his groin. She felt the bulge of his erection through four layers of material, and wriggled a bit. 'Mmm, feels nice,' she murmured softly, her mouth inches away from his, before running her tongue around Johnathan's lips. As she did so, she gyrated her hips, causing Johnathan to wonder briefly whether the sensation he was feeling in his nether regions was intense pleasure or intense pain.

Kibby resolved the problem by sitting back. It was pain. Johnathan stifled a yelp. What happens when an irresistible force meets an almost immovable object? The almost immovable object gets squashed. And then it deflates.

Kibby had now begun to lick her own lips. She began to unbutton her shirt, staring all the time into Johnathan's eyes. Johnathan stared back, hypnotized, too frightened to think about the damage she had just inflicted on his rapidly shrinking genitals. When she had undone the last button, Kibby pulled the front of her shirt open and shrugged it off her shoulders and on to the floor. Johnathan apologetically broke off from looking at her face to have a closer look at her chest.

Kibby was wearing a black satin bra, which had small lace details along the top of each cup. She thrust her chest towards him eagerly.

'I rather think that needs to come off, don't you?' she panted.

Johnathan gulped, and nodded mutely. Bras incorporate a particular release mechanism which can only be operated by the owners of at least two X chromosomes. Men just cannot do it. But they are always made to try.

Staring at the small nubs of her erect nipples through the black fabric, Johnathan took a deep breath and reached behind Kibby and ran his hands over the bare skin of her back. His hands descended on the bra hook. He felt tentatively along the line of the strap. It was particularly unfair that he wasn't even allowed to see what he was supposed to be doing. He wrestled with the clasp, which refused to yield to his clumsy touch. After a few moments of silent struggle, his tongue sticking half out of his mouth in concentration, he looked up at Kibby. She smiled down at him and pushed her breasts towards his face in encouragement. The sight of so much flesh spurred Johnathan on. He began fiddling like a man possessed. Kibby yawned. Eventually she said, 'Would you like me to do it?'

Johnathan nodded. Three seconds later the bra was on the floor. Kibby had effortlessly unhooked it with one deft swoop of a single hand. Johnathan didn't mind. Kibby had beautiful breasts, and they were now swaying gently in front of him, about six inches from his face. His erection was staging something of a recovery.

Johnathan reached up, gently cupped one of Kibby's

36

breasts in each hand, and squeezed. Kibby let out a small sigh. She ran her hands through Johnathan's hair, and when they were clasped firmly around his head she pulled him fiercely towards her right nipple, urging it into his mouth.

Startled, Johnathan began to flick the end of his tongue over Kibby's nipple, but as she continued to pull his head closer he took it wholly into his mouth and began to suck it, stopping occasionally to take quick gasps of air. Kibby sighed again, more deeply this time.

Eventually she pulled back. Her face was flushed.

'Time for bed,' she said.

Some time later, Kibby said, 'Well.'

'Sorry,' said Johnathan.

'Don't be,' said Kibby. 'It was nice. Have you got an ashtray?'

'Somewhere. Hang on.' Johnathan rolled off the bed. He pulled on his dressing gown which was lying by the door and went to the kitchen. There he took a plate from the drying rack and brought it back to the bedroom. He presented it to Kibby.

'Thanks,' said Kibby, who had retrieved her cigarettes from her handbag and was now puffing away contentedly. 'I always enjoy my post-shag fag more than any other,' she said. 'It's an integral part of the whole process. Of bonking.'

'It probably takes longer, too, if that performance is anything to go by,' said Johnathan gloomily.

Kibby eyed him critically. 'Are you one of these men who worry about their sexual performance so much that unless he can keep it up for an hour and a half and the woman has nineteen multiple orgasms he considers himself a failure?'

'Yes,' said Johnathan.

'Oh God,' said Kibby.

'Sorry,' said Johnathan again.

Kibby rolled over to face him. 'Look, there is nothing to apologize about, really. It was *fine*. It was nice. It was cuddly. *Please* don't start torturing yourself about it. I enjoyed it.'

'Cuddly'? thought Johnathan, appalled. Since when was sex supposed to be cuddly? Weren't words like 'magnificent' in the more traditional lexicon of sexual epithets? Or at least 'passionate'? But 'cuddly'. Johnathan felt as if he had been compared in bedroom prowess and technique to Humpty Dumpty.

It *had* been nice. It had also been very quick, and rather humiliating. They had repaired to Johnathan's bedroom, and undressed as quickly as they could. Kibby had straddled Johnathan and lowered herself on to him. She bent forwards to kiss him softly on his mouth and then whispered in his ear in her best Clint Eastwood voice, 'Go on, spunk, make my day.'

Johnathan had duly obliged, there and then.

As he came, the pleasure was somewhat eclipsed by his horror of an ejaculation so premature as to be in the wrong time zone. Kibby saw the look of mortified despair which passed over his face. She stopped moving.

'What's wrong? Am I hurting you?' she asked.

'Not exactly.'

'What then?'

'Ah.' Johnathan had rolled his eyes nervously, silently praying that she wasn't going to make him say it. She wasn't. Instead she said:

'Oh.'

'Sorry.'

*   *   *

38

Kibby exhaled languorously, studying the glowing end of her cigarette. 'You really mustn't worry,' she said. She stubbed out her cigarette and carefully put the plate by the side of the bed. She rolled over on to her front and looked at Johnathan. 'So. Are you going to ask me to stay the night or are you proposing to banish me outside at this ungodly hour?'

'Well, you can stay, of course. I was hoping you would.'

'Good,' said Kibby. 'In that case do you think I might have something to wear? An old T-shirt or something?'

'Let me go and see,' said Johnathan, wearily whipping back the duvet a second time. He was starting to feel very tired. He rummaged around in the corner of his bedroom and found a T-shirt, which he passed to Kibby.

'Thanks,' said Kibby, slipping it over her head. She reached out and held Johnathan's hand. 'I don't have to go anywhere tomorrow morning, so I think we should have another go then. OK?'

'OK.'

'Got any breakfast?'

'Cornflakes, but no milk.'

'Is that all?'

'Don't worry, there's a shop nearby. It sells most things. You can have whatever you want for breakfast.'

'Goody. I'll start off with some more of your delicious sausage.' Kibby laughed again, more softly this time. She kissed Johnathan tenderly on the cheek, and then moved to the other side of the bed and settled down with her back to him. 'Night.'

Johnathan stared up at the ceiling. He thought of how Chloe would have reacted to his performance. She would doubtless have begun explaining compassionately how he should not be embarrassed by this sort of thing, but should confront it – indeed, here was just the book to help him – *90s Man in the Bedroom: Placid and Flaccid.*

'Night,' he said absent-mindedly. Who was this woman who cared so little for social etiquette, the politics of sexual encounters? Who was this woman with the finely-honed bullshit detector? Who was this woman who didn't mind sexual failure on a truly epic scale? And, above all, what on earth was she doing in his bed?

Ever since his university days, Sunday mornings in Johnathan Burlip's life had been reserved for doing precisely nothing, except possibly for taking some pills to temper the Saturday night hangover, and then lying very still until it went away.

When Johnathan woke on this particular Sunday morning he was alone in the bed. From the kitchen came the clanking sound of pots and pans. Johnathan swung his feet on to the floor and went into the kitchen. Kibby was standing by the fridge, fully dressed, surrounded by green plastic bags. Schroedinger was sitting on his bean bag, watching her with benign interest.

'Hello,' said Johnathan.

Kibby smiled at him. 'I've been to the shop.'

'So I see.'

'Do you want some coffee? I'm going to do scrambled eggs with mushrooms, bacon and sausages. Sound OK?'

Johnathan nodded. He surreptitiously pinched himself.

'I think I've worked out how to use your coffee machine,' continued Kibby as she began to unpack the bags. 'Why don't you go next door and let me deal with all this, and I'll bring you a coffee and some mango and guava juice. Sounds disgusting, but it was all they had.'

'Right,' said Johnathan, feeling a little overwhelmed. He went into the sitting room and switched on the television. A very old children's show which had been popular fifteen years earlier was on. He watched distractedly. A few minutes later Kibby came in with a glass of juice and a steaming cup of coffee. She put them on the table and came and sat down next to him.

'Hello,' she said, and kissed him on the lips.

'Hello,' said Johnathan, immediately worried about the danger of his incipient hard-on manifesting itself through the lightweight towelling of his dressing gown.

'Are you hungry?'

Johnathan looked at her as innocently as he could. 'Not particularly.'

'Good,' said Kibby. 'Come on then.' She took his hand and led him back to the bedroom.

Johnathan eyed the over-laden plate with ill-disguised glee. Mushroom, sausage, egg, bacon and fried bread were heaped on top of each other, jostling for space. He looked carefully for a spot to put his tomato ketchup.

'Wow,' he said.

Kibby grinned. 'I don't know about you, but I've worked up quite an appetite.' She paused. 'You'd better enjoy it though. Don't think I make it a habit to cook men breakfast. Strictly first-time shags only, birthdays excepted. From now on it'll be back to cornflakes.'

A carefully constructed forkful went into Johnathan's mouth. He chewed contentedly.

Kibby watched him eat. 'Tell me something,' she said. 'Do you really not mind people like Gavin having a go at you? Doesn't it rankle?'

41

'Not really,' said Johnathan cheerfully. He thought. 'Well, sometimes it does. Sometimes it pisses me off hugely.'

'Because they're right or because they're wrong?'

'God, I don't know. It just pisses me off.'

'Oh, come on.'

'All right then, both. They may be right. But what really infuriates me about people who criticize lawyers is that they don't have a clue what they're talking about. Lawyers are pretty easy targets, after all. People just make assumptions about how awful and greedy we are. That's what really irritates me.'

'Not the fact that most of you actually *are* awful and greedy?'

'No. *That* I can live with.'

Kibby looked around his sitting room. 'You don't seem to be doing too badly for yourself.'

Johnathan put down his knife and fork. 'Look, I'm not saying I'm particularly proud of what I do. I'm not. I don't even enjoy it, really. I never wanted to be a lawyer. I never used to dream about a life of fighting injustice when I was younger. I just sort of fell into it. I work all the hours God sends and it's usually pretty bloody boring. I won't deny that the money isn't bad, but there should be more to it than that.'

'Such as?'

'Recognition. Respect. More personable colleagues. Prospects. Better coffee.'

'If it's so awful, why don't you leave?' said Kibby.

There was a heavy silence. Then Johnathan said, 'I can't.'

'Why not?'

'I just can't.'

'You're scared,' observed Kibby.

Johnathan looked at her. 'Correct,' he said.

'Can't you get another job? One that's more fulfilling?'

Johnathan rolled his eyes. 'They don't exist.'

'Have you tried?'

'Well. No. No, I haven't actually tried. But I know people who have.'

'Perhaps you should try yourself.'

'Perhaps I should.' Johnathan began to eat again.

'Bet you won't,' said Kibby.

'I bet I won't, too,' agreed Johnathan with his mouth full.

'Shame, though.'

'Yes, isn't it?'

There was a pause while Johnathan busied himself in skewering the last mushroom with the end of his fork, jabbing at it half-heartedly as it skidded around the plate. Kibby watched him closely as she sipped her mango and guava juice.

'You only get one chance at this,' she said eventually.

'At what?'

'Life. It's not a dress rehearsal. You can't come back and have another go. It's now or never. Aren't you worried that you're going to wake up one day when you're sixty and ask yourself what you've ever achieved in your life and arrive at the rather awkward conclusion that the answer is probably nothing? And by then it will all be too late. You're right when you say that there are more important things in life than money. There are.'

'Breakfast,' suggested Johnathan.

Kibby ignored him. 'It's pointless spending your life running after money if you're empty inside. At least if you enjoyed your work that would be a reason for doing it, but you don't. You're a nice bloke, Johnathan. You deserve better, you really do. You should at least think about it.'

'I will,' said Johnathan.

'Bet you don't give it another thought.'

'I will. I promise,' said Johnathan.

'We'll see,' said Kibby. She drained her glass, and looked at her watch. 'I should really go.'

'Oh. Right,' said Johnathan, suddenly realizing that he desperately wanted her to stay. He watched helplessly as she got up and began collecting her things.

'Thank you for a nice evening,' she said. 'And a nice morning.'

'Thank *you*,' said Johnathan.

'Here's where I am,' said Kibby, writing down a number. 'It would be nice to see you again, so give me a ring.'

Five minutes later Kibby was gone, after a slightly embarrassing goodbye kiss. Johnathan had aimed for Kibby's mouth and she had gone for his cheek, resulting in an awkward clash. Johnathan had only narrowly avoided poking out Kibby's left eye with his nose.

Alone in the flat, Johnathan stood in the middle of the sitting room with a broad smile on his face. After a while he became bored, and so instead sat on the sofa with a broad smile on his face.

Kibby Kibby Kibby, he thought. Nice name. Kibby what? He realized that he did not know her second name. Who was she, actually? He had slept with someone without knowing their surname. Johnathan felt appalled and then felt an unstoppable rush of elation. Kibby. Kibby Something. Kibby Something with whom I have recently had sex. Twice. Johnathan nodded with satisfaction. It sounded good.

Johnathan walked into the kitchen where the dishes from breakfast were stacked up neatly by the sink. He would do them later, he thought. Perhaps on Wednesday. Just then he didn't want to spoil his moment of glory.

He leaned down towards Schroedinger's bean bag. 'Oi,' he said. 'I *scored*.'

Schroedinger looked up at Johnathan, unimpressed. 'Suit yourself,' said Johnathan. He beamed. Schroedinger emitted the sigh of the long-suffering self-righteous, and closed his eyes.

Johnathan remembered the winking answer-phone. He went into the hall and reluctantly pressed the button. After a brief crackle of static, a familiar voice echoed through the flat.

'Hello? I know you're there. I do. I can sense it. Why won't you pick up the phone? Johnathan, we need to talk. I'm worried about you. After Troilus. I know you're upset. I just want to talk to you. I want to check you're all right.' There was a small pause, followed by an artfully controlled sob. 'I think you need help. I wish you'd call me. Soon. Please.'

Johnathan let out a low whistle of appreciation. Some performance. Brilliant. He had fallen for this sort of thing before, but no longer. Chloe was history. He made some more coffee and walked through the flat thinking about Kibby and what she had said about his job. It was, he reflected, nothing new. Such thoughts had been lurking at the back of his mind for years. He had learned to ignore such ideas when they fought their way to the front of his consciousness. Dissatisfaction was all part of the job package, along with private health insurance and gym membership.

Money. The root of all evil. Also the root of quite a lot of pleasure, thought Johnathan. A thought began to nag at the back of his mind that if that was true, he should be getting a lot more pleasure from it than he actually was. He began to wonder where his salary went. He stared at the ceiling, trying to remember what he had spent money on in the previous week.

Johnathan went to the hall table where the last few months' bank statements had amassed, unopened. He found the most recent one and opened it. He was hugely, cripplingly overdrawn. Johnathan scanned the column headed 'withdrawals'. He sat down and began systematically to account for each figure on the sheet.

Half an hour, later the awful truth had sunk in. The electricity bill, council tax, mortgage, house contents insurance, income protection plan, water rates, telephone, television licence, car insurance, credit card repayments, interest charges on some long-standing loans and membership of a few university clubs whose standing order he had never got around to cancelling left him with a net income per month which just made it into three figures. His life had been hijacked by a never-ending stream of pleasureless bills which had set him firmly on the road to financial ruin.

Johnathan threw the treacherous bank statement into the wastepaper basket. Perhaps Kibby was right after all. Something was clearly wrong. There seemed little point in carrying on like this. Something had to be done.

He thought about what Kibby had said. Life was not a dress rehearsal. He thought about his money, or lack of it. He thought about his job. He thought about Gavin's self-righteous preaching of the night before. Maybe, he

46

thought, the time has come to actually do something about all of this.

Ah, sod it, he said to himself. What have I got to lose?

FIVE

Johnathan arrived at work the following Monday morning burning brightly, full of resolve. Resolve to do what, exactly, he did not yet know. The first thing he needed to do was to check his employment contract and see how much notice he had to give before he could leave.

As Johnathan walked through the marble-encrusted reception area he heard a voice call his name. His heart sank. He stopped, and turned to face Derek, the security guard.

'Derek, hello. How are you?' he asked with as much grace as he could muster.

'Not bad, Corporal, not bad,' said Derek.

'Oh good,' said Johnathan shortly. He detested Derek.

To compensate for spending his entire career behind a desk, Derek, who was about forty, had created a glamorous past for himself. He claimed to have spent several years in a crack unit of the SAS – the Official Secrets Act meaning, conveniently, that he couldn't go into any details about what he had purportedly done. Instead of walking, he performed a peculiar strut, one arm outstretched in front of him, buttocks fiercely clenched together, a mix of goose-step and quickstep. Presumably this was how people marched in the SAS, like effete nazis.

Derek addressed everyone by military title, according to

his perception of their seniority. He cringed respectfully in front of the firm's partners as if they were generals, whereas, to his chagrin, Johnathan rarely rose above the rank of sergeant. Not even officer material. Johnathan's lowly rank was accompanied by a patronizing chumminess that he found rather aggravating.

'Ere,' said Derek, beckoning Johnathan forward.

Johnathan approached the desk. Derek leaned forward conspiratorially.

'D'you see what happened this weekend?' he asked.

'What?' said Johnathan.

'Those poofters,' said Derek.

'What?' said Johnathan.

'Them little arse-bandits.'

'What are you talking about?' asked Johnathan. He could feel his enthusiasm for the challenges of the day wane, as if Derek was sucking it out of him like a leech.

'You know. Faggots.'

'Homosexuals?' suggested Johnathan.

'Yeah.' Derek sat back, satisfied.

'What about them?' asked Johnathan after a pause.

'Well, they're all queer, aren't they?' said Derek reasonably.

'Derek, what's your point?'

'My point is, my point *is*, right, that another one of them got beaten up in Soho this weekend. There's been a series of attacks.'

'Really?'

Derek nodded. 'Yeah. Quite right too. About bloody time if you ask me. They're just getting what they deserve. This bloke had his arm broken in three places. I know the technique.' Derek grimaced, serious. 'We used a similar

49

method in Cambodia.' He paused for effect. Johnathan sighed. 'Course, you'll have to take my word for that. I've said too much already.' Derek sat back in his chair and pretended to look contrite.

'Was there anything else?' asked Johnathan.

'No, son, that's it. Just thought you should know. Be informed. Ear to the ground. Reconnaissance is the key to success. Just watch those benders. Nothing's safe when they're around.'

'Well, thanks for that. As edifying as ever,' said Johnathan, picking up his briefcase and marvelling that nobody had ever complained about Derek. His rather reactionary approach to a whole range of matters would have even the most radical right-wing policy think-tank quivering in excited apprehension.

Johnathan wandered along to his office and followed the usual routine. Put down briefcase on desk. Open briefcase. Stare inside morosely. (It is empty.) Shut briefcase. Sigh, with feeling. Hang jacket on back of chair. Ask: what am I doing here?

Johnathan wandered out of his room and peered around the next corner towards the secretarial pool. His heart sank. Charlotte was at her desk, bolt upright, typing furiously.

Charlotte had been Johnathan's secretary for five months. In that time they had barely exchanged a word more than was absolutely necessary for their professional relationship to survive. This was not for want of trying on Johnathan's part, but Charlotte was unwilling to be drawn into conversation about anything at all. And yet she did her job with an unnerving efficiency. She was never late. She never forgot anything. She never made mistakes. She never smiled.

Charlotte was also the thinnest person Johnathan had ever

seen. All she ever ate was a small plastic tub of green salad (without dressing), which she brought in every morning and would pick at throughout the day. She looked like an under-nourished Giacometti sculpture. Her hair was always scraped fiercely back into a flaccid pony-tail, which Johnathan had thought accounted for the permanently sardonic look she wore, her eyebrows forever hoisted towards the heavens. It had soon become apparent though that their sky-bound appearance had nothing to do with her hair. Charlotte looked witheringly cynical because she *was* witheringly cynical. She had a fantastically low opinion of lawyers.

Johnathan and Charlotte were now embarked upon a bitter war of attrition. Charlotte was always sullen, taciturn and grossly unhelpful, but typed like the wind.

As Johnathan approached her desk that morning, Charlotte did not take her eyes off the screen. Johnathan looked at where her hands should have been. All he saw was a blur of motion over the keyboard.

'Good morning,' he said.

The blur of motion got blurrier.

'Any messages?' said Johnathan.

Charlotte sneered silently.

'Right. No. Good. I'll just have a quick look in my in tray, I think.' In the tray were a glossy pamphlet from the Law Society offering beneficial rates for life assurance policies, and various internal memos. 'No, nothing,' he reported, and turned to retreat to his office.

'Can you take those with you?' said Charlotte.

'Take what?' asked Johnathan.

'The stuff in your tray. I don't want it cluttering up my desk.'

'Well I don't really want it cluttering up mine either.'

Charlotte glared at him. 'Right.' She picked up the tray and emptied its contents into the waste-paper basket.

'Oh brilliant, thanks,' said Johnathan, wondering whether the stuff about the life assurance would have been worth reading. He returned to his office and slumped in his chair, exhausted before work had even begun. He wanted to think hard about how best to implement his proposed life change, but first he had some work to do.

Johnathan began to think about his meeting that morning. His client was a gruff industrialist from Halifax who, over the last twenty-five years, had built up a profitable business making plastic children's dolls, known for their vacuous expressions and improbably proportioned torsos. The gruff industrialist had decided that he had made more money than he would ever be able to spend before he died, and so had decided to retire and sell the business to a massive American corporation, Dolls and Guise Inc.

Johnathan was being supervised on the matter by one of the firm's partners, a man called Gerald Buchanan. 'Supervised' in this context meant that once a week Gerald would wander into Johnathan's room for thirty seconds in between a lunch appointment and a game of golf to see what was going on. Exceptionally, Gerald had decided to come to the meeting this morning. His golf game had probably been cancelled, Johnathan reasoned.

While Johnathan was aimlessly reading the file, Gerald put his head around the door. As always he gave a strong impression of unruffled calm. He wore a pristine dark blue double-breasted suit with a loud chalk stripe running through it, a crisp white shirt and a pink silk tie which was tied with an enormous knot. His pungent aftershave filled the room.

'Are the Yanks here yet?' asked Gerald. He spoke in a languid, self-satisfied drawl which betrayed a life of pampered opulence.

Johnathan looked at his watch. 'Not yet. They should be here in about ten minutes.'

'Good,' said Gerald. 'I'm just off for a dump, so if they arrive while I'm gone just go ahead and start without me.'

'OK,' said Johnathan, wondering how long he was anticipating spending on the toilet.

As soon as Gerald had left, Johnathan's telephone rang. It was Derek.

'I've got a bunch of Americans in reception for you,' he said, in the sort of tone which sounded as if he was announcing an outbreak of scabies.

'A bunch?' said Johnathan. 'What do you call a bunch?'

There was a brief pause while Derek did a quick head count. 'I reckon about five or six,' he said.

'God. OK, tell them I'm on my way.'

Johnathan gathered up his papers and set off to the reception area, which was filled with the low nasal drone of transatlantic accents, as people huddled together in small groups talking urgently. As he approached, a short tubby man in a shiny light grey suit waved at him heartily. This was Gary Schlongheist III, the lawyer running the deal for the Americans. He was evil.

'John, hi, thanks for agreeing to see us so soon,' said Gary Schlongheist III. He gestured expansively behind him. 'As you can see, we've got a few more troops today.'

'Yes,' said Johnathan, hating him. Everyone else had stopped talking and was looking at him critically.

'The reason for everyone's being here today is that we have something to discuss which is in our view sufficiently serious as to merit the attendance of all these various individuals for one reason or another as you will see when we get down to business but of course prior to that I will be introducing you to everybody here and explaining to you their roles in this transaction to date and the roles which they will adopt from now on, once of course we've all got some coffee down our throats, hey folks?' said Gary Schlongheist III. Johnathan rapidly felt himself losing control in the face of such officious and long-winded pedantry. He opened his mouth but no noise came out. Schlongheist looked at him questioningly for a few moments and then slapped him on the back and prompted, 'So, lead on, Macbeth. Which of your rooms do we get to see today?'

Johnathan cast a desperate eye over the group of people. 'If you'd just like to follow me.' Feeling like a tour guide, he turned and set off down the corridor which led to the rabbit warren of conference rooms.

The Americans filed into the appointed room and seated themselves along one edge of the long table. Johnathan awkwardly put his papers in the middle of the table opposite the row of faces. Just as he was about to speak, Gary Schlongheist III began again.

'OK everybody, time for formal introductions. The gentleman sitting opposite you is John Burlip, who represents Mr Rocastle in the current transaction.'

Johnathan shifted in his seat. The row of heads nodded ever so slightly in his direction. My name is Johnathan, you fat American turd, he said to himself as he smiled weakly.

54

'Now, John. Can I introduce, from left to right, the following ladies and gentlemen: Ulverton Lovestick, Aaron Bostick, Randy Merrick, Brandy Jordan, and lastly Harry Sawyer.' Gary Schlongheist III beamed.

In perfect synchrony each person reached into an inside pocket and withdrew a business card which was then pushed over the table at Johnathan like a poker hand. He arranged the cards in front of him in the same order as the people opposite him. He looked up at Gary Schlongheist III, who was playing with his expensive-looking pen.

'First of all, John,' said Schlongheist, 'I'd like you to listen to the managing director of Dolls and Guise Inc., Harry Sawyer.'

The man sitting next to Schlongheist cleared his throat and began to shuffle papers busily. Johnathan glanced down at his business card. It said: 'H.D.(Harry) Sawyer, Managing Director' in overly florid typescript.

'Good morning,' said H.D.(Harry) sombrely. 'The reason that I asked Gary to arrange this meeting today is that we appear to have encountered a problem which might seriously affect the viability of the proposed transaction for us.'

Johnathan's heart lurched. 'Oh?' he said.

'Yeah,' agreed H.D.(Harry), 'and we just wanted to talk the issue through with you to see if we could arrive at some happy compromise.'

'I see,' said Johnathan.

There was an awkward pause.

'The thing is,' said H.D.(Harry), 'we've been having a look at those dolls your client produces. And while they're real cute, we've spotted a problem with them. It has always been a point of commercial concern and indeed pride for

55

Dolls and Guise Inc. that all of the little dolls that we make are as lifelike as possible so as to provide young girls with a genuine learning tool as well as a terrific toy.' H.D.(Harry) was looking round the table, acknowledging the enthusiastic nods of his colleagues. 'As a result of this policy our dolls have certain features which perhaps are not what you in England might ordinarily expect to see. And there is one thing in particular which we hold to be especially important which you certainly don't see on Mr Rocastle's dolls.'

'Which is?' said Johnathan.

The American glanced at Brandy Jordan, who was sitting next to him. 'Pubic hair.'

Johnathan blinked.

Brandy Jordan spoke for the first time. 'Mr Burlip, we at Dolls and Guise Inc. firmly believe that we have a social obligation to educate the young of America in the mysterious ways of nature. Hence our product lines of Pregnant Penelope and Menstruating Melissa.' She paused. Randy Merrick coughed supportively. Randy and Brandy exchanged smiles of such cloying sweetness that Johnathan felt a little queasy.

Brandy continued. 'We have conducted a great deal of research into this and we do believe that to manufacture dolls with pubic hair prepares young girls for the often shocking trial that puberty represents. It means that when they begin to grow *their* pubic hair they will have already familiarized themselves with the concept and above all the *sight* of pubic hair in general.'

'Pubic hair,' repeated Johnathan dully.

Brandy Jordan's cheaply peroxided head disappeared beneath the table top. 'Let me show you,' she said. There was the unclicking of a briefcase. Brandy Jordan reappeared, clutching a doll about twelve inches high with long red hair. She thrust it across the table towards Johnathan. Johnathan eyed it suspiciously.

'And Mr Burlip, *look*,' said Brandy Jordan. With no further ceremony she hooked her little finger underneath the doll's knee-length skirt and hiked it upwards over its hips. She deftly spread the doll's legs as wide as the little plastic joints would allow, and placed it in the middle of the table, its parted legs pointing wantonly at Johnathan. Johnathan looked, appalled. At the top of the doll's legs sat what looked like a small Brillo pad.

'Right,' he said eventually.

'John, if my client is to adhere to company policy then all future dolls coming from Mr Rocastle's factory will have to be fitted with pubic hair, and that may be quite an expensive addition,' said Schlongheist. It sounded a bit like getting a car fitted with a sun-roof. 'Unless we can come to some sort of arrangement then I fear we shall have to reconsider our current negotiating position.'

Johnathan tried to think. He began to feel very uncomfortable. He tried hard to look somewhere other than at the doll's grisly pudendum, which seemed to have fixed him with its evil eye. 'Wouldn't it be a feasible option to leave these dolls as they are?' he said desperately. 'If you like it could represent another option open to women. After all, not every woman *has* pubic hair.'

Harry Sawyer considered this. 'So you're suggesting that the English dolls could just be dolls of women who have chosen to shave their pubis?' He seemed enchanted. He looked down the length of the table enquiringly. 'It certainly is an option. Anybody got any comments?'

Ulverton Lovestick raised his hand, as if in school. He spoke with a mellifluous southern twang. 'I guess that'd work as long as we made it clear from the marketing that the choice to depilate had been made, and that it wasn't some oversight on our part.'

There was an enthusiastic nodding around the table as people began to murmur quietly to each other. Ulverton Lovestick began to sketch something on a piece of paper.

Gary Schlongheist III raised his hands in protest. 'Ladies and gentlemen, I suspect we may be getting slightly off the point of today's meeting –'

He was ignored. The other Americans had descended into a huddle. '. . . We could package in such a way as to explain the health benefits of depilation, the convenience . . .'

'. . . It would be a radical departure for us . . .'

'We could call her Depilating Donna.'

'Or Hairless Helen.'

'I've got it. What about Shaving Sharon?'

Aaron Bostick was not convinced, however. 'It'll just make our products like everyone else's,' he complained. 'We'll lose the male market, that's for sure.'

Johnathan blinked.

The Americans began to discuss the marketing possibilities which Johnathan's suggestion had unwittingly presented. Schlongheist flapped ineffectually around his clients. Johnathan eyed the half-naked doll. Some deep-seated sense of decorum urged him to straighten its legs and restore its dress to the proper position, but he couldn't bring himself to touch it.

Gerald Buchanan then breezed in. Johnathan got up from his chair and led him to the far corner of the room, out of earshot of the others.

'What's the prob?' demanded Gerald. Johnathan told him.

Gerald blinked.

When Johnathan explained his proposed solution to the problem Gerald let out a low whistle. 'I'm surprised they didn't lynch you on the spot, old boy,' he said. 'Americans don't like people taking the piss.'

Johnathan leant forward. 'But Gerald, that's what they're discussing. They think it might be a feasible option.'

'Are you serious?' asked Gerald. Johnathan nodded. 'Well I'll be buggered,' whispered Gerald, 'they're even madder than we thought. Extraordinary.'

Gary Schlongheist III bustled up. 'Excuse me, gentlemen,' he said peevishly. 'I don't really think it appropriate that you be present while my clients are making this sort of sensitive commercial decision. Would you mind . . . ?' He gestured towards the door. Gerald slowly turned and left. Johnathan followed him out.

They stood in the deserted corridor. 'Pubic hair?' said Gerald. Johnathan nodded. 'Christ, what next? Next they'll be having dolls that menstruate.'

'Actually, they already do,' said Johnathan.

Some minutes later the door to the meeting room opened and Schlongheist came out. 'It appears that my clients have reached a consensus of opinion in respect of the problem which we have identified this morning,' he said, trying to hide his disappointment.

'Yes?' said Gerald.

'Won't you come in?' Schlongheist held the door open sulkily.

Gerald and Johnathan filed inside and sat down opposite a row of flushed, excited faces. Gary Schlongheist III coughed.

'Well, we do appear to have arrived at a suitable compromise solution to the difficulty identified –'

'Cut the crap, Gary,' suggested H.D.(Harry) Sawyer amicably.

Schlongheist reddened. 'Yes, as I was *saying*, my clients are prepared to run with the idea that Mr Burlip suggested and on that basis I think that we can now proceed on the terms as we had originally planned.' He looked crestfallen.

Gerald looked at him sourly from across the table. He leant forward and said, 'Are you tweaking my twinky?'

'Pardon?' said Schlongheist.

'You heard. Are you pulling my plonker? Jiggling my joystick? Yanking my yard? Beating my meat?'

'I'm sorry, Gerald, I really have no idea what you're referring to,' said the American, glancing at the assembled company nervously.

Gerald was in full flow now. 'Come off it, *Gary*,' he said, with some venom. 'I've been in this business long enough to know when someone is schlapping my schnitzel.'

Johnathan frowned, quite lost. The Americans had begun to murmur amongst themselves.

'Your schnitzel?' asked Schlongheist doubtfully.

Gerald looked at the Americans and gestured helplessly. He seemed genuinely upset. Without warning he slammed down his hand on to the table top. Brandy Jordan jumped. The doll jumped. 'Dammit Gary! Come on. Be reasonable.' Gerald stood up and began pacing the room. He appeared to be struggling to find the words he wanted to say. 'I'm not prepared,' he said, 'to be treated like this, have you

60

manipulate my manhood, let you play cat's-cradle with my cock.' He slumped back into his chair, emotionally wrung out. The Americans looked impressed. Schlongheist, hopelessly confused, waited.

Eventually Gerald said, 'Have you nothing to say?'

Schlongheist looked at him through slitted eyes. 'About what, exactly?'

Gerald looked at Schlongheist for a moment. 'I see,' he said suddenly, and began gathering up his papers to leave. Turning away from Schlongheist, he winked cheerfully at Johnathan.

'Wait, wait,' said Schlongheist, panicking. 'Whatever it is you have to say, please say it. In words of one syllable,' he added.

'Well it seems pretty obvious to me,' said Gerald, putting his papers back down on the table. 'Our client is offering your client a marvellous, not to say unique, opportunity to expand their product range to encompass a totally new – to them, anyway – concept in doll manufacture. Think about it. Don't you think my client deserves to receive greater compensation as a result?'

Gary Schlongheist III now went purple. 'I'm quite sure –'

Gerald interrupted smoothly. 'Why don't we ask your clients what *they* think?'

H.D.(Harry) Sawyer stood up. 'Hell, yes,' he said, 'that sounds reasonable enough to me. If we're going to benefit from this breakthrough I don't see why we shouldn't share a little of it around.' He looked down the table munificently, ignoring Schlongheist who remained rooted to his seat, opening and closing his mouth soundlessly. The Americans gazed adoringly up at their leader, and burst into spontaneous applause.

Some time later Gary Schlongheist III recovered his power of speech. He said: 'What an *asshole*.'

SIX

When Johnathan arrived back at his office after the meeting, Charlotte smiled shyly at him. Immediately he sensed something was wrong.

'There's a message for you,' she said, brandishing a small piece of paper.

'Oh. Thanks,' said Johnathan, and took it. On it was written,

Could we have a word? 2.30 this afternoon, my office.

E.J.S-J.

It was not a request, it was a command. And it was no ordinary command: it came from Edward Stenhouse-Jellicoe, the ancient and somewhat batty senior partner. Johnathan frowned. He had been at the firm for six and a half years, and had always believed that Stenhouse-Jellicoe didn't have the faintest idea who he was. Each time Johnathan met him in the corridor or in the lift he would bow and scrape in obsequious reverence as expected but all he ever got in return was a rather puzzled, far-away smile.

Stenhouse-Jellicoe had given up practising any law long ago. He was too much in the grip of addling senility for that. Instead he now usually arrived at eleven o'clock each day to sign some letters, perhaps chair a meeting or two of the partners to which he would contribute nothing other than a few irrelevant Latin maxims, before going into lunch in the partners' dining room, where he would stay for most of the afternoon cuddling the port decanter and dozing fitfully.

Under his benign and useless sovereignty, the real power was wielded ruthlessly by a small group of partners. Johnathan suspected that the balance of blood to port coursing through Stenhouse-Jellicoe's veins had now tipped in favour of the port, and that as a result he no longer knew what actions were being taken in his name; he just signed whatever he was asked to sign and only complained when things made him late for lunch.

Johnathan looked at his watch. It was 2.20. Why would Stenhouse-Jellicoe want to see him? His brain rioted with unpleasant theories. Suddenly Johnathan realized that whatever happened, it didn't matter: he was going to resign anyway. He must remember: *he no longer cared*.

At 2.30 he knocked on the door of Edward Stenhouse-Jellicoe's office. There was a clearing of throats and then a strangled 'Come' from within. Stenhouse-Jellicoe was slumped like an abandoned rag doll in his old leather chair behind his mahogany desk, which was about the same size as Johnathan's office. He was flanked by two of his henchmen, Richard O'Donnell, head of the corporate department, and Trevor Bailey, the partnership secretary. Some time ago the dog had stopped wagging its two tails and the tails had begun to wag the dog, even though the dog was now too sozzled to notice. And when they wagged, they wagged hard, and without pity or remorse.

'Johnathan, Johnathan,' cooed Trevor Bailey, 'come in.'

Johnathan closed the door behind him and approached the table.

'Sit down, please,' said Bailey, gesturing towards the single chair opposite Edward Stenhouse-Jellicoe.

Johnathan sat. He waited. He shifted uneasily in his chair and made a farting noise as the material of his suit rubbed against the chair's upholstered leather. He shifted again, just to show that it wasn't a fart. The ensuing noise sounded even more like a fart than the first one. Johnathan decided to stay still.

Richard O'Donnell placed one hand on the back of Edward Stenhouse-Jellicoe's chair in a proprietorial way. 'Edward, you of course know Johnathan Burlip.'

Stenhouse-Jellicoe peered mistily at Johnathan. 'Ears,' he said enigmatically.

Johnathan wondered what was wrong with his ears.

'Johnathan works in our Company Department,' continued O'Donnell.

'Ears, ears,' said Stenhouse-Jellicoe again, nodding slowly. Johnathan realized that he was agreeing with O'Donnell.

Stenhouse-Jellicoe riffled his sheaf of notes without looking at them. He gave Johnathan a beatific if unfocused smile over the top of his half-moon glasses. 'Well,' he began. Then he stopped, and stared off into space over Johnathan's right shoulder, lost in thought. Johnathan waited. Bailey and O'Donnell exchanged glances.

'Yes?' said Johnathan politely.

The old man woke up. 'Ah, yes, *alea jacta est,*' he said, and then took off his glasses and began polishing them with the end of his tie.

Johnathan looked at O'Donnell.

O'Donnell said, 'Johnathan, as I'm sure you will have noticed, the recession has hit the firm hard.'

'*Res ipsa loquitur,*' declared Stenhouse-Jellicoe without looking up.

'Quite. Anyway, in such times it is clearly beholden on the managers of any enterprise, be they lawyers, accountants, or manufacturers of fork-lift trucks, to enter into a structured programme of damage limitation and rationalization with a view to streamlining the business, maximizing efficiency and minimizing extraneous and overhead-enhancing superfluities.'

'Yes,' said Johnathan uncertainly.

'Now in recent months Trevor and I have been involved in the conceptualization and implementation of just such an operation on behalf of the firm, which, I may say, has been an exercise of no little complexity and soul-searching. We have had to take some difficult decisions that have caused us much heartache.'

There was a well-orchestrated pause while all three men behind the desk nodded.

O'Donnell continued. 'What we have done is to come up with a set of suggested scenarios within the context of which the firm can regroup and begin to work its way organically out of the recession. We have put these various scenarios to Edward, who after much thought and no little angst has arrived at some very tough decisions, which only he, as senior partner, could legitimately make.'

Stenhouse-Jellicoe looked at Johnathan with an air of fatherly concern, happily unaware that he was being manipulated and used as a scapegoat.

'Inevitably with this sort of rationalization, Johnathan, there always have to be losers,' said Richard O'Donnell. 'And this time, unfortunately, the loser is you.'

'What?' said Johnathan.

'I'm sorry, Johnathan, but we're going to have to rationalize you.'

'What?' said Johnathan again.

'I realize that this will have come as a terrible shock to you,' said Trevor Bailey as he left Stenhouse-Jellicoe's side and began the long trek around to the other side of the table. Compassion oozed from every pore of his body. 'And you must appreciate that we're no happier about this than you are. But these are hard times and we're faced with hard choices. And you my friend,' he said, as he put a strong hand on Johnathan's sagging shoulder, 'were the hardest choice of all.'

'I am being rationalized,' said Johnathan. Trevor Bailey nodded. 'Without wishing to appear obtuse,' said Johnathan, 'what exactly does that mean?'

There was a pause. O'Donnell and Bailey exchanged glances. 'What it means, Johnathan, is that the firm's train is pulling out of the station, and you're staying on the platform.'

Something in Johnathan's brain refused to allow this information to register. 'On the platform?' he said helplessly.

Trevor nodded sadly.

'What do you mean, "on the platform"?' said Johnathan. Trevor Bailey frowned.

'Johnathan,' he said, 'you're fired.'

'Ah,' said Johnathan. 'Right.'

Bailey and O'Donnell watched for some other reaction. There was none. Johnathan sat rigidly upright in his chair, staring unseeingly ahead, numbed into inactivity. Stenhouse-Jellicoe had begun to hum 'The Surrey with the Fringe on Top' quietly to himself.

'I'm fired,' said Johnathan after a while.

O'Donnell nodded.

'Now what?' asked Johnathan.

67

O'Donnell replied. 'Well, as you know, it is a *sine qua non* that every lawyer here has a three months notice provision in his contract of employment. However in the circumstances we feel justified in proposing a waiver of that provision, the *quid pro quo* for which will be two months' salary.' The Latin was obviously contagious. 'You leave at the end of the week.'

Johnathan reeled. 'The end of the week?' he stammered. 'Do I have a choice?'

'No,' said Bailey.

'But what am I going to *do*?' whined Johnathan, his plans for resignation long forgotten.

O'Donnell said, 'Johnathan, it's an exciting time. The rules have been rewritten.'

'Quite right. In this day and age, there *are* no rules,' said Bailey unhelpfully. O'Donnell shot him a dirty look.

'You can go out there and make a splash,' continued O'Donnell. 'The world is your oyster. Grasp the nettle.'

'Grab the bull by the horns,' suggested Bailey.

'*Carpe diem*,' croaked Stenhouse-Jellicoe.

Johnathan got up shakily. 'Thank you,' he said. He walked to the door in as dignified a manner as he could. The three partners watched him go. Johnathan heaved open the door and tottered out without another word.

'Extraordinary,' said Trevor Bailey. 'No gumption at all.'

'*Quod*,' said Edward Stenhouse-Jellicoe, '*erat demonstrandum*.'

The rest of the week passed in a vague haze of panic.

Johnathan wasn't sure whether to tell his colleagues about his imminent departure or not. He eventually decided to wait until one of the other casualties of the redundancy initiative took the plunge and went public with the news. As the week continued however, nobody else announced their leaving drinks. Nobody else appeared to be packing up their personal belongings into cardboard boxes. Johnathan reasoned that the hatchet-men must be rationalizing in stages so as not to cause too much upset to the remaining staff.

By the Wednesday evening Johnathan decided that he should probably mention his impending departure to someone. He told one of the solicitors in his corridor, who didn't appear very surprised by the news.

'We were wondering when you were going to tell us,' she said.

'You knew?' said Johnathan.

'Of course. It's been common knowledge for the last three weeks. We thought you would let us know in your own time.' She scanned a page of tightly-packed print while she spoke.

'Three weeks?' said Johnathan.

'Well, maybe four.'

'Who else is leaving?' asked Johnathan.

The woman looked up from her work. 'Who else? Nobody else as far as I know.'

Nobody else?

'Oh,' said Johnathan.

'Anyway, best of luck,' said the woman, taking the cap off her pen and looking intently at the papers in front of her.

'Right, well, thanks. It's actually quite a relief, you know. I'll be able to go and do something more fulfilling.'

His colleague looked up. 'What sort of thing did you have in mind?' she asked.

'Work with real people,' said Johnathan grandly, more grandly than he felt. There was an enquiring pause. He ploughed on. 'I thought I might go for work in the voluntary sector. Charities, Legal Aid work, you know, that sort of thing. Give a bit back to the community. Do my bit to help.'

The woman looked at him curiously. 'Well, that's jolly nice,' she said eventually.

Once it became public knowledge that news of Johnathan's departure was now public knowledge, a few people popped their heads into his office briefly to say goodbye. Charlotte said nothing. Johnathan wondered how long she had known.

On Friday he called around his colleagues to see if they were available for a final night of revelry to see him off into his new life. They weren't. There was an unparalleled outbreak of family birthdays, weddings in the provinces and unavoidable dinner engagements. At a quarter past five in the afternoon Johnathan sat at his desk, his briefcase packed, and stared at his telephone. He debated whether to call Kibby. He hadn't spoken to her all week.

He decided against it. Telephone conversations with people you have only slept with once are dangerous affairs. Picking your way carefully through the potentially lethal minefield of small-talk, there was always the risk of inadvertently tripping an unseen wire which could imperil the delicate negotiations. Johnathan didn't want to risk it.

At half past five exactly Johnathan walked through the reception area with his briefcase for the last time. He went to say a last farewell to Derek.

'Orright, Private Burlip?' said Derek. He saluted.

'Oh.' Johnathan looked down. 'You know.'

'Anything planned for the weekend? Har har har,' said Derek.

'Not really, Derek.' Johnathan paused. 'I just wanted to say . . . goodbye.'

'Yup. 'Bye then,' said Derek briskly.

'And . . . thanks. Thanks for everything.'

'No worries. See you on Monday, then. Be good. And if you can't be good, be careful, know what I mean? Hur, hur.'

Johnathan turned to go, leaving Derek to his guffaws. Bloody man.

Johnathan joined the bleating herds of secretaries as they funnelled down the corridors towards the weekend.

Johnathan arrived home feeling empty. He hung up his suit. He felt an overwhelming sensation of anticlimax. In theory, this should have been cataclysmic, a real-life horror story. In practice, the reality was proving crushingly mundane. Johnathan was still there. He would not wither up and die without his job, no matter how tempting or dramatically apt that sounded. He padded around the flat, unsure what he should do or how he should feel. Apathy threatened to smother him.

He decided to telephone Jake.

'Jake,' said Johnathan, climbing on to the stool next to his friend.

Jake looked up from the sodden beer mat in front of him, and smiled in an unfocused way. 'Hello, mate. You well?'

'Been better. You?'

'Yeah, not bad.' He scratched his tousled head. 'I tell you,

I do enjoy this journalism stuff. I've spent all day investigating vampire cults in Surrey.'

'Oh?' said Johnathan, girding himself for Jake's obtuse musings. Jake's brain did not follow even the most fundamental rules of cerebral activity. Years of consuming vast quantities of finest Moroccan hashish had permanently scrambled it. Talking to him was a bit like watching the television when someone else has the remote control: he had a habit of unpredictably switching his train of thought between unrelated topics without drawing breath, and without bothering to tell you he had done so. To complicate matters further, Jake's spin on things was often so weird that it was usually impossible to make sense of what he was saying *before* he began switching subjects. It was actually like watching Swedish television when someone else has the remote control. Unless, of course, you were Swedish.

'Yeah,' said Jake. 'There's a whole batch of vampire covens all the way around the M25. The principal area of activity seems to be in Hertfordshire. There are unconfirmed reports of bodies turning up with two small red holes in the neck outside the Sainsbury's in Potter's Bar.'

'Dead bodies or live bodies?' asked Johnathan.

Jake shrugged. 'It doesn't matter, really. Obviously it would be better if they were dead.'

'And what about Surrey, then?'

'Surrey is looking hopeful. I've found a mad old crone who lives near Dorking who keeps bats.'

'And?'

'Well, and nothing, as yet, but it's a start. I mean, why else would you keep bats unless you were a vampire?'

To his irritation Johnathan couldn't answer this question. 'What are these vampires supposed to do?' he asked.

'You know. Vampire stuff. Prowling around Leatherhead at midnight in dark flowing capes, sharpening their teeth, and drinking blood.' Jake waved his pint at Johnathan.

Johnathan shut his eyes. Nobody he knew had less of a grasp on the distinction between fiction and reality than Jake. The strange thing was that Jake *knew* what he wrote wasn't true. However, in order to preserve some sort of integrity he had adopted the logically untenable position of nonetheless choosing to believe it. It must have taken some resilience of mind and conscience, but Jake managed to live with the duplicity with no apparent difficulty. On that basis, reflected Johnathan, he could have made a fine lawyer.

Johnathan had known Jake from his first week at university. Jake had been reading English; Johnathan had been reading law. Johnathan always felt slightly jealous of the English undergraduates. While he toiled in the law library reading turgid case reports and abstruse legal treatises, Jake and his fellow English students sunned themselves on the lawn behind the hall of residence with a fat spliff in one hand and a can of beer in the other, an unopened text lying beside them for the sake of good form, discussing anything except the work that they weren't doing.

To be fair to most of the English students, they did eventually leave such hedonistic pursuits behind them and knuckled down to the serious business of getting a degree. This would usually happen about three weeks before their final exams. The lawyers, in contrast, never stopped working. About three months before finals, though, they stopped sleeping and eating. There wasn't enough time.

Jake had been laid-back, even for an English student. He arrived half an hour late for his first exam having forgotten to set his alarm-clock and overslept. By the time their exams arrived, even the English undergraduates were buying cartons of Pro-plus from pharmaceutical wholesalers and swallowing them by the bucket-load, drinking gallons of coffee, and taking uppers, downers, beta-blockers, amphetamines, and anything else within reach. Jake, though, meandered calmly from exam to exam, only once becoming slightly agitated when he realized after the start of his Elizabethan poetry paper that he had forgotten to bring anything to write with. One of the invigilators lent him a pencil.

Had he been a real genius, Jake would have got a first. He didn't. He passed, just. After university Johnathan went to law school and began to acquire all the accoutrements of grown-up respectability. Jake, on the other hand, had refused to accept any sort of responsibility and instead spent several years flitting around the world doing an eclectic selection of jobs. He had worked for a while in a wildlife reserve in Mozambique where his job had been to manually stimulate a homosexual giraffe which refused to mate with its designated partner. Then, during a trip through Bangladesh, he acquired a job teaching music at a school where the previous music teacher had got into an unfortunate altercation with an angry cow, and had been admitted to the local hospital. Jake's legacy when he left some weeks later was a school full of Bangladeshi children who could all play the opening notes of 'Smoke on the Water' on the sitar.

On his return to London Jake had become a freelance journalist. Occasionally he wrote short items which appeared in one of the more pretentious sections of a heavy Sunday newspaper. Such articles tended to coincide with demands for arrears of rent from irate landlords. What was apparent from the few pieces that Jake ever got around to producing was that he was in fact very good at it. His writing was astute, witty, clever, and original. And of course nobody ever read it.

Recently, though, Jake had changed course and was now involved in some of the more fantastic areas of investigative journalism, reasoning (correctly) that there was a significantly greater market for trashy drivel than for high-minded drivel. Johnathan listened to Jake ramble on about dental records he had uncovered in Basingstoke, which suggested that a number of people in the region had extended canine teeth. He gazed into his pint glass and wondered what on earth he was going to do about his own enforced career move.

Jake eventually drew breath to take a large swig of beer. 'So what's your news, then?' he asked.

'Funny you should ask. I just lost my job.'

'Kidding.'

'I wish. Today was my last day.'

'Wow. Bummer.'

'Uh-huh.' Johnathan nodded morosely.

'What are you going to do?'

'Good question. Get pissed, for starters.'

Jake brightened. 'Good idea.' He paused. 'By the way. Talking about bats. Was Batman bitten by a bat?'

'Sorry?' said Johnathan.

'Well. I need some facts about bats. You know, "Twenty things you never knew about bats." And I was wondering if Batman was bitten by one.'

'When?' asked Johnathan.

'Not on any particular occasion. But before he became Batman. Which, you know, *made* him Batman.'

Johnathan thought. 'No, I don't think so. Spiderman was bitten by a radio-active spider, though, wasn't he?'

'Exactly,' said Jake. 'That's why I asked. Spiderman was bitten by a spider and that explained why he could climb up and down buildings and spin webs. But you don't think Batman was bitten by a bat?'

'No I don't,' said Johnathan, slightly aggrieved that they had got off the subject of his unemployment quite so quickly. 'Anyway, it's not as if he had any special bat-powers or anything, did he? Like radar or night vision.'

Jake looked at his pint thoughtfully. 'Good point.'

Johnathan continued, 'And I'm pretty sure Robin wasn't pecked by a robin.' Jake nodded, conceding this.

'So why was he called Batman, then?' he asked.

'Well, he had to be called something,' said Johnathan.

'Maybe Bruce Wayne had a thing about vampires as well,' suggested Jake.

Johnathan raised his eyebrows. 'Maybe. Perhaps there's some allegorical significance to bats that we've both missed.'

'I reckon he was just a pervert,' said Jake. 'Any excuse to wear his underpants outside his tights. More beer?'

Johnathan cheered up a little.

SEVEN

Johnathan emerged from beneath the duvet the following morning earlier than usual and cooked himself bacon and eggs with the remains of Kibby's feast of a week earlier, which were still festering in the fridge.

As he watched the eggs cook in the crusty frying pan, Johnathan turned his thoughts to his immediate future. There was little in his life which could be described as concrete. There was now little linking him to the rest of the world or it to him. Without the prosaic solidity of his job, there was a risk that he might just drift away. As the misshapen ovals of egg spat and wiggled at him in the pan, Johnathan wondered whether Kibby might hold the key to the problem, whether she might be able to drag him back from the brink of whatever it was he was on the brink of.

After his breakfast he found her telephone number. After three long, deep breaths, he picked up the telephone and dialled. It rang twice.

'Hello?' said a voice at the other end.

'Kibby?' said Johnathan hopefully.

'No, it's Tibby,' said the voice. 'Hang on. I think she's still in bed.' Johnathan tapped his foot. He looked at Kibby's handwriting on the piece of paper. It was neat and considered, with short, heavy strokes. There were no unnecessary flourishes. Very business-like. To the point.

Eventually there was a rattle as the receiver was picked up.

'Hello?' yawned Kibby.

All of Johnathan's thoughts simultaneously evacuated his brain. He said, 'Er, Kibby?'

'Yes?'

'It's Johnathan. Burlip. Johnathan Burlip.'

There was a low whistle. 'Hallelujah. It's Erroll fucking Flynn himself.'

Johnathan considered this response.

'Look, I'm sorry I didn't ring before,' he said.

'Oh, don't worry, I can understand what sort of pressures you men with God-like physiques and dicks the size of well-nourished aubergines must be under, what with the entire female population of the species to satisfy. You have to spread yourselves thinly.'

Johnathan shifted uncomfortably from one foot to the other. He looked balefully at Schroedinger, who had emerged from beneath the kitchen sink to watch him make the call. For someone who had been half-asleep thirty seconds earlier, Kibby had made an impressive, if startling, transformation from sleepy harmlessness to venom-spitting ferocity. 'Please,' said Johnathan, 'don't be like that.'

'Don't tell me, you've been busy.'

'Well, yes, actually, I have.'

'Doing what, exactly? No, let me guess: you've left your job, and you're now having repatriation orders for legions of Nigerian cleaning ladies overturned.'

'Half right.'

There was a pause.

'Which half?' asked Kibby.

'Well, not the bit about the Nigerian cleaning ladies.'

'You've left your job?' said Kibby.

'I no longer work where I used to work,' confirmed Johnathan.

'Really?' asked Kibby.

'Really,' said Johnathan.

'God.' Another pause. 'You actually did it. I'm impressed.'

'Well, don't be,' said Johnathan.

'Why not?'

'I got sacked.'

There was a pause.

'Really?'

'Really.'

'Oh Christ, Johnathan, I'm so sorry. When?'

'Monday.'

'Shit. How long have you got before you leave?'

'I've left. Yesterday was my last day.'

'*Shit*. What about your notice period?'

'It was decided to dispense with that small formality in the interests of expediency,' explained Johnathan.

'They can't do that,' exclaimed Kibby angrily.

'They already have,' said Johnathan.

There was another pause.

'Where are you now?' said Kibby. 'At home?'

'Yes.'

'Give me forty minutes,' she said. 'I'm on my way.'

That evening Kibby cooked roast chicken which they ate with a bottle of quite good white wine, and then she took Johnathan to bed. Later, as he watched her smoke her cigarette, he wondered why he had waited for a week

79

before telephoning her. Kibby stubbed out her cigarette, and farted loudly. With a delighted gasp she pulled up the duvet and plunged beneath it, giggling uncontrollably. A low groan came from where Johnathan supposed her head must be.

·'Oh wow, this you have *got* to experience for yourself,' came the muffled shout.

Johnathan balked. 'Tempting offer, but no thanks.'

Kibby's head reappeared. 'Are you chicken? If you're not prepared to smell my farts we're not going to get very far. I fart like a dyspeptic cow on a mung bean diet. Come on.' And with that she flung the duvet over Johnathan's head. Against his better instincts, Johnathan breathed in. The smell was truly awful. About three inches away from his nose he could just see Kibby's face which was cracked with a gleeful smile. Johnathan realized as he lay with his head under his duvet, sniffing someone else's fart, that something extraordinary was happening.

The next day they went to the National Gallery. As a boy Johnathan had been dragged round it by his parents on numerous occasions, and had not returned since. He obediently followed Kibby around the paintings, and listened to her explain about some of the famous ones. He tried to pay attention, but had difficulty keeping his mind off Kibby's breasts.

Afterwards they sat in a café on St Martin's Lane, and ordered red wine and large wodges of chocolate gateau from a waiter with a dirty apron and an unconvincing French accent.

'So,' said Kibby, twiddling her fork between her fingers. 'What now for the great Mr Burlip?'

Johnathan sighed. 'Find another job, I suppose.'

'No shit, Sherlock,' said Kibby. 'I mean, what sort of job?'

Johnathan contemplated his wine glass. 'I really don't know. Perhaps I should try something a bit different.'

'Different how?'

'Christ knows. Something that would shut Gavin up, maybe. Anything. Divorces, personal injury, selling houses, that sort of thing. More everyday stuff.' He paused. 'The fact is that at the moment I haven't decided, I suppose,' said Johnathan. 'I'm not ruling anything out just yet.'

'Quite right. You'll find something suitable, I'm sure,' said Kibby, leaning over and kissing him full on the mouth. The couple on the next table turned fractionally in towards themselves.

That evening they went to the cinema, and Kibby showed Johnathan her work.

As the first trailer ended, Johnathan whistled. 'You did that? Christ, it looks amazing. When is it out? I definitely think we should go and see that.'

'You seem to forget,' said Kibby prodding him gently in the ribs, 'that I have seen that film at least seven or eight times, and I would rather have my toe nails pulled out than sit through it again. Anyway, it's rubbish.'

'But it looks *brilliant*,' protested Johnathan.

Kibby looked smug. 'Of course it does,' she whispered. 'That's what I get paid for. The cinematic alchemist. I take piles of crap and turn it into heaps of incandescent gold.' She rolled her eyes.

Johnathan smiled at Kibby in the flickering semi-darkness. She reached for his hand, gave it a squeeze, and settled down to watch the film. Something went ping deep inside Johnathan. He blinked. He wasn't quite sure what was going on, but he had a vague suspicion that he might be falling in love.

Monday morning came and went like any other. Johnathan eventually got out of bed at half past two in the afternoon. As he looked out of his kitchen window he saw the usual stationary lines of traffic in the street outside, shimmering in the haze of exhaust fumes. The rest of the world, he saw, was going to carry on without him. There would be no period of mourning for anyone except him.

Johnathan had a plan. He knew what he had to do. After some thought, he had decided to put his aspirations of politically correct employment to one side for the immediate future. Being sacked had rather spoiled all that. These things were much easier when you worked to your own timetable. The most important thing right now was to get a job, any job. Virtue is all very well, but it helps if you can afford it. At that particular moment, Johnathan could not. Much as he wanted to impress Kibby, he also wanted to be able to eat.

Johnathan dressed quickly and, bidding Schroedinger goodbye, strode purposefully towards the tube station, where he did not get on a train but instead bought copies of *The Times*, the *Telegraph*, the *Independent*, and, after some debate, the *Guardian*.

Two hours later he returned to buy *Investors' Chronicle*, *The Economist*, *Newsweek*, and *Private Eye*.

Two hours after that he bought the *Evening Standard* and the *Sun*.

He telephoned Kibby.

'Nothing,' he said.

'Nothing?'

'Nothing.'

'Now what?'

'Now I start to do some serious letter writing.'

Dear Mr Bowles

I am a solicitor with several years of high quality training
and company law experience, and as such I believe that I
represent a major asset to any law firm. I have pleasure in
enclosing herewith my curriculum vitae for your perusal, in
which you will find a more detailed résumé of some of the
work I have undertaken to date. I am presently looking for
new opportunities to expand my professional horizons and to
seek new and exciting challenges which the practice of law
offers. I feel that your firm represents one of the most dynamic
and proactive practices currently operating in the London area,
and in view of this feel that there are many exciting synergies
whose potential, if realized, could be mutually beneficial to
both of us.

I look forward to hearing from you shortly with a view to
arranging an interview to discuss matters further.

Yours sincerely

Johnathan Burlip

Dear Mr Burlip

*I was somewhat surprised to receive your letter dated last Tuesday,
for which many thanks. Your curriculum vitae was beautifully typed.*

Wishing you every success for the future.

Yours etc.

Eric Bowles

Dear Mr Croft

I am a solicitor with several years of high quality training and
company law experience, and as such I believe that I represent

a major asset to any law firm. I have pleasure in enclosing my curriculum vitae for your perusal, in which you will find a more detailed résumé of some of the work I have undertaken to date. I am presently looking for new opportunities to expand my professional horizons and to seek new and exciting challenges which the practice of law offers. I feel that your firm represents one of the most dynamic and proactive practices currently operating in the London area, and in view of this feel that there are many exciting synergies whose potential, if realized, could be mutually beneficial to both of us.

I look forward to hearing from you shortly with a view to arranging an interview where we can discuss these matters further.

Yours sincerely
Johnathan Burlip

Dear Mr Burlip

Thank you for your letter enquiring after the possibility of employment with Croft & Co. Unfortunately I regret to have to inform you that my husband has been very ill of late and, being a sole practitioner, the firm ceased operating when he first went into hospital for his hernia operation.

Yours sincerely
Alice Croft (Mrs)

Dear Mr Keighley

I am a solicitor with several years of high quality training and company law experience, and as such I believe that I represent a major asset to any law firm. I have pleasure in enclosing herewith my curriculum vitae for your perusal, in which you will find a more detailed résumé of some of the work I have undertaken to date. I am presently looking for new opportunities to expand my professional horizons and to seek new and exciting challenges which the practice of law offers. I feel that your firm represents one of the most dynamic and proactive practices currently operating in the Nottingham area, and in view of this feel that there are many exciting synergies whose potential, if realized, could be mutually beneficial to both of us.

I look forward to hearing from you shortly with a view to arranging an interview to discuss these matters further.

Yours sincerely

Johnathan Burlip

Dear Mr Burlip

It was with frustration and no little despair that I read your recent letter to me. Whilst being, I suspect, a masterpiece of oblique circumlocution, it was, I felt, all too indicative of the saddening trend amongst the members of our profession nowadays to indulge in superfluous verbosity, to over-egg the syntactical omelette, to use ten words when two will suffice. At Keighley Mendip Morris we actively participate in 'Good English' schemes whereby our practitioners are actively encouraged to utilize clearer, less ambiguous and more easily understandable language, with particular emphasis placed on avoiding the use of old-fashioned, archaic forms such as your unfortunate 'herewith', and on avoiding tautological phrases where the same thing is said more than once. By way of example, might I take this opportunity to point out that the expression 'mutually beneficial to both of us' is tautological? The last four words are otiose and contribute nothing to the sense of the phrase.

Yours sincerely

Nigel Keighley

Dear Mr Scott

I am a solicitor with several years of high quality company law experience. I enclose my curriculum vitae. I am looking for new opportunities to expand my professional horizons. I feel that your firm is one of the most dynamic practices in the Chepstow area, and feel that there are many synergies whose potential could be mutually beneficial.

I look forward to hearing from you.

Yours sincerely

Johnathan Burlip

Dear Jonathon,

Thanks for your letter, which I enjoyed a lot.

Best wishes

Tom Scott

Dear Mr Ashworth

I am a solicitor with several years of high quality company law experience. I enclose my curriculum vitae. I am looking for new opportunities to expand my professional horizons. I feel that your firm is one of the most dynamic practices in the Skegness area. I would like a job.

Yours sincerely

Johnathan Burlip

Dear Mr Burlip

Thank you for your letter. Unfortunately Skegness is not exactly renowned for the quality of company law work available there. I tend to work in the less glamorous world of wills, residential conveyancing and disputes between neighbours about boundary fences, and the like.

*It is with some regret, therefore, that I must inform you that at
present there is no vacancy at my firm for someone like you. However
in the event that in the forthcoming years Skegness becomes the home
of a number of significant multi-national conglomerates, I will keep
your letter on file and contact you then.*

  Yours sincerely
  Jeremy Ashworth

Letters began to arrive from Johnathan's bank, enquiring
why his monthly pay cheque, the sole entry on an otherwise
barren 'deposits' column on his statements, had not arrived
that month. After some thought Johnathan decided that the
most responsible way to deal with these letters was to ignore
them, and he stopped opening them. This technique seemed
to work in the short term, and so he tried it with the letters
from the telephone and electricity companies too. He threw
unopened envelopes of increasingly angry hues – red, purple,
and ultimately black – into the bin.

That this approach might have been misconceived first
occurred to him one evening when he tried to switch the
kitchen light on and discovered that there was no electricity
in the flat. With the indignant self-righteousness of one who
knows, but is unwilling to admit, that he is to blame, he
immediately lifted the telephone receiver to dial the number
of the electricity company, only to find it ominously silent.
His last lines of communication with the outside world had
been severed.

Johnathan went to Kibby's flat where he used her telephone to persuade the utility companies to reconnect him.
Reluctantly he paid the outstanding bills, conscious of his
ever-increasing overdraft.

Each day Johnathan scanned the classified ads in every

publication he could think of in the hope of finding work. In his desperation, he had even started reading the *Law Society Gazette*. One morning he noticed a small announcement at the bottom of one of the pages of classified advertisements.

WANTED. Dynamic young solicitor who enjoys a challenge to participate in the workload and management of highly motivated and exciting city legal practice. Wide variety of work undertaken. Fluent Greek helpful, but not essential.

Johnathan reached for his pen and ringed the announcement. Presumably the Greek was because they did a lot of work for shipping magnates. Johnathan allowed himself briefly to picture himself flying first class to Athens to negotiate multi-million pound shipping deals on board luxury cruisers harboured on the glimmering waters of the Aegean. That he had never done shipping law and his knowledge of Greek was limited to the word 'mousaka', did not deter him. He had long ago stopped applying any sorts of meaningful criteria in his search for a job. There was a telephone number at the bottom of the announcement. Johnathan reached for the telephone and dialled.

The phone rang for about half a minute. Just as Johnathan was about to hang up, there was a rattle as the receiver was unhooked.

'Hello, yes,' said a breathless female voice. 'Er, sorry, Kyriakedes and Podymotopolos. How can I help you?'

Johnathan paused, staring straight ahead.

'Hello?' said the voice. 'Is there anyone there?'

Johnathan woke from his reverie. 'Yes, good morning,' he began. 'I'm calling in relation to —'

'Sorry, caller,' said the voice. 'Please hold.'

There was an abrupt click and the earpiece blossomed with the sound of 'Eleanor Rigby' played by the Tijuana Jazz ensemble. Eventually there was another click and the voice said, 'Thank you, caller. Who was it you wanted to speak to?' The voice did not sound very interested.

'Ah, well,' said Johnathan. 'I'm calling in relation to the advertisement —'

There was a piercing scream down the telephone. 'Where's Eddie?' cried the voice.

There was a thunk as the phone was dropped. Johnathan could hear an urgent discussion taking place at the other end of the line.

'But he was there a minute ago.'

'I don't bloody care where he was a minute ago. I want to know where he is now,' said a gruff male voice.

'He must have escaped.'

'I can see that. The question is where did he escape to?'

'I don't know,' whined the first voice.

'Tremendous. Brilliant. Our prize piece of evidence and you let him just wander off for a quick jaunt around the office.'

There was a pause. The first voice asked, 'He's not *poisonous*, is he?'

'Luckily for you, no.'

Johnathan had begun to listen with interest. The first voice remembered he was there. 'Some bloke on the telephone,' it said.

'What does he want?'

'Dunno.'

'Well *ask* him, then,' said the second voice. 'And then start looking for Eddie.'

'Right. Hello, caller,' breezed the voice. 'How may I help you?'

Johnathan started. 'Er, sorry, yes,' he stammered. 'I'm telephoning in relation to the advertisement placed in the *Law Society Gazette* last week.'

There was a pause.

'Advertisement?' said the voice. 'Hang on.'

There was a click. Trombones shimmied their way through 'Ob-la-di, Ob-la-da' behind the insistent cha-cha-cha of an incongruous bossa nova rhythm section. There was another click.

'Right, caller,' said the voice. 'Are you available this afternoon for an interview?'

Johnathan stood rooted to the spot. 'Don't you want to see my details first?'

'No, that won't be necessary. Just turn up,' said the voice. It gave an address in North London. 'Nearest station is Finsbury Park,' said the voice. 'We'll expect you for three.' The line went dead.

'Right, thank you,' said Johnathan into the buzzing phone. He looked at his watch. Four hours to clean his shoes.

EIGHT

Johnathan emerged from the cool, curving tunnel which delivered passengers from the depths of Finsbury Park station, into the bright afternoon sunlight, right on time for his interview. Across the concrete forecourt, lines of bored people waited for a bus. A rotting smell wafted from a nearby waste-bin, which was overflowing with crushed beer cans. It was surrounded by small fortifications of lollipop wrappers and angrily crumpled lottery tickets. A squadron of wasps was inspecting its contents.

Johnathan passed a pub outside which people lay sprawled over wooden tables and benches, roasting themselves in the sun like lizards, nursing their pints lethargically. Further along, he passed a dingy grocer's shop. Vaguely erotic vegetables of dubious genealogy sprouted obscenely from battered cardboard boxes.

An endless tide of fag ends and empty crisp packets swept down the hill towards the station. Johnathan turned off the main road. After some minutes, he reached the address he had been given. It was a halal butcher.

He stuck his head around the door.

'Hello,' he said politely. 'Kyriakedes and Podymotopolos?'

'Who?' said a youth who was wielding a massive meat cleaver in a menacing way behind the counter.

'Er, solicitors? Law firm?' tried Johnathan.

'Oh, yeah,' said the youth. 'Greek ponces. Down the side.' He waved the cleaver to show the way.

'Right. Thanks,' said Johnathan, beating a hasty retreat. He scooted down the side of the butcher's shop and found a dark blue door. Next to it was a doorbell and a tarnished brass plaque with the word 'Solicitor' on it.

Johnathan pressed the bell. Nothing happened.

After a pause, he tried again. Still nothing happened. Johnathan pushed the door. It swung creakily back to reveal some narrow stairs. Nobody was in sight. Glancing surreptitiously back into the street, Johnathan walked in and shut the door behind him. He adjusted his tie.

Resting on the bottom step of the stairs was a handwritten cardboard sign wrapped in polythene: 'Kyriakedes and Podymotópolos, Solicitors. Ascend the stairs to the First Floor.' Johnathan climbed the stairs.

The carpet in the reception area of Kyriakedes and Podymotopolos was an assault of swirling oranges and browns. There were several armchairs, each a cat's cradle of chrome tubing into which had been inserted two large square cushions covered in light grey plastic and punctuated by a shiny button the size of a tennis ball. Next to each armchair stood hemispherical chrome ash-trays, which looked like discarded props from early episodes of *Star Trek*. On the low table in the middle of the room sat a pile of dog-eared magazines. To the right of the table hovered a large woman's bottom, over which was stretched an acre or two of scarlet and gold lycra. The woman to whom the bottom belonged was looking underneath one of the armchairs.

'Bollocks,' said the woman without moving.

Johnathan coughed politely.

The woman pulled her head out from beneath the chair and looked over her shoulder at Johnathan. She inspected him calmly as she chewed some gum.

'Hello,' said Johnathan.

'Hello,' replied the woman.

There was a pause.

'Have you lost something?' asked Johnathan.

'I haven't, no,' said the woman, straightening up. 'My . . . *colleague* has lost an important exhibit, which I am trying to find.'

'What is it?' asked Johnathan.

'Eddie. He's a spider. A tarantula, actually. Horrible thing, although apparently he's harmless. De-fanged. Bloody hope so.'

Johnathan looked around him in alarm.

'You didn't see him on your way up, did you?' asked the woman, masticating remorselessly like a pensive cow. 'It's just that he's been missing for a few hours now.'

'I didn't, no,' said Johnathan. There was a pause. 'What sort of case is Eddie involved in?' asked Johnathan.

'Divorce,' said the woman, walking back towards the desk at the far end of the room. 'Mental cruelty. The husband bought him to scare his wife, who is terrified of spiders. Agoraphobia, they call it. He had a lot of fun with Eddie, as you can imagine.'

'Amazing what people will do,' said Johnathan blandly.

The woman sat down primly behind the desk. 'Disgusting.' She looked up at Johnathan. 'What can I do for you?'

'I'm here for an interview. For a job,' Johnathan said.

'Right,' said the woman. 'Hold on.' She picked up the telephone, hit a button and put the receiver to her ear. They both waited. Trapping the phone between shoulder

93

and neck, the woman put up her right hand and examined her nails critically.

Finally there was an audible click and Johnathan heard a voice answer.

'Bloke here for you. Says he's got an interview.'

There was a brief pause as the voice on the other end spoke.

'Hang on.' The woman covered the receiver with her hand. 'When did you call?' she asked.

'This morning, ' said Johnathan. 'I don't think I spoke to you.'

'You won't of,' said the woman. 'I'm afternoons only. This morning,' she said into the telephone, sniffing. She listened some more to the voice at the other end of the line.

'All right,' she said, and put the phone down with such ferocity that it rattled slightly in its cradle. 'You're in luck,' she said to Johnathan. 'He'll see you now.'

The receptionist led Johnathan up another set of stairs. They stopped outside a large door. 'Here we are,' she said, and opened the door.

They both peered into the room. Everything was obscured by a billowing wall of smoke. Johnathan blinked as his eyes started to prickle. The receptionist vanished without another word.

'Greetings, my friend. Efthymios Kyriakedes.' There was a scraping of furniture and Johnathan heard the clump of heavy footsteps. Gradually, from out of the surrounding mists, the silhouetted figure of Efthymios Kyriakedes emerged, wheezing slightly, with a stubby cigarette clutched firmly between the podgy fingers of his right hand.

'Er, hello,' said Johnathan.

'You're here about the ad?'

'Yes. I rang earlier.'

'I see.' Efthymios Kyriakedes stood with his hands on his hips and looked Johnathan up and down appraisingly. Mainly up. (Efthymios Kyriakedes was very short.)

'Well, it's good to meet you,' he said. 'Come and sit down. Let's see if we can get to know each other a little better, shall we?' He smiled widely and disappeared into the opaque wall of smoke, waddling slightly as he went. (Efthymios Kyriakedes was very fat.)

Johnathan advanced uncertainly. A cheap-looking desk covered with mountains of bulging files materialized ahead of him. In front of the desk was a chair.

'Take a seat,' came a voice from somewhere in front of him. Johnathan sat down. The chair was ludicrously uncomfortable. There was a brief pause, during which the smoke began to clear. After a while Johnathan could make out the shape of his interviewer on the other side of the desk, and little by little, he was able to see him relatively clearly. After a brief inspection Johnathan wished the smoke would come back. (Efthymios Kyriakedes was very ugly.)

He had very black, very greasy hair which badly needed a cut. Beneath his swarthy and bejowled face hung an indeterminate number of chins which quivered when he spoke. The flagging bristles of a tired moustache were clustered together unevenly on his upper lip. His eyes, sunk deep into fatty recesses, shone with a crafty intelligence. He wore a striped shirt, sleeves rolled up to just below his elbows and top button undone. His tie hung limply around his neck, its over-sized knot resting a few inches below where it should have been. Johnathan noticed that the shirt's buttons were

95

straining under the pressure of trying to rein in and contain the Greek's enormous gut.

Efthymios Kyriakedes settled comfortably back in his chair and looked at Johnathan keenly. 'So you want a job?' he said.

Johnathan nodded.

'Where were you working before?'

Johnathan mentioned the name of his firm.

Kyriakedes whistled. 'Oh, right,' he said. 'Very big swinging dicks, aren't they?'

'I suppose so,' said Johnathan, suddenly missing his erstwhile colleagues greatly.

'So why'd you leave?' asked the Greek. 'Didn't your dick swing big enough?' He began to chortle in an unattractive way.

'Differences of opinion,' said Johnathan, who had been waiting for this question. 'I felt that my career wasn't progressing as I had hoped, and I felt that a change of scenery was needed, a new challenge to reawaken my –'

'Hold on,' said Efthymios Kyriakedes. 'Pardon me for interrupting. What sort of work do you think we do here?'

Johnathan gestured expansively. 'I firmly believe, Mr, er,' he said earnestly, 'that as a solicitor with several years of high quality training and company law experience, I represent a major asset to any law firm. I'm presently looking for new opportunities to expand my professional horizons and to seek new and exciting challenges which the practice of law offers. I feel that your firm represents one of the most dynamic and proactive practices currently operating in the, um, North London area, and in view of this I feel that there are many exciting synergies whose potential, if realized, could be mutually beneficial.' He paused. 'To both of us.'

The man on the other side of the desk looked confused. 'I'll give you one thing,' he said. 'You can't be that bad a lawyer because you managed to spew all that stuff and look as if you mean it, and what's more, you totally failed to answer the question.'

Johnathan looked pleased.

'The thing is,' he continued, 'there's not a great call for your sort of stuff in Finsbury Park. It's all a bit more down to earth.'

'No shipping law?' asked Johnathan, his hopes of completing million dollar deals on the decks of huge yachts dissolving.

Kyriakedes snorted. 'Nah. The last time I encountered a boat in this job it was a plastic toy one and was the alleged weapon with which my client was alleged to have clobbered his girlfriend, who had just started to sleep with one of his mates. So she had it coming to her anyway. A clear case of provocation. He was totally innocent, of course. Never laid a finger on her.' He paused. 'Anyway, it wasn't a big boat.' He absent-mindedly lit a cigarette.

'Where was I?' he said after a few moments.

'The sort of law you do,' said Johnathan helpfully.

'Oh yeah. Anyway, we handle everyday issues for everyday people. It's like this. At some point in all of our lives a certain amount of shit is thrown our way. What we do here is either help our clients to avoid the shit that has been thrown at them, or at least get them as far out of the way as possible. Comprende?'

'Oh, absolutely,' nodded Johnathan.

'So we do lots of divorce, that sort of stuff. Sell a few houses, write snotty letters to the Council when people don't pay their Poll Tax, do some wills. And of course we do criminal stuff. That is, we act for people who do criminal stuff.

Allegedly. A lot of what we do is dependent upon human beings' basic inability to coexist peacefully with one another. Voices are raised, tempers fray, a bottle gets smashed – and bingo: more sponduliks for us as we've got to get the buggers off.' He paused. 'Or not. It doesn't really matter whether they win or not as we get paid anyway. Which is just as well, I suppose.' He smiled smugly at Johnathan. 'The joys of the welfare state are manifold and great, my friend. Free access to justice for all. Wonderful idea. Especially for lawyers. Have you ever done any Legal Aid work?'

'Not really, no,' conceded Johnathan.

Efthymios Kyriakedes leaned forward. His chair groaned beneath him. 'It's brilliant,' he said. 'This is how it works. I get paid for every letter I write, no matter how long, short or useless it is. Same for everyone. So we all spend all day writing totally useless letters. Rather than send three documents in one envelope, you send three separate letters with one document each, and triple your money. And then the chap who gets them sends three letters back to you acknowledging receipt of each of the letters, and then you send three letters back acknowledging receipt of the letters acknowledging receipt . . . it's easy.'

'Doesn't it all take rather a long time to get anything done?' asked Johnathan.

'It does. Bloody ages. The longer the better.'

'What about your clients?' asked Johnathan.

Kyriakedes looked baffled. 'What about them?'

'Well don't they mind about the delay?'

'Listen, mate,' said Kyriakedes. 'It's not as if they're actually *paying* for any of it. They should be grateful. Why should they be the only ones to benefit from the Government's generosity? We've all got livings to earn.' He paused.

'Of course, if they're in prison they can't complain much anyway.'

'I suppose not,' said Johnathan.

Efthymios Kyriakedes looked across his desk at Johnathan thoughtfully. 'So do you still want a job here?'

'Well,' said Johnathan, 'it's different.'

Kyriakedes opened his hands towards Johnathan. 'We like it. We're one happy little family here, dispensing justice to the good folk of Finsbury Park and surrounding postal districts. We like to think we make a difference.'

There was a pause.

'Listen, hombre,' said the Greek, 'you're not exactly what I was looking for, but I am a bit desperate at the moment. Nobody else seems to have seen the advert. If you want the job, it's yours.'

Johnathan beamed. 'Thanks.'

'Subject to a three month trial period.'

'Oh,' said Johnathan. 'All right.'

'Now,' said Efthymios Kyriakedes, 'what are we going to pay you?'

Johnathan shrugged affably. He was already thinking about breaking the good news to Kibby.

Kyriakedes named a figure. It was so low Johnathan was not sure whether this was a monthly or annual sum. 'Per year?' he asked.

Kyriakedes chuckled. 'No, per month, actually. Yes, per year.'

'I was hoping for a little more,' said Johnathan meekly.

'Yeah, don't we all. Take it or leave it. I'll review it at the end of your probationary period and we'll see what we can do. But the recession is hitting us hard, too. People are committing less crime. People have got less things worth stealing.'

Johnathan considered his options.

'All right,' he said.

'Good.' Efthymios Kyriakedes rose from his chair and stretched out his ring-encrusted right hand. 'Can you start on Monday?'

'Yes,' said Johnathan.

'See you then, then. Can you see yourself out?'

'Right,' said Johnathan, and turned towards the door.

'Oh by the way,' called Johnathan's new boss as he was stepping into the corridor.

Johnathan turned back into the room.

'What's your name?' asked Efthymios Kyriakedes.

NINE

The rest of Johnathan's day was hectic. He went to the supermarket to buy some champagne to celebrate his new job, and spent the rest of the day on the telephone. His bank manager, the faceless voice of dour reason and the slasher of exotic schemes, almost sounded glad to hear his news, until Johnathan told him how much he would be earning.

'Is that per month or per year?' he had asked.

He called Kibby and asked her to come to his flat after work. When she arrived they celebrated by drinking the champagne too quickly. Kibby was genuinely delighted – not least, Johnathan reflected the following morning in the aching clarity engendered by an award-winning hangover, because he would soon be able to afford to pay his own way again.

Jake was delighted at Johnathan's career move, too, probably because he sensed that close links with a criminal lawyer might prove useful in getting an occasional exclusive story. A few nights later Johnathan and Jake sat in Jake's kitchen and got roaringly drunk on Malibu and milk. Johnathan drunkenly tried to explain the principle of client-solicitor confidentiality which would make it unethical for him to tip Jake off whenever a good story popped up. As soon as Jake heard the word 'unethical', however, he began giggling uncontrollably.

The following Sunday evening, Kibby arrived at Johnathan's flat clutching a large good luck card and a bright orange pencil case with Donald Duck laminated on its front. It was full of brand new pencils. Johnathan couldn't remember the last time he had seen a pencil, let alone used one.

After two glasses of wine Kibby briskly rose from Johnathan's sofa, startling Schroedinger with the rapidity of her movement. She bent down to ruffle his head. Immediately Schroedinger rolled over on to his back to display his genitals. 'Not tonight, sunshine,' said Kibby cheerfully. Johnathan stood up.

'Please stay,' he said.

Kibby looked at him, mock serious. 'Best not,' she said. 'You must preserve your vital juices. You need to be bouncing around the office tomorrow like a randy goat, not stumbling around like a shagged-out rhinoceros. I'll call you tomorrow evening. Good luck.' She kissed him firmly on the mouth, in a tender, don't-even-think-about-getting-your-tongue-out kind of way. Johnathan responded half-heartedly.

'Um,' he said miserably.

'Bye. Good luck!' With a wave Kibby hoiked her rucksack on to her shoulders and was gone.

Johnathan began to iron his shirts for the week. He tried not to feel irked at the apparent ease with which Kibby seemed able to spend significant periods of time out of his company. He failed.

The problem was simple. Johnathan wanted to spend every moment of every day with Kibby. Kibby, however, did not want to spend every moment of every day with Johnathan. At least she gave no indication that she did. The truth was that Johnathan actually had very little idea how Kibby felt about him, whereas he was by now pretty sure that he had fallen in love with her. Which was awkward, really.

One of Johnathan's difficulties was that he was quite incapable of telling Kibby how he felt. He had already tried several times, only to discover himself rambling inconsequentially about the first thing to come into his head, while Kibby listened politely with a bemused look in her eye.

His inability to confess everything to Kibby had made him dissatisfied with the way things were. Johnathan fancied that what was required was ardent declarations of undying love, a lot more sex than was presently on the agenda, and then a quiet wedding in a pretty country church. The problem lay with the first bit, the ardent declarations of undying love. After that, the sex and marriage stuff would be easy.

The ironing finished, Johnathan sat on the sofa next to Schroedinger and stared at the television until it was time to go to bed. He had always hated Sunday evenings.

Johnathan awoke early the following morning moments before his alarm clock erupted in his ear. He had slept a deep but troubled sleep. He knew that he had dreamed vividly but was unable to remember what he had dreamed of. Reluctantly relinquishing the comfort of his duvet, he staggered to the kitchen to switch on the coffee machine.

Bidding Schroedinger goodbye with a wave more positive than he really felt, Johnathan set off towards the tube station, his new pencil case sticking out of his pocket, incongruously bright against the dull grey of his suit.

Entering the reception area of Kyriakedes and Podymotopolos an hour later, he saw there was a different receptionist. She seemed a better bet than the dour, fingernail-inspecting afternoon version. A bobbing mass of peroxided ringlets cascaded in a chaotic way around a pretty face which had been heavily slathered with lipstick and more blue eye shadow than a chorus line of dancing girls. Beneath her tight-fitting orange top, Johnathan could see two very large breasts.

'Good morning,' said the girl.

'Hello,' said Johnathan. 'My name is Johnathan Burlip. I'm starting work with you today.'

The girl looked surprised. 'With me?' she said.

'Well, with all of you,' explained Johnathan. 'With the firm.'

'Oh, I see,' said the girl brightly. 'What's your name?'

'Johnathan. What's yours?'

'Sonya. With a "y". Not with an "i". That's the afternoon girl.' Sonya with a y wrinkled her nose in distaste.

'With a "y". OK,' said Johnathan, grinning stupidly.

'So,' said Sonya leaning forwards on the desk in front of her and resting her chin in her upturned hands. She contemplated him mistily. 'Are you a lawyer, then?'

'Well, yes, I suppose so,' said Johnathan.

'Any good?'

'Sorry?'

'Are you any good at being a lawyer?' she asked patiently.

'Oh crumbs, I don't know. Not bad I suppose,' gushed Johnathan. 'I suppose we'll find out soon enough.'

'You *look* like a good lawyer,' said Sonya kindly.

'Thank you,' said Johnathan.

'Now,' she said, suddenly business-like. 'Who would you like to see?'

'Mr Kyriakedes, I suppose.'

'Mr Kyriakedes won't be in until about eleven. He's usually a bit of a late starter.'

'Oh,' said Johnathan.

'Actually,' said Sonya, 'the only person here at the moment is Clark. Shall I call him? He's nice. He'll show you round.'

'Please,' said Johnathan.

Still smiling at him, Sonya picked up the telephone and dialled. She spoke quietly into the receiver, nodded, and put it down carefully. 'Clark'll be with you in a minute,' she said.

There was a pause. Johnathan hovered in front of the desk. He tried to think of something to say.

'Have you worked here long?' he said eventually.

'Oh no,' replied Sonya. 'About a month now.'

'Do you enjoy it?'

'Oh, you know.'

'Fun people?' he tried.

Sonya snorted, amused. 'Oh, you *know*.'

The door opened and an old man dressed in slightly tatty corduroy trousers and an open-necked shirt walked in. As he saw Johnathan he extended a wrinkled, liver-spotted hand.

'This is Clark,' stage-whispered Sonya.

'Hello, Mr Burlip,' said Clark across the reception room as he approached. 'My name is Clark Kent.' He announced this totally without irony.

'Hello Clark,' said Johnathan, shaking his clammy hand. 'Nice to meet you.'

'I'll show you around. Thanks Sonya. See you later.' Clark winked at Sonya. He guided Johnathan through the door. As it shut behind them Clark said simply, 'Fantastic tits.'

Johnathan nodded, surprised. 'Not bad,' he confessed.

'Makes my day, I can tell you,' said Clark as he walked down the corridor. 'Shit, if only I'd been thirty years younger. But a good look's better than nothing at all. She isn't exactly Brain of Britain, though,' he added as an afterthought. 'But Mr Kyriakedes is a liberal-minded employer. He's prepared to overlook certain deficiencies in the job requirements if other areas are amply filled. And I do mean amply.' Clark chortled. He stopped in front of a door badly in need of a new coat of paint. 'First things first. This is where *I* work,' he said proudly, and pushed the door open. Johnathan peered in. It was a small, windowless room. Every inch of wall was covered by unsteady-looking wooden shelving, on which were stacked piles of dusty files. Most of the floor was covered in files as well, save for a space in the middle of the room which was occupied by a small table. The table was also covered in files.

'What exactly is it you do, Clark?' asked Johnathan.

'This and that. I'm responsible for looking after old files and making sure they're stored properly once cases are over. But also I do anything else that needs doing. Mending plugs, changing light bulbs, that sort of thing.' He stood for a few moments with his hands on his hips, looking into his dusty domain.

They continued through the deserted office. In contrast to the glossily high-tech atmosphere of Johnathan's former firm, where lawyers worked on a raised floor above a spaghetti-like mass of electronic wires and cables, the premises of Kyriakedes and Podymotopolos were rather old-fashioned. They occupied the first and second floors of the building. The entire place was in need of a coat of paint and was permeated by the dank smell of old paper.

Finally they arrived at a small room which was totally bare. There were not even any files on the floor. Nor was there a light bulb, a desk, or a chair.

'And this,' said Clark, 'is your room.'

Johnathan looked in. 'Very nice,' he said uncertainly.

'Your furniture should be arriving later today,' said Clark. 'It only got ordered on Friday because everyone thought that everyone else was doing it. And frankly if it arrives before the end of the week, it'll be a miracle. We buy our office furniture from Mr Kyriakedes's little brother. He should of been a lawyer too, the amount his promises are worth.' Clark chuckled. Johnathan's spirits dipped a little lower.

At the back of the building on the second floor was a small and dirty-looking kitchen with a tiny, humming fridge. On top of the fridge sat five open cartons of milk. A kettle with a frayed electric flex sat next to the sink. Clark turned to face Johnathan.

'Well,' he said. 'That's about it.'

'What about Mr Podymotopolos?' asked Johnathan. 'Where does he work?'

'Mr Podymotopolos runs a small taverna on Mikonos.'

'Gave up the law, did he?'

'Naw,' said Clark. 'He was never *in* the law. He's Mr Kyriakedes's cousin.'

Johnathan was confused. 'So why . . . ?' he gestured vaguely around him.

'Mr Kyriakedes thought it would sound better with two Greek names rather than one. More impressive.'

'Great,' said Johnathan limply.

'Well,' said Clark, 'I'd better leave you to it. I'll take you back to your room. The boss is usually in by eleven or so and I guess he'll be able to give you some work, or something.' He led Johnathan back to his office.

Johnathan wandered over to the window of the empty room and looked out. About twenty yards away was a decaying brick wall which blocked off almost all natural light. In the alleyway below sat a line of battered iron dustbins, with their lids dislodged. A mangy cat padded lazily around them, scavenging for scraps. Johnathan tried not to feel despondent. He failed.

About an hour later Efthymios Kyriakedes disturbed Johnathan's reverie. Without knocking he pushed open the door and stuck his head around it with a wide grin on his face. 'All right,' he said. He came in with his arm outstretched. 'Welcome, er,' he said. 'Glad to see you here. Didn't change your mind, then?'

Johnathan laughed dutifully, heartily wishing that he had.

'I gather Clark has shown you around,' said Kyriakedes. Johnathan nodded. 'What do you think?'

'Oh, well, very nice,' said Johnathan.

'It's not much,' said Kyriakedes, 'but it's home.'

'I understand my furniture will be here later today,' said Johnathan.

'Should be, if my little brother gets his act together. Which, between you and me, is highly unlikely.' Kyriakedes found this very amusing. Johnathan's heart sank.

'When do you want me to start?' he asked.

'Right away, old son, right away,' said his new boss, punching him playfully on the arm. 'There's a whole pile of cases waiting for you in my room. You'll just have to make do without a desk for the moment, but I'm sure you'll manage.'

Johnathan shrugged, defeated.

Kyriakedes leant forward conspiratorially. 'Listen. Did you see the receptionist?' he asked.

'Sonya? Yes, I met her when I came in.'

'Have you ever seen a pair of tits like that before?' asked

the Greek. 'Smashing. Thick as shit, but what the hell. Just don't ask her to do anything more taxing than licking a stamp on to an envelope.'

'OK,' said Johnathan.

'Mind you, she brings a little sunshine into the lives of all those sad old farts who come in. Puts a bit of a strain on their pace-makers I should imagine.' He laughed leerily. 'Listen. Bloke has three girlfriends, right? And he decides he wants to get married. But he can't choose which of his girlfriends he wants to marry. With me so far?'

'With you so far,' said Johnathan.

'Good. So anyway he gives them each £5,000 and tells them to go away and spend it on whatever they like. The first one comes back and she's spent it all on new clothes, beauty treatment, new hair, the lot. She looks fantastic. And she says, "I spent the money like that because I love you and I knew this would make you happy." The second girl goes out and buys a new set of golf clubs, and the best stereo she can get, and gives them to him. "I spent the money like that because I knew you would like those things and I love you and all I want to do is to make you happy." So. The last girl goes and invests the money on the Stock Exchange. She does really well and doubles her money in a month. And she hands the original £5,000 back to the guy and keeps the other £5,000 in a high-interest account at the bank, saying "I'm putting it aside for our wonderful future together because I love you so much." OK. So.

'Here's this guy with these three amazing women. He thinks long and hard about how they have all spent the money, and decides to marry the one with the biggest tits.

Think about it. Come on.' He slapped Johnathan on the back and set off up the corridor.

'OK,' said Johnathan lamely, and followed him out of the door.

TEN

Rosa Gloria Dei (popular name, 'peace' rose) is a vigorous, bush rose. It has scented, fully double flowers (pale yellow with a pinkish tinge), which are approximately 15 cm in diameter, borne freely in clusters throughout the summer months. It grows to an average of 1.2 metres, and prefers sunny environments, close to walls. It prospers best on well-drained soil. Also it hurts like hell when shoved up your jacksie.

Johnathan sighed and pushed the buff coloured file away from him. He shut his eyes and massaged his temples. His first case at Kyriakedes and Podymotopolos had not begun auspiciously. Menendes v. Menendes would have been a nightmare even if he had known what he was doing. In his present situation, not so much wet behind the ears as submerged and going down for the third time, it was far, far worse. Efthymios Kyriakedes had winked at him as he handed him the file. 'This'll be a good one to start you off,' he had said. 'Cracking stuff. Got a bit of everything.'

And a bit of everything it had. Divorce, Grievous Bodily Harm, Theft, and a few more spicy bits for good measure, all slung into the legal boiling pot and allowed to cook over an unnecessarily inflammatory heat. As a result,

Johnathan's cup, to mix culinary metaphors, ranneth over, and had spilled.

His client was a Spanish lady called Dolores Menendes. She had initially approached Kyriakedes and Podymotopolos for legal advice about her divorce. She had discovered that her improbably moustachioed husband, Oscar, had been having an affair with one of the wide-eyed waitresses who worked at their tapas bar in Walthamstow. The illicit romance had blossomed among the chorizo sausages, until one evening Mrs Menendes had walked into the kitchen, inadvertently disturbing the lovers' evening tryst amidst steaming bowls of paella. Without saying a word she delivered a well-aimed spit at the nearest bowl and stormed out of the restaurant.

The next day Dolores returned to the tapas bar, and carried on as if nothing had happened. Throughout the day Oscar's moustache quivered in apprehension, worried that she was going to use her much-celebrated skill with a filleting knife to separate his *cojones* from the rest of his body.

In fact, Dolores had something else in mind. She spent much of the day winking in a rather pornographic way at her husband and occasionally whispering in his ear what she intended to do to him when they got home, obscenities of such verve and imagination that Oscar was unable to concentrate on his cooking.

That night Oscar drove home with barely suppressed excitement. Dolores stripped him naked and then tied his hands to the bed-posts of their conjugal bed. At this point (it is alleged) Oscar began to bellow triumphantly, whooping with anticipation. The fact that he had been tied to the bed face down did not at the time strike him as significant. He allowed his wife to tie his feet to the bed as well. This was, in retrospect, a miscalculation. If there is one lesson to be learnt from Oscar Menendes's story, it is: never allow yourself to be put in a position where you are (a) physically helpless and (b) in very close proximity to a woman who has just found out that you have been cheating on her.

Having got her husband exactly where she wanted him, Dolores left him on the bed and went through their house, packing everything of value into two suitcases, and then went to sleep in the spare bedroom. In the early hours of the following morning Dolores went into the garden and picked a bunch of the finest examples of *Rosa Gloria Dei* she could find. She then returned to the bedroom where her husband lay. Oscar by that time had fallen asleep, even though he was still spread-eagled on the bed like a latter-day crucifixion victim. While he was sleeping, Dolores began to insert the roses, stalk first, into her husband's bottom. Only as the third one went in did Oscar fully wake up and realize that something deeply unpleasant was happening to him. Dolores carried on despite his protests. When she had finished she stormed out of the house with the two suitcases, her floral tribute left standing proud.

Oscar had little choice but to wait to be rescued. This eventually happened thirty-six hours later, when the restaurant staff became worried about his continued absence and persuaded the police to pay a visit to the Menendes home to check that everything was well. Oscar was found where Dolores had left him. The roses, still in place, had begun to wilt.

Oscar vowed a fearful revenge on his wife. He had become the laughing stock of Walthamstow. Business fell off. His shoulders drooped. His moustache drooped. Just as he was going to see his solicitor about getting a divorce, he received a divorce petition from Dolores. At this point, the ignominy became too much to bear. He went to the police and brought charges against her for Grievous Bodily Harm, and theft of the various items from the house.

Dolores Menendes was loud, brittle, defiant, and clearly not remotely worried about the possibility of a criminal conviction for her gardening exploits. She had spent a few hours being questioned by the police, who had had difficulties concealing their disbelieving laughter. She was released without bail, pending further enquiries. Dolores believed that no court in the country would convict her of such a *crime passionel*, particularly one of such eye-watering inventiveness. Johnathan had tried to explain to her that the argument was unlikely to be successful in an English court. Dolores Menendes didn't care. She was unapologetic. She lived her life like an up-tempo, high octane version of *Carmen*. She was the most exhausting person Johnathan had ever met. And she didn't speak English.

Johnathan wandered along the corridor to the kitchen and switched on the kettle. After the bustle of his old job, with its never-ending chorus of insistent telephones and slammed doors, Kyriakedes and Podymotopolos seemed like a ghost firm.

The kettle spluttered anxiously for a minute or two and eventually clicked off. Johnathan carefully spooned two heaped teaspoons of dried, odourless brown flakes from a dirty Tupperware box into his mug. He didn't know what the stuff was. It could have been coffee. It could have been a new breakfast cereal or dried dog food. It didn't taste much like coffee, but then it didn't taste much like cereal or dog food either. He watched the steam rise from his mug. Dolores Menendes was due in shortly for another excruciating question and answer session. Johnathan dreaded these meetings. Dolores was always accompanied by her enormous brother Pablo, who translated her ramblings into broken English. Pablo seemed to enjoy playing the macho protective brother of his vulnerable, defenceless sister. He watched Johnathan during these meetings as might an officious mother at a party of hormonally-charged fifteen-year-olds. He seemed to believe that having been hurt once, Dolores was now at constant risk from all men, which suggested that someone had judiciously decided not to tell him about the roses. It also made it rather hard to talk about the impending criminal charge against Dolores, as Johnathan didn't know what to say to her brother. At some point it was going to prove necessary to address the matter in some detail, and Johnathan did not wish to be present when Pablo finally learned the painful truth about his sister.

An hour later Dolores and Pablo were sitting in Johnathan's office. The atmosphere was tense. Johnathan had had his skills in circumlocution pushed to their limits. They had spent the last ten minutes skirting cautiously around the issue of how Dolores was intending to plead to the Grievous Bodily Harm charge. Pablo was becoming more suspicious. His forehead was creased in confusion. His huge single eyebrow, which spanned his face like a monstrous centipede, had concertinaed up in concentration. Johnathan shifted uncomfortably in his seat, as Dolores and her brother spoke quickly to each other. Pablo's face was becoming increasingly red. The centipede was getting smaller by the minute as his whole face seemed to scrunch up in disbelief.

Eventually Pablo turned from his sister and looked darkly

at Johnathan. 'These . . . *ting* with the plant,' he said eventually. 'Ees true?'

Johnathan shrugged. 'Allegedly.'

Pablo shook his head and looked uncomfortable. He spoke again to Dolores, who nodded and folded her arms defiantly.

Pablo shook his head. 'Ees horrible,' he said. 'Ees bad.' He paused. 'My hown sister.' He looked dismayed. 'Such a ting to do to a man. Ees *horreeble*,' he repeated.

Johnathan understood. It was quite acceptable to steal valuables from your cheating husband. It would probably have been acceptable, perhaps even honourable, to have cut his *cojones* off. But to use your husband as a makeshift flowerpot was something that could never be justified. At that point Pablo's masculine sensibilities trumped whatever righteous indignation he might be feeling as Dolores's brother, and he found his allegiances radically altered as a result. Not even his sister was entitled to inflict such indignity on another man.

Pablo stood up. 'I go now,' he explained to Johnathan. He turned and spoke to his sister with the heaviness of a man whose most deeply-held belief has just been shattered. Dolores looked away and did not respond. With a curt nod to Johnathan, whom he obviously felt was somehow responsible for his sister's behaviour, Pablo left the room.

As the door shut behind him Dolores snorted contemptuously, and muttered something to herself in Spanish. Johnathan looked at her apprehensively. He waited a few moments, and then said, very slowly, 'Do you understand me?'

'*Si*,' nodded Dolores.

'We need to establish the precise reasons why you decided to tie up your husband.'

Dolores frowned.

'We need to establish why you decided to, er, insert the roses, um, where you did.'

Dolores looked at Johnathan blankly.

'Do you understand me?' asked Johnathan again.

After a pause, Dolores shook her head.

Johnathan stood up. He extended his hand to his client as graciously as he could. 'Thank you, Mrs Menendes,' he said. 'Please do come again when you've found someone else in your family who can actually speak English.'

Dolores Menendes did a small curtsey in return and daintily shook Johnathan's hand.

'Don't hurry back,' said Johnathan. 'In fact,' he said, 'why don't you boil that fat Spanish head of yours and put us all out of our misery?'

Dolores looked at him coyly and waggled her finger in admonition. 'No honderstand,' she murmured.

'Just do us all a favour and fall under a bus,' said Johnathan, smiling as he held the door open for Dolores to bustle through. He waved cheerily. 'See what you can do, all right? No preference as to which bus. As long as it's big, and going fast.' Dolores nodded and set off down the corridor.

Silently cursing Dolores Menendes, Johnathan went back into his room. He walked over to the corner of his new rug and angrily trod on a small lump which had been bothering him ever since the carpet had been laid a week earlier. There was a peculiar scrunching sound. Johnathan got on to his knees and gingerly lifted up the corner of the carpet. On the floor lay a small squashed mass of hair and limbs. He had just found Eddie the spider, the star exhibit.

ELEVEN

After a few weeks, Johnathan had begun to get used to his new routine. He learned how to concoct reasons for writing wholly unnecessary letters which were full of legal pomposities but extremely short on anything approaching substance. He became a master of procrastination, equivocation, obfuscation, and noncooperation. Efthymios Kyriakedes was delighted.

There had been an awkward moment when Johnathan had squashed Eddie. Johnathan's protestations that Eddie had already been sitting under the rug for a week and so must have already been dead fell on deaf ears. Kyriakedes seemed to take Johnathan's mistake as a personal affront.

'Christ knows what we'll do now,' he said. 'That poor woman probably won't get a bean and'll end up squatting penniless under Waterloo Bridge in a cardboard box, all thanks to you. We were relying on Eddie. Cruelty to animals goes down *very* well. You know what the British are like. Hit a defenceless old granny over the head with an iron bar and you get a smacked wrist, but you're liable to get banged up for years if you hurt a cat or a dog.'

'Or a spider, apparently,' said Johnathan.

'Well, granted, a spider isn't quite so effective, but it was all we had.'

'But I thought the point was that this guy used Eddie to scare his wife. So it had to be a spider. You can't inflict mental cruelty on someone with a poodle.'

Kyriakedes sighed. 'The mental cruelty thing was bollocks,' he said. 'I mean, it was all true, of course, but that wasn't what was going to help us. The important thing was to show that he'd been cruel to the *spider*, not his wife. After that, it's easy. Cruelty to Animals means Total Bastard means Loads of Money. It's a proven technique. As opposed to Cruelty to Wife means Nasty Bastard but Probably Quite Justified means Less Money.' He sighed again.

'Look, it's only a tarantula,' said Johnathan, feeling ridiculously guilty. 'Can't you just get another one? No one will be able to tell the difference. A spider's a spider. It's not like a dog. Just get one with the same markings and you're away.'

Kyriakedes regarded Johnathan levelly. 'Are you suggesting that I replace Eddie and produce a false exhibit to the Court?'

'It was just a thought,' said Johnathan meekly.

'And a *good* one,' said Kyriakedes. 'My cousin's sister-in-law works in a pet shop in Crouch End. I'll have a word with her. Shouldn't be too hard to find another tarantula, should it?' He rubbed his podgy hands together gleefully. 'Johnathan, I do believe you're learning a thing or two.' He picked up the phone and began to dial.

One Friday afternoon Johnathan was sitting at his desk trying to understand the complexities of a bitter boundary dispute between two neighbouring families which had been dragging on for years. The problem centred around the precise location of the fence which divided their two gardens. The area in dispute was a strip of not-exactly-prime North

London real estate approximately four inches wide, but it had engendered feuding which put the Capulets and Montagues to shame. One of the families was systematically working its way through every solicitor in the postal district, moving on to a new one every time it was advised that the matter simply did not merit the time or effort. It was now Johnathan's turn to reach this inevitable conclusion, but not of course before he had incurred a hefty fee for considering the full facts and merits of the case.

While he was reading, Efthymios Kyriakedes put his head around the door.

'All right pal,' he said pleasantly.

'Hello,' said Johnathan, relieved to be interrupted for a moment.

'You live in Tooting, don't you?' said Kyriakedes. Johnathan nodded. 'I wonder if you'd mind delivering a small package for me. It's in the area.'

'Sure,' said Johnathan. 'Happy to.'

'Smashing,' said Kyriakedes. He named an address. Johnathan did not know it. Once they had inspected the tattered *A to Z* which was kept behind the reception desk, it transpired that it wasn't in Tooting at all, but was actually in Balham. 'Never mind,' said Kyriakedes cheerfully. 'Close enough. I'll go and fetch it.'

'Right,' said Johnathan, making a mental note not to agree to do any more favours for his boss. A few moments later Kyriakedes bustled back into the room.

'There you go,' he said, handing over a sealed envelope. He winked. 'Make sure it gets there safely. Matter of life and death.' He grinned.

'What's inside?' asked Johnathan as he weighed the envelope in his hand.

'Good grief, I can't tell you that. Well, I could, but if I did I'd have to kill you.' A grin spread over Kyriakedes's chubby face. 'Nah. Just kidding. A few papers. Just tell them the Greek sent you.' He clapped Johnathan on the back. 'Thanks again. They like a personal service, these people. They don't trust the post much, to be honest. Make sure that you give it personally to a guy called Spike.' He paused. 'Interesting bloke, Spike. Bit of a character.' He winked at Johnathan. 'Anyway. I'm off. I've had enough. See you on Monday. Have a good weekend.' With a wave he disappeared.

Johnathan looked the envelope sourly. Stopping off in Balham would add a significant amount of time to his journey home.

Might as well make an evening of it, he thought. Jake lived in the area, and so Johnathan telephoned him to arrange a drink.

A few hours later Johnathan emerged from Balham underground station and studied the map of the area which was peeling away from the wall by the station exit. Soon he was standing in front of the address which Efthymios Kyriakedes had given him. It was an innocuous looking terraced house in a quiet residential street with a small but well-tended front garden. In the street a small gang of children aimlessly kicked a football at each other without much enthusiasm, scattering for the safety of the pavement every time a car passed and hurling lazy insults at the drivers for disturbing their game.

Johnathan checked his watch and pressed the doorbell. He would be slightly early for his drink with Jake. Just as he was contemplating the pleasures of enjoying a solitary pint of beer, the front door of the house opened a fraction and a man peered suspiciously out from behind it.

'Hello,' said Johnathan.

The beady scrutiny continued unabated. Finally the man said, 'Yeah?'

'Is, er, Spike there, by any chance?' asked Johnathan politely.

Suddenly there was a flurry of movement. The door swung fully open and the man stepped across the threshold and grabbed Johnathan firmly by his lapels. What Johnathan had not appreciated from his hitherto concealed position behind the door was that the man was enormous, being the approximate size of two Efthymios Kyriakedeses stacked one on top of the other. Without another word he hauled Johnathan into the house and slammed the door shut.

'Spike?' demanded the man, maintaining his grip on Johnathan's lapels. 'Who the fuck are you?'

'Oh, well,' stammered Johnathan, who was slightly lost for words after the unexpected velocity of his entrance. 'You see, the Greek sent me.'

There was an immediate change in the man's demeanour. He let go of Johnathan's suit and took three steps backwards. 'Oh. Right. I see. Sorry.'

Johnathan brushed himself down. 'Quite all right,' he said. Before he could explain about the envelope he had brought, the large man moved off down the corridor, indicating that Johnathan should follow. They went into a room at the back of the house, where two other men sat at a bare wooden table. They looked up as he walked in.

'This is our man,' said the giant who had opened the door. 'The Greek sent him.'

Without saying another word the smaller of the two

got up from his chair and left the room. There was an awkward silence as Johnathan eyed the two remaining men with trepidation. They showed little interest in Johnathan. They looked at him in a bored way, and showed no signs of wishing to start a conversation.

Johnathan was about to mention Kyriakedes's letter when the door opened and the smaller man re-entered. He was followed by another man in a burgundy coloured jacket and grey silk shirt with a metallic sheen to it, which was buttoned right up to the neck. The sleeves of his jacket were rolled up to his elbows. Diamond rings twinkled from every finger of both of his hands. His hair was streaked with peroxided flashes. It wobbled ever so slightly when he moved but otherwise maintained its implausible shape to perfection. An intense aroma of horse shit wafted up Johnathan's nostrils, which he took to be some manner of pungent aftershave. The man walked up to Johnathan and looked him directly in the eye for a few seconds. Then, without warning, a truly horrible grin spread across his face, revealing a set of teeth so white and so uniformly perfect that there was not the remotest possibility that they might be real.

'You're early,' he said.

Johnathan shrugged. 'I came when I was told to come.'

The man regarded Johnathan thoughtfully. 'Well, you do what you're told, which is a good thing, I suppose,' he said. He thrust out his hand towards Johnathan. 'Spike,' he said. 'And you are?'

Johnathan was about to open his mouth to explain why he had come when Spike held up a warning hand. 'Sorry pal. Stupid of me. I don't want to know. And you won't want me to know. Wasn't thinking. Long day.' He shrugged. 'So,' he continued. 'The Greek sent you.'

'Er, yes,' said Johnathan, by now quite mystified.

'Been with him long?' asked the man.

'A few weeks,' replied Johnathan.

'Having fun so far?'

'Well there's certainly a lot to learn.'

The man laughed harshly. 'Isn't there just. Listen.' He reached into his horrible jacket and extracted a thin envelope from his inside pocket. 'There you go,' he said. He held the envelope out. Uncertainly, Johnathan took it. He was supposed to be delivering a package rather than receiving one. He examined the envelope. There was nothing written on the outside. He looked questioningly at Spike.

'Everything you need to know's inside,' he said. He moved a step closer to Johnathan. 'Name. Address. Where you can find him. I want you to get this guy good. Usual sort of thing. You know the ropes. I don't want him to sit down for a good while without thinking of me. This little prick has one very large lesson to learn.'

Oh dear, thought Johnathan.

Spike continued. 'This guy has made a prat out of me. I don't like being taken for a fool. People like you and me, we got to maintain respect, right? Can't have people thinking they can treat us like silly buggers, can we?'

There was a pause. Spike leant even closer towards Johnathan, whose eyes had begun to prickle with tears at the onslaught of the aftershave. '*Can we?*' he demanded in a low voice.

Johnathan started. 'No,' he squeaked.

Spike stepped back, satisfied. 'I want this sorted by the end of next week. Usual payment terms. Any questions?' he asked.

Funny you should say that, thought Johnathan, but yes,

I did have the odd one or two. Who the fuck are you? for starters, followed by Who the fuck do you think I am? What the fuck is inside the envelope you've just given me, and What the fuck am I supposed to do with it, precisely?

Johnathan saw that the men, whoever they were and whatever they were involved with, would not react favourably if he were suddenly to whip out Efthymios Kyriakedes's envelope and try and explain that there must have been some misunderstanding as to who he was. He would leave the delivery of his own letter for another day.

'No,' he said. 'No questions.'

'Good,' said Spike. He put his hand out to be shaken. 'You'll let me know as soon as you have something to report?' he asked.

Johnathan shook the proffered hand limply. 'Of course,' he said, wondering what on earth was happening to him.

'Right. Look forward to hearing from you. Cheers.' He nodded towards the man who had opened the front door. 'Terry'll see you out.' Spike turned swiftly on his heel and strode out of the room.

Once Spike had left, Terry gestured that Johnathan should follow him, and before long he was wandering in a daze to the pub where he had arranged to meet Jake.

Jake was uncharacteristically early, and was already installed at the bar when Johnathan arrived. Idly they discussed the journalistic projects Jake was working on, one of which was an exposé of a prominent politician and his penchant for sexual congress with soft fruit.

'Is any of this stuff actually true?' asked Johnathan.

'Well,' said Jake, 'obviously that's a bit of a theoretical question.'

'It is? In what way?'

'It is in the sense that truth is a relative concept in journalism. I mean, what is Truth? Do any of us really know? In philosophical terms, the question transcends much of what we do and what actually appears on the printed page.'

Johnathan thought about this. 'I don't have a clue what you're talking about,' he said.

'Good.' Jake took another swig of beer.

'Let me put it another way,' tried Johnathan. 'Can you actually *prove* any of this stuff?'

'Oh yeah,' said Jake. 'Although, if you want to get technical about it, just because we can prove it doesn't necessarily mean that it's true.'

'It doesn't?'

'God, no. Anyway,' said Jake, 'what's happening with you? Any good stories for me yet?'

'Funny you should say that. The weirdest thing happened to me just before I got here.' Johnathan explained briefly about his trip to deliver the letter.

Jake sat up. 'Christ. Sounds like a contract job. Hardly something for a mild-mannered solicitor.'

'I know,' said Johnathan gloomily. 'Obviously a case of mistaken identity, but I wasn't going to tell them that. I just wanted to get out in one piece.'

'Quite right,' agreed Jake. 'So where's the envelope?'

Johnathan patted his jacket pocket. 'In here.'

'Aren't you going to open it?'

'Of course not,' said Johnathan. 'I want nothing to do with this. As soon as I get home I'm going to throw it away and forget any of this ever happened. These people can lead their seedy little lives of crime and revenge without my help.'

'Hang on a second,' said Jake. 'In your pocket is the name

of a man who has made somebody very unhappy and who is
– whatever you do – about to enjoy a prolonged stay in his
local hospital by the sounds of it.'

'And?'

'Well look, don't you think you have a responsibility to
warn him that someone's after him?' asked Jake.

'Frankly, no.'

Jake sighed. 'I don't believe this. You have the chance to
act to reduce the sum of human misery and violence and
you're not interested.'

'Not remotely,' confirmed Johnathan. 'It's nothing to do
with me. I don't want to get involved. And anyway, it sounds
as if the guy has it coming to him.'

'So let me just check I've understood this correctly,' said
Jake. 'You are condoning the use of violence against the guy
whose name is in that envelope because you believe, on the
basis of what you've been told by an obviously extremely
shady criminal type, that he deserves it.'

'I'm not *condoning* it,' snapped Johnathan. 'I just want
nothing to do with it.'

'And you're prepared to sit back and allow this Spike and
his cronies to beat merry hell out of some poor bastard who
for all we know has done nothing wrong.'

Johnathan brooded silently. To his annoyance, he could
see that Jake had a point.

'After all,' continued Jake, 'supposing you did nothing and
the poor guy ends up dead. Then how would you feel?'

Johnathan held up his hands in defeat. 'All right, all right,'
he said. 'I give in. You win.' He pulled the envelope out of
his pocket and put it on the bar. He looked at it for a few
moments.

'Go on, then,' said Jake.

Reluctantly Johnathan picked up the envelope and opened it. Inside was a single sheet of paper, which he unfolded and spread out on the bar in front of them. Johnathan and Jake inspected it together.

'Wow,' said Jake after a while. 'Weird coincidence.'

Johnathan did not reply.

'After all,' continued Jake, 'it's a pretty unusual name.'

Johnathan still did not reply.

'D'you know the guy?' asked Jake.

'Sort of,' said Johnathan. 'He's my brother.'

TWELVE

There was a pause.

'You have a brother?' said Jake eventually.

'Well. Half brother, actually,' said Johnathan dully, still staring at the piece of paper in front of him.

'You've never mentioned him before,' said Jake, bewildered.

'We don't talk. He hates me, actually.'

'Why?'

Johnathan sighed.

Gregory Burlip was four and a half years older than Johnathan. Gregory's birth at St Mary's Hospital in Paddington had been long and complicated. His mother had been in labour for thirty-six hours. His father had been pacing the corridors of the hospital when the young attractive woman obstetrician came out to give him a progress report. Over the hours that followed this became a regular occurrence, and when at last Gregory had been born and mother and baby were resting comfortably, the proud new father asked the obstetrician out for a celebratory drink.

A year later, on Gregory's first birthday, the proud new father asked the obstetrician to marry him, and filed for divorce the following day.

Johnathan had been the sole product of his father's second

marriage. Gregory, never the most intellectually robust of people, held his younger brother personally responsible for his father's defection and had come to hate Johnathan with the sort of fervour that made Cain look like a wuss.

Soon after Johnathan's birth Gregory's mother had re-married as well, to a successful businessman, who died a few years later. Mother and son had been left with a huge inheritance, which they had immediately begun to fritter away as assiduously they could.

Perhaps not entirely surprisingly in the circumstances, when Gregory left school having achieved the worst set of academic exam results in his school's history, his inclination to go to university or find gainful employment was not strong. Fifteen or so years on, he had never, to Johnathan's knowledge, had a job.

Their father had kept in touch with his elder son in a desultory, grudging way for the first few years of his second marriage. Once his ex-wife had remarried he no longer needed to make any maintenance payments, and gradually he had begun to see less and less of Gregory, particularly once Johnathan was born. Finally, just after Gregory's eleventh birthday, he had given up visiting altogether, instead sending hurriedly written cards on birthdays and Christmases, until these too had petered out. For years there had been no contact between father and son.

Unfortunately for Gregory, no amount of flashy cars or luxury holidays could relieve the pain of rejection that he felt at his father's desertion. Johnathan believed that Gregory's insecurity was actually growing as the years passed, and that his jealousy of Johnathan was growing with it. There was a certain irony to it all: all Gregory wanted was to be loved and accepted by his father; he could take or leave his immense wealth. All Johnathan wanted was immense wealth; he could take or leave his father.

Gregory had kept in sporadic and ill-natured contact with Johnathan for several years in the hope that his brother would put in a good word for him with their father. He had failed to understand that Johnathan hardly ever saw his parents either, although this was Johnathan's choice: the generation gap between father and younger son was vast, uncrossable. (Well-intentioned conversation always descended into a confusion of misunderstandings and awkwardness, eventually settling into uncomfortable exchanges of halting banalities.) Finally Gregory had realized that Johnathan was not going to help him achieve any reconciliation with his father, and had stopped calling him. Since then, Johnathan had heard nothing of him. Until now.

Johnathan explained all this to Jake, who sat back and listened, occasionally taking disbelieving swigs of beer.

'That,' said Jake when Johnathan had finished, 'is *seriously* fucked up.'

Johnathan nodded. 'It would be helpful to have a fantastically rich brother who owned a properly functioning fraternal love facility. He could so easily be the answer to so many of my problems. Like my mortgage. It wouldn't even make a dent in his pile.'

'Have you tried to bury the hatchet?' asked Jake.

'Haven't had the chance, really,' said Johnathan. 'Every time he sees me his first reaction *is* to try and bury the hatchet, but between my shoulder blades.'

Jake thought. 'Surely he must be able to see that all this isn't your fault,' he said. 'If anything, you're the most innocent party of all. You came along after everything else had already happened.'

'I know. But what you have to remember, Jake, is that my brother is very, *very* stupid. And that,' continued Johnathan as he motioned towards the barman for two more beers, 'probably explains why his name is on this piece of paper and why some oikish South London thug is prepared to pay someone to hurt him.'

'I was wondering about that,' said Jake.

Johnathan sighed. 'It's probably some innocent misunderstanding which Gregory has managed to turn into something far worse.' He paused as the drinks were presented to them. 'He's not what you might call a "people person".'

'I see.'

Johnathan stared at piece of paper morosely. 'I suppose this means I ought to go and warn him about this.'

'Christ, yes. Of course you should. Like now.'

'God. Do you think so?'

'Johnathan,' said Jake. 'Put yourself in his shoes. Wouldn't you want to know about this? Wouldn't you like the chance to try and do something about it instead of just waiting for them to turn up on your doorstep? I mean, OK, I realize that you two aren't exactly close or anything, but he *is* still your brother. I think you should tell him, and I actually think you should tell him right away, on the basis that your new friends are at some point going to realize that they asked the wrong man to do their dirty work.'

Johnathan nodded. 'I suppose you're right.'

'Of course I'm right. Go on. Call him now.'

'What, now?'

'*Now.*' Jake pointed at the telephone by the door of the pub.

Reluctantly Johnathan rose and went to the phone. Looking around self-consciously, he picked up the receiver and dialled Gregory's number, unsure of quite what to say or quite how Gregory would react to hearing his voice — whether, indeed, he would have the chance to say what he needed to say before Gregory slammed the phone down. As the ringing tone echoed in the receiver, Johnathan tried to prepare himself.

There was no need. The ringing continued for half a minute. Gregory was not at home, and had not switched on his answer-phone. Relieved, Johnathan replaced the handset and returned to Jake.

'No reply,' he reported.

'Leave a message?'

'No machine.' Johnathan paused. 'I'll try later.'

'You can't,' said Jake.

'I can't?'

'No. You need to do something *now*. Go round to his house. Maybe he was asleep and didn't hear the telephone. Leave a message. Stick it through the door. At least let him know so he can do something as soon as he returns.'

'But he lives in Chelsea,' complained Johnathan.

'And?'

'It's miles away.'

'*And?*'

'All right, all right. You're right, I know. I'll go. It's just that-well, we *really* don't get on.' He sighed.

'Right, well, I'm coming too,' announced Jake. 'This sounds as if it might be something worth seeing.' He finished his pint in one long swig.

Johnathan looked at Jake sourly. A nagging suspicion lingered in the back of his mind that Jake's insistence might be born out of something less than concern for his best friend's half brother whom he had never met. The possibility of a good story, for example.

'OK,' said Jake. 'Shall we go?'

Johnathan and Jake took a train to Victoria station and then clambered on board a bus which took them to Sloane Square and down the King's Road. As they alighted on the pavement a gaggle of pretty girls, none of whom looked more than sixteen, emerged from an unmarked door from behind which the remorseless thud of a stereo system blasted out trauma-inducing dance music. The girls seemed to be wearing little more than bikini tops and skimpy patches of lycra wrapped around their midriffs. In perfect synchrony, they each delved into their handbag, withdrew a packet of Marlboro Lights, and coolly lit one as they surveyed the scene before them.

One of the components of that scene was Jake, salivating like one of Pavlov's dogs listening to a troop of campanologists. 'Jesus,' he said. 'I can see why your brother lives around here.'

Ordinarily, Johnathan would have joined in with this rite of male bonding with enthusiasm. To his surprise, though, he found that he wasn't at all interested in the girls. He thought about Kibby and how very much more attractive and interesting she was than any of them would ever be. It simultaneously occurred to him that such a reaction was not perhaps entirely normal or healthy. During his relationship with Chloe he would never have thought twice about leering at teenagers. Once again he resigned himself to the growing realization that Kibby was causing something rather serious to happen to him. He began walking towards the street where Gregory lived.

Jake scuttled up behind him. 'Mate?' he asked.

Johnathan looked around. 'What?'

'Is something wrong?'

'What do you mean?'

'Well,' said Jake, 'you just walked right past a posse of *very* foxy girls without so much as a blink. Are you ill?'

'No.'

'What then?'

'Actually,' said Johnathan, trying not to sound smug but failing completely, 'I've got a new girlfriend.'

'What? You finally got rid of thingy?'

'Chloe,' said Johnathan, a shade irritably. 'Yes. Finally.'

'Thank Christ. Good for you. When did this happen?'

'A few weeks ago,' said Johnathan. 'We're playing it very gently,' he said, hoping that he was hiding his disappointment about this.

'Wow. What's her name?'

'Kibby.' Johnathan felt a small rush of warmth as he said her name, and said to himself, This is ridiculous.

'Kibby,' repeated Jake thoughtfully. 'Interesting name.'

Johnathan was immediately worried. Interesting? What did that mean? Stupid?

'You'll like her,' he said hopefully.

'Course I will,' replied Jake. 'She can't be any worse than the last one.'

After a few minutes they turned down a quiet road, flanked on both sides by spotlessly white houses. On the road was parked an impressive range of expensive new cars. Jake whistled. He turned towards Johnathan. 'Your brother lives *here*?' he whispered. *With all these cars and girls?* ran the sub-text.

Johnathan shrugged. 'With the amount of money he's got, this might be considered as slumming it.'

'But a flat round here must cost a fortune.'

Johnathan laughed humourlessly. 'He doesn't live in a flat. He lives in a whole bloody house.'

'Unbelievable.' Jake shook his head.

'And this is the whole bloody house in question.' Johnathan stopped and looked up at a four storey town house. There were no lights on except for a dim glow from a third floor window.

Jake looked up. 'Someone might be home,' he said, nodding to the third floor.

'Only one way to find out, I suppose,' said Johnathan unenthusiastically, and walked up to the front door. He pressed the large brass doorbell. The ring echoed shrilly out on to the street. Nothing happened. Johnathan waited. Jake stood further back on the pavement, hands dug deep in his pockets, humming quietly to himself.

After about a minute, Johnathan turned to Jake. 'Nobody's home,' he said, trying to hide the relief in his voice. 'I'd better leave a message for him. Have you got a pen?'

'Hang on a sec,' said Jake. 'Those lights have gone off.'

Johnathan stepped back from the front door and looked up at the front of the house again. Sure enough, the third floor windows were now as dark as those in the rest of the house. Johnathan frowned. 'Well somebody must be there, then,' he said. He went back up to the front door and pressed the bell again, this time for longer. Still there was no noise from within. Johnathan bent down and pushed open the letter box in the middle of the door. Inside was darkness. After a while he returned to where Jake was standing.

'This is very weird,' he said.

Jake nodded. Johnathan thought. 'That trick of turning the lights off once I'd rung the doorbell is classic Gregory,' he said. 'He's managed to do the one thing which is guaranteed to show there *is* somebody home.' He tapped the side of his forehead with his finger. 'Like I said, not the brightest of boys.'

'Now what?' asked Jake. 'Is it worth trying the bell again?'

'I wouldn't have thought so.'

'What about trying the telephone?'

Johnathan shook his head. 'Not even Gregory would pick up the telephone if he's pretending he's not there.'

Jake thought. 'I suppose if he doesn't want to play, he won't play. Maybe he knows about Spike already.'

'There's one thing we haven't tried, I suppose,' said Johnathan. He turned and walked into the middle of the street, looked upwards at the house, and took a deep breath.

'Oi,' he shouted at the top of his voice. 'Gregory.'

There was silence.

'Gregory,' began Johnathan again. 'It's me. Johnathan.' He paused. 'Your brother,' he shouted by way of clarification.

Jake and Johnathan looked up at the house for some sign of movement. There was none. In a few of the neighbouring houses inquisitive lights were turned on and curtains began to twitch. 'We know you're there,' shouted Johnathan. 'We saw you turn the lights off.'

They waited a few more moments. Jake turned to Johnathan. He shrugged. 'Nice try.'

Suddenly a strangled noise came from the house.

Johnathan looked at Jake. 'Did you hear that?' he asked.

'Yeah,' said Jake.

'What did that sound like to you?'

They both listened as the same sound came again.

'Sounded a bit like "Fuck off" to me,' said Jake.

'That's what I thought,' agreed Johnathan. 'That's definitely my brother. Always had a telling way with words. Hold on,' he said, peering towards the house. The flap of the letter box appeared to be moving. 'Back in a tick,' he said, and walked up to the door.

'Bend down,' whispered a voice through the letter box as he approached. 'Pretend you're tying your shoelace.'

Johnathan did so, keeping his head level with the letter box as he fiddled with his shoes. He looked through the hole and saw a pair of eyes staring back at him. 'Hello, Gregory,' he said amicably. 'How's tricks?'

'Who's we?' said the voice, ignoring his question.

'What?'

'Who's we? As in "We know you're there."'

'Oh, me and my friend Jake.'

'What's he doing here? What are you doing here, come to that?'

'Look,' said Johnathan, 'I don't mean to be rude, but can we come in? We've come all the way over from Balham to see you.'

'Can't you just fuck off?' said the voice. 'It's not a good time.'

'Not until we've spoken to you,' said Johnathan. 'I've got something important to tell you, and I'm not going anywhere until you hear me out. *Then* we will both happily fuck off. And if you don't let us in then I shall stay out here shouting at your house.'

Gregory swore under his breath. 'Shit. All right, I give in. Get your friend up to the door and then I'll open it. You'll have to move quickly.'

Johnathan turned around and beckoned Jake to approach.

Jake sauntered casually up to the door. He bent down to address the letter box. 'All right?' he said conversationally. He was greeted with a frosty silence.

There was the sound of two keys being turned in their locks, followed by the scraping back of several security chains and an unclicking of automatic safety devices. Finally the large door creaked open to reveal a gap of about six inches. There was a pause as Johnathan and Jake looked at the open door.

'Well come on then,' whispered the voice from the other side of the door. 'What are you waiting for?'

'Would you mind opening the door a bit more?' said Johnathan mildly.

'Oh. Right.' The door opened sufficiently for them to squeeze inside. As soon as they had entered, the door slammed shut and Gregory set about resecuring it. There was no light in the hall, but a faint glow emanated from further down the corridor.

When he had finished, Gregory turned to face Johnathan and Jake. He eyed them with distaste. 'Well,' he said. 'This *is* a surprise. Follow me.' He set off towards the light.

Johnathan and Jake exchanged looks. 'He's got your easy charm,' whispered Jake.

'Oh yes. He's a poppet,' replied Johnathan.

THIRTEEN

Johnathan and Jake followed Gregory down the corridor and into a massive kitchen. The curtains were drawn tightly over the windows. On an impressive oak table in the middle of the room stood a single candle which was the sole source of light. Its flickering flame threw shadows against the walls, the mutating shapes dancing eerily around the three men.

Gregory stood at one end of the table with his arms crossed. He watched his visitors with ill-disguised suspicion. Johnathan looked at his brother. Time had not been kind to Gregory since they had last seen each other. He looked terrible. He had put on weight and, Johnathan was secretly pleased to see, his hairline had begun to recede drastically.

'So,' said Gregory. 'What was it you had to tell me? Make it quick. This isn't a good time.'

'Have you had a power strike?' asked Johnathan, gesturing towards the candle. 'Or is this some sort of economy drive?'

'Look, prat,' replied Gregory, 'I really don't have time for this at the moment. As a matter of fact, your being here is placing us all in danger.'

'Are you hiding from someone?' asked Jake.

'In a manner of speaking,' said Gregory.

'In an affirmative manner of speaking?' asked Jake.

'What?' said Gregory, his face clouding with confusion.

'Don't worry,' said Johnathan. 'Look, Gregory, what's the reason for all this cloak and dagger stuff?'

'Oh, you wouldn't understand,' answered Gregory.

'Try me.'

'Well, I think someone may want to hurt me.'

'Good heavens,' said Johnathan. 'Tell me, this person who wants to hurt you. He wouldn't be called Spike, by any chance, would he?'

Gregory's reaction was electric. He went, almost literally, white. He took a couple of steps backwards. His eyes grew impressively large. 'How did you know?' he whispered.

'Well you won't believe this,' replied Johnathan conversationally, 'but Spike actually asked *me* to come round and beat you up. Some coincidence, isn't it? It's a small world, when you think about it, really.'

All this had exactly the effect Johnathan had wanted. Panic and blind terror were now etched large across his brother's face. Jake, who had quickly realized what Johnathan had in mind, casually walked over to the stove and began inspecting the collection of large kitchen knives.

'He asked *you* to come?' shrilled Gregory. He began to moan pitifully. 'Oh God. Oh God, no. Not by my own brother. Jesus.' A thought occurred to him. 'Look. I've got an idea.' Gregory had a slightly crazed glint in his eye. 'Now I know you and I have never exactly seen eye to eye in the past. But that can change.'

This was a surprise. Interesting what terror can do to a person, thought Johnathan. 'Go on,' he said coolly.

'I'm rich,' said Gregory.

'I know,' said Johnathan. 'And?'

'Well. I can give you money. We can do a deal. Should

have done it ages ago, obviously, and I really am very sorry I never did, but we can let bygones be bygones, can't we, yeah, and tomorrow I can sort you something out and we can just forget about what Spike asked you to do. How does that sound?' He beamed hopefully at Johnathan.

Johnathan closed his eyes and tried to think. This was something he had not anticipated. A small amount – say £30,000 – would have no effect on Gregory's lifestyle, but would radically change Johnathan's for the better, particularly in view of the massive pay cut – pay *slash* was a better term for it – that he had accepted on moving to Kyriakedes and Podymotopolos. But there was a moral issue here. As a general principle, accepting bribes was probably immoral, he thought. Accepting money to perform criminal acts on behalf of others was definitely immoral. Accepting bribes *not* to perform criminal acts on behalf of others was an interesting conundrum. Better or worse? Debatable. Accepting bribes not to perform criminal acts when you hadn't actually been going to perform the criminal acts in the first place was too complicated to think about.

How to play this? he wondered. Get the money first, he told himself. Then you can worry about the other stuff. He closed his eyes and took a deep breath.

'We don't want your money,' said Jake.

Johnathan's eyes shot open.

'You don't?' said Gregory.

'We're not going to hurt you,' continued Jake. 'We're here to help you.'

Johnathan looked furiously at Jake.

'Help me how?' asked Gregory.

Johnathan sighed, seeing the opportunity had been lost. He explained to his brother about the case of mistaken identity and how Spike had given him the envelope with Gregory's name on it.

'So obviously the first thing I wanted to do was to come and see if you were all right and to warn you that you were in danger. You are my brother, after all.'

Jake coughed in discreet disbelief.

'So you're not going to hurt me?' asked Gregory nervously.

Johnathan shook his head. 'Tell me, what have you done to piss Spike off so much?'

'He thinks I owe him some money.'

'What for?'

'Just a gambling debt.'

'Jesus. How much are we talking here?'

'A hundred and twenty thousand quid.'

'Jesus,' breathed Johnathan. 'That's some debt.'

Gregory nodded. 'It was some bet.'

'What was it on?'

'Well, it's a long story. Me and Spike belong to the same little group of poker players. We meet once a fortnight or so and play for pretty high stakes, you know, a couple of grand a hand, usually. And one evening after the other guys had left and we were waiting for our cars, Spike suggested a few games of highest cut – you know the sort of thing, you both cut to a card and the winner is the guy who cuts to the highest card.'

'OK,' said Johnathan. 'Sounds harmless enough.'

'Yeah, well. It started off all right. We were bored. We were betting small amounts, a hundred quid a cut. And it was weird, because I kept winning, and Spike was getting more and more angry. He hates to lose. *Hates* it. And so he starts to raise the stakes to give him a chance to recover all

144

the money he's lost so far, and to win some back as well. Still he keeps losing, until he owes me eighty thousand quid. And finally he offers to bet two hundred grand on one cut of the pack.'

'Sweet Jesus on a lollipop,' said Jake.

'You actually agreed to this?' asked Johnathan.

Gregory shrugged. 'Yeah. It's only money, after all. Anyway,' he continued, 'when Spike gets into that sort of mood, it gets kind of difficult to say no. If I'd tried to back out I would have got into all sorts of trouble.'

'As opposed to your present predicament,' observed Johnathan.

'So what happened?' asked Jake.

'Well, we cut. I went first, and got a jack, which was pretty good. But when Spike cut he came up with the ace of diamonds.'

'So he won,' said Johnathan. 'Why don't you just pay the guy? You've got the money.'

'I'm not paying him because he cheated,' replied Gregory furiously.

'What?' said Johnathan.

'He cheated. I saw when he showed me his card. There was a little nick in the corner of the ace. He could see where to cut to.'

'Are you sure?'

'Course I'm sure. If he'd won fair and square then I would have paid him, obviously. But this is a matter of principle. If you ask me, he owes me eighty thousand quid. At least.'

'Is it really worth getting beaten up on a matter of principle?' asked Johnathan.

Gregory looked defiant. 'I don't intend to get beaten up.'

145

'Gregory, are you aware of how much trouble you're in?' said Johnathan. 'This guy is very, very pissed off.'

'He would be, wouldn't he? He wants his money. But what's worse, and why he's so angry with me, is because I found him out. He cheated, and I caught him. He's embarrassed. Cretin.'

'Well, look,' said Johnathan. 'What are you going to do?'

'What can I do? Stay here and hide, I suppose.'

'Is that wise? I don't think you should expect everyone to be as polite as we were. If you don't answer the door they won't just go away and try again later. They'll break in and do a bit of damage, just to let you know they're on to you. And if you happen to be hiding under the bed at the time, they'll find you.'

Gregory blinked. 'Do you think?'

'Of course. Isn't it obvious? You need to move out for a while.'

Gregory looked around in panic. 'But all of my things are here,' he whined.

'You'll just have to take what you need and leave the rest,' said Johnathan. Gregory looked appalled at this prospect.

'What do you suggest I do, then?' he asked.

'Have you got anywhere you can stay?'

'I could go to a hotel,' mused Gregory.

Jake shook his head. 'Bad idea. Hotels are public places. Notoriously difficult places to hide. Your name's on the register, you have to walk in and out through the front lobby.' He paused. 'I've found lots of people when they've been staying in hotels,' he explained.

'What does he do?' asked Gregory.

'Journalist,' replied Johnathan.

'Oh, perfect.' Gregory put his head in his hands.

'Anyway,' said Johnathan, 'OK, we've ruled the hotel option out. Haven't you got any friends you could stay with just for tonight?'

Gregory shook his head. 'Not really. No friends as such.'

There was a small pause as Johnathan and Jake digested this.

'OK,' said Johnathan. 'Well, I would offer to put you up myself, but I'll need a day or so to arrange things.'

Two pairs of eyes swivelled towards Jake.

Jake looked at the two brothers and sighed.

The next day was a Saturday. In the taxi back to South London the previous night it had been agreed that Jake and Gregory would come around to Johnathan's flat just before lunch.

During the morning Johnathan performed his usual round of Saturday morning chores, and went to buy an uncharacteristically expensive bottle of white wine from the local off licence. Desperate to impress Kibby, he had recklessly offered to cook for her, and she was coming for supper that evening. Jake had suggested a fool-proof recipe which involved a chicken and large amounts of brandy. Johnathan had planned to cook some carrots too, until he had dismissed the idea as fanciful. Vegetables you got when you were fed elsewhere. Johnathan had never really progressed from the student gastronomy of his youth. He ignored the received wisdom that a man who cooks is attractive. A man who can afford to take women out to expensive restaurants must be *more* attractive, he reasoned, although he had never really had the financial wherewithal to test his theory properly. He had in the past tried to impress women by taking them to terribly *chic* restaurants only to spoil the effect by being rendered speechless on the presentation of the bill and then asking the manager if he might borrow a calculator.

At around eleven o'clock Jake and Gregory arrived. Jake looked exhausted. Gregory wrinkled up his nose as he walked into Johnathan's flat. 'So this is it, then,' he observed as he looked around with obvious distaste. 'Interesting.' He went over to the sofa and ran a finger along its arm to feel the fabric. 'In a sort of a ghastly kind of way. And a *dog*. How delightful.' Schroedinger responded by giving Gregory's groin a disdainful sniff before retiring to his bean bag beneath the kitchen sink.

'Coffee?' offered Johnathan.

'Please,' said Gregory, who was still examining the sitting room.

'Let me help,' said Jake, and followed Johnathan into the kitchen, where he shut the door and turned to face his friend.

'Johnathan. You're my mate, right?'

Johnathan nodded as he switched on the coffee machine. 'Of course.'

'And as a mate I would normally do everything I could to help, you know that, don't you?'

'Of course you would,' said Johnathan in a resigned way.

'Right.' He paused. 'It's just that I do have a bit of a problem with your brother.'

'You do?'

'Yeah.' Jake looked awkward.

'What's the problem?'

'Well, basically, he's a complete arse.'

There was a pause.

'I know,' said Johnathan.

148

'He's driving me nuts. He has spent all morning wandering around my flat criticizing everything from my coffee to my record collection.'

'Well,' said Johnathan, 'your coffee *is* awful.'

'Yeah, well, maybe, but that's not the point. I'm doing him a favour, for Christ's sake. He can't come into my house and behave like fucking royalty. I swear, I've come within seconds of thumping him too often for comfort. I've half a mind to go and see that guy and offer to beat him up for free.'

'So it's not going that well, then?' said Johnathan. 'You haven't seen his good side yet?'

'The only good side he has is his back, when it's going in any direction away from me,' fumed Jake.

'I see. Well, in that case, it makes your willingness to help all the more laudable.'

'Yeah, well, that was what I wanted to talk to you about, actually,' said Jake.

'Oh?'

'I don't think I can in all honesty bear another evening with that git in my flat, if I'm honest.'

'And if you lie?'

'I never lie, as you know,' replied Jake. 'I'm a journalist, remember?'

'Listen,' said Johnathan. 'All I'm asking is a couple more nights. Please. As a friend. No. Not just as a friend. *As my best friend.*' Johnathan smiled weakly.

'Can I ask why it's so important that he doesn't come here tonight?'

Johnathan reminded Jake about Kibby's visit for supper that evening. 'Can you imagine what would happen if Gregory's here?' he said. 'It would be a disaster. I might as well not bother.'

Jake nodded. 'All right, then. God, I must be mad. But that's it. After that he's out on the street.'

There was a shout from the sitting room. 'Have you two quite finished chatting in there?'

'I won't forget this,' said Johnathan seriously.

'Don't worry,' replied Jake. 'I won't let you.'

Back in the sitting room Johnathan distributed the coffee cups, and they began to discuss what Gregory's best course of action was.

'I think we need to assume that your house will probably be being watched from now on. At least during the day. So it would really be safest if you went nowhere near it for a while,' said Johnathan.

'So the question,' said Jake pointedly, 'is where you should stay in the meantime.'

'Jake has kindly insisted that you stay with him again tonight,' said Johnathan.

'Oh. Thanks.' Gregory looked almost as crestfallen as Jake.

'And I think it's best if you didn't leave the house at all.'

'What?' said Jake and Gregory together, looking equally dismayed.

'Just as a precaution,' explained Johnathan. 'You can't be too careful after all. You wouldn't want to bump into any unsavoury characters by chance, would you?'

'I suppose not,' said Gregory doubtfully.

'And after a few days,' continued Johnathan with less enthusiasm, 'you will come and stay with me until we work out what to do.'

'With you?' asked Gregory.

'Is that all right?'

Gregory slumped back into the sofa like a sulking child. 'Suppose so,' he said.

'That's settled then.' The three men looked at each other with equally miserable expressions.

That evening, after Jake had reluctantly taken Gregory back to his flat, Johnathan wandered aimlessly about the kitchen while the chicken fizzled in the frying pan, taking the odd swig from the brandy bottle. He had, inevitably, been thinking about Kibby and the unpredictable nature of their relationship to date. He resented the fact that he never knew whether she was going to jump on him with gratifying ardour, or whether he would have to attempt to lure her into his bed with a well prepared tactical campaign, with detailed plans of action, counter-offensives and damage limitation procedures all carefully set out in advance. Depending on Kibby's behaviour, he could appear anywhere on the spectrum of male functions, from Complete Irrelevance to Occasional Shag to Potential Life-Long Partner. It was an unsatisfactory state of affairs, particularly as Johnathan's feelings for Kibby had more or less reached stasis at around the Should be My Wife level.

Johnathan peered at the chicken. According to Jake's recipe, it should have been well cooked, but it lay lamely in the frying pan, anaemic and rubbery. Johnathan sniffed at it tentatively, and pulled a face. He sliced a bit in two with a sharp knife. The flesh of the chicken was an angry pink. Johnathan sighed. He suspected that something wasn't quite right, but didn't know what. Judging it more prudent to swallow his pride than his chicken, he tipped the contents of the pan into Schroedinger's bowl and called the local Chinese take-away. Schroedinger cautiously emerged from underneath the sink and sniffed at his bowl. After a few moments' contemplation he slunk back to his bean bag, leaving the chicken untouched. Settling back down, he looked at Johnathan with reproach.

Johnathan made a decision. Enough was enough. Tonight he would tell Kibby how he really felt. Tonight she would know just how much he really loved her. He took another swig of brandy, and burped.

By the time Kibby arrived half an hour later, a third of the brandy had gone in Johnathan's efforts to sustain his resolve. He was feeling decidedly more positive, if also less focused. Five aluminium containers sat on the kitchen bench. Johnathan gestured to them apologetically.

'Chinese,' he said. 'I did try and cook, but not even the dog will touch it.'

Kibby inspected the contents of Schroedinger's bowl. Kindly she said nothing.

The meal was dispatched within minutes. 'It's a funny thing,' said Kibby as she lay back on the sofa, resting her stomach in cupped hands as if she was pregnant. 'Chinese food always looks so filling, and I suppose it is in a way, but why do we eat it five times more quickly than everything else?' She prodded Johnathan. 'What do you reckon? Does the human Hoover have an opinion on the subject?'

Johnathan shook his head. He was thinking about other things. He was thinking, to be precise, about how to declare his love for Kibby and ask her to move in, marry him, have his children. As he skewered the last imperfect orange golf ball of sweet and sour pork and deposited it whole into his mouth, he experienced a moment of aching clarity amidst the slippery fog of alcohol. He saw that this was a perfect opportunity: he was drunk enough to say what he wanted to say, but sober enough to be able to string his words together in such a way that Kibby would at least get the general drift.

With the careful deliberation of the half-pissed, he poured more wine into their glasses. He handed Kibby's to her gravely.

'Kibby,' he began.

Kibby looked at Johnathan with tender interest. 'Yes, Johnathan,' she said.

'I've got something quite important to say. Well, I say quite important, but I suppose it's not really, not in the greater scheme of things. Still, it is quite important to me, as you would probably have guessed anyway, as I'm hardly going to call something quite important if I didn't think it was, even if objectively it was obvious that it *was* quite important.' He paused.

'Go on,' said Kibby cautiously. 'I think.'

'Right.' Johnathan took a mouthful of wine. 'Right. Where was I. Um.'

'Are you all right?' asked Kibby. 'You don't look very well.'

'No, no, I'm fine. Fine fine fine. Fine. Right,' said Johnathan, aware that this wasn't perhaps going as well it might have been. 'OK. What I wanted to say was. Um. About us. And what we were doing. Because I have something quite important to say.' He suddenly raised his head and looked Kibby in the eye for the first time since they had sat down to eat. 'Look, Kibby, I don't want to unduly worry you or put you off or anything but there's something I'm going to have to tell you or else I'll burst.'

Kibby was now looking worried. She watched him closely, her lips slightly pursed. 'I'm all ears,' she said quietly, shifting slightly into the back of the sofa.

'There's no easy way of saying this,' said Johnathan. 'So I'll just come out with it.' He closed his eyes and took a deep breath. 'Kibby –'

The telephone rang.

Johnathan sprang off the sofa as if he had been electrocuted. 'Hold on. Sorry.' He grabbed the receiver roughly and with as much good grace as he could muster said, 'Yes?'

'It's me,' said Jake.

'What is it?' demanded Johnathan, bitterly seeing his opportunity slipping from his hands. The moment for intimate revelations had been lost. He smiled wanly at Kibby, who had settled back into the sofa and was sipping her wine, a frown ghosting across her face. He realized that he was sweating freely.

'It's your bloody brother,' said Jake.

'What about him?'

'He's disappeared.'

FOURTEEN

Johnathan put the phone down and looked at Kibby.

'What is it?' she asked, looking worried.

'My brother.'

'What about him?'

'He's disappeared.'

'Where?'

Johnathan looked at Kibby oddly. 'I don't know.'

'What can you possibly do now? It's late.'

Johnathan thought. 'I'm going to go round to Jake's. Trouble is,' he confessed, 'I'm a bit pissed.' He looked around the sitting room bewildered. 'God knows where he is. They might have tracked him down. He might be lying at the bottom of some disused pit shaft by now. You stay here. Once we've found him I'll come right back. OK?'

Kibby put up her hands. 'Whatever. Where's the nearest disused pit shaft to Tooting, do you think?'

Johnathan ignored her question and pulled on his coat. 'I won't be long, I promise,' he said. He went out to the deserted street. Ten minutes later an empty taxi passed and Johnathan clambered in. He tried to collect his thoughts as he sped towards Jake's flat. Things didn't look good. People didn't just disappear for no good reason. It was too much of a coincidence to ignore. Johnathan sighed. He had done his best. He hoped Gregory's injuries would be very painful, but not permanently debilitating.

When he arrived at Jake's flat, he found his friend standing by the front door, clutching his telephone in one hand and a cigarette in the other.

'Your fucking brother,' said Jake by way of hellos, 'is a stupid shit.'

'He's only my half-brother,' said Johnathan defensively.

'Bad enough,' retorted Jake. 'I've been calling all the casualty units in London. Asking if they've admitted a tall, stupid, selfish fuckwit with only half the injuries he's going to have by the end of the evening once I've got my hands on him.' He inhaled deeply. 'No luck yet.'

'What happened?' asked Johnathan.

'Well, I went to see a film. I told Gregory he should stay at home as we agreed. He just nodded and said he'd prefer that anyway. I got back about an hour ago and he wasn't here.'

'Any sign of a struggle?'

Jake shook his head. 'Nothing. No forced entry. No chippings of broken teeth along the skirting board. No clues.' He shrugged. 'I really don't know what else to do,' he said. 'Perhaps when I've gone through the list of hospitals I should start calling the mortuaries.' He thought. 'I shall be *extremely* pissed off if they've killed him. I want to do that myself.'

Johnathan sat down heavily on the sofa. 'Surely they couldn't have tracked him down here. He must have gone out looking for trouble.'

'Ironic, really,' observed Jake. 'If he was looking for grief I would have been more than happy to oblige.'

Johnathan looked at his friend closely. He had never seen anyone get Jake as worked up as Gregory had managed. Jake's mood stood as a glowing testament to his brother's extra-ordinary ability to get up the noses of everyone he met.

'Can we call the police?' asked Johnathan.

'To report what? That a man in his mid-thirties hasn't come home for a couple of hours? We'd get prosecuted for wasting police time.'

'I'd defend you,' said Johnathan gallantly.

Jake turned away. 'It gets better and better.'

Johnathan sat back in the sofa, crushed. 'What, then?' he asked in a small voice.

'We wait, either for his body parts to be delivered in a small sack, or for one of us to have a brainwave.'

They waited. Nothing happened. Johnathan thought of Kibby alone in his flat and wanted to howl in frustration. This just wasn't fair. Bloody Gregory. Finally the brandy and wine started to catch up with him and he fell into an undisturbed sleep on Jake's sofa.

Undisturbed, that is, until he was shaken roughly awake by Jake's hand on his shoulder. 'Wha?' he said groggily.

'There's someone at the front door,' whispered Jake urgently. 'Come on.'

'What time is it?' asked Johnathan, as he tried to regain control of his brain.

'About four in the morning,' said Jake.

'Christ almighty.' Johnathan staggered to his feet and followed Jake unsteadily across the room and out to the front door. Jake looked at him, concerned.

'Are you ready for this?' he asked.

'No,' admitted Johnathan. He was expecting a sombre policeman bearing bad news and didn't really feel equipped to deal with it.

Jake opened the door.

Before them stood Gregory, dressed in black jeans and an orange lycra top which clung to his torso like a second skin. He regarded them sardonically.

'Hello,' he said. 'You didn't give me a key.'

Jake and Johnathan looked at him, speechless, as he walked past them into the flat. He went into the kitchen, opened the fridge and drank the remains of the only carton of milk in it. Jake and Johnathan wordlessly followed him and watched him as he drank. 'That's better. Needed that.' Gregory noticed the others' stares. 'What's wrong?' He put a hand up to his mouth. 'Do I have milk on my face?'

'Where,' asked Johnathan, 'the fuck have you been?'

'Just my usual Saturday night club round. Start off near Charing Cross, move on to a new place in Soho, and then finish off the night at this groovy rave club in Pimlico.'

'I thought we agreed you wouldn't leave the house,' said Jake.

'Oh.' Gregory considered. 'We did say that, yes. I changed my mind.'

'You could have left a note,' said Jake. 'If you're going to go and take stupid risks then you could have told us first. We've been phoning the hospitals. Thought Spike and his friends must have found you.'

Gregory was not the slightest bit apologetic. 'Christ, you old maid,' he said to Jake, giving him a prod. 'If anyone should have been worried, then it should have been Boy Wonder over there.' He pointed at Johnathan, who was blinking sleep out of his eyes.

'I was worried too,' said Johnathan defensively.

'Yeah, right,' snapped Gregory. 'As if you ever cared about what happened to me. You and your perfect family all sitting pretty in your tragic middle class Hampstead house.'

Johnathan reeled. 'What?' he stammered.

'Oh, come on,' said Gregory, angry now. 'Just admit it. You never liked me. You never cared about me. You're only doing this now so you can gloat and act all superior. Mr perfect lawyer. You make me sick.'

Well, the first bit was easy enough: guilty as charged. I never did like you, thought Johnathan. 'You think I'm *gloating*?' he said. 'About what, exactly?'

'About Dad, of course. About the fact that it was your home he came back to every night. You were the one he took on holiday with him. You were the one he saw every day. You're the one who still sees him now.' The bitterness was audible.

'But Gregory, tell me something. Have you actually tried to get back in touch with him lately?'

Gregory looked defensive. 'Not exactly.'

'Why not?'

'Because he obviously hates me,' exclaimed Gregory.

'But he hasn't *seen* you for years,' said Johnathan.

'He always hated me,' whined Gregory.

Johnathan's head had started to hurt. He rubbed his temples as he tried to concentrate. 'Why do you say that?'

'Well, he always loved you more.'

'Oh?'

'Obviously.'

'Why? Give me an example.'

'All right,' said Gregory. 'What about the bikes?'

'What *about* the bikes?' asked Jake.

'What bikes?' asked Johnathan.

'The bikes. You know, those Chopper bikes.' Gregory looked at Johnathan expectantly, waiting for him to remember.

Johnathan frowned. 'Yes.'

'We had strict rules about those bikes. It was agreed that we got them on our tenth birthdays. Set in stone, that rule was.'

Johnathan shrugged. 'And?'

'You got yours on your *eighth*,' hissed Gregory.

'I did?'

'Oh, don't try and pretend that you don't remember,' said Gregory scornfully. 'That's just insulting my intelligence. And yours had gears, and a dynamo.' Gregory's eyes blazed with the zeal of a man deeply wronged.

'This is ridiculous,' said Johnathan. 'I've just stayed up half the night waiting for you to come home when I should have been in bed with my girlfriend, and this is all the thanks I get.'

'Ooh, Johnathan's got a girlfriend,' minced Gregory. 'How spiffing.'

'I'm going,' said Johnathan.

'What's her name?' asked Gregory.

Johnathan looked at Jake. 'Can you try and make sure he doesn't go anywhere tomorrow?'

Jake nodded. 'I'll do my best, but no promises.'

'Is she pretty?' asked Gregory.

'Look,' said Johnathan to Jake, 'do you want to go for a drink tomorrow night? You can meet Kibby.'

'Yeah. That would be cool.'

'Hah! Kibby. What does she do?'

Johnathan named a pub. 'Around eight?'

Jake nodded. 'See you then.'

'Can I come?'

'No, you most definitely can't. You have to stay at home and keep your head down.'

'Anyone would think you were shy,' observed Gregory.

Johnathan put on his coat and turned to go. He was very tired. 'Gregory, could you just do me one favour?' he asked.

'What?'

'Please,' said Johnathan, 'shut up.'

He shut the front door behind him.

Johnathan went home and crawled into bed next to Kibby without waking her. He fell into a deep and dreamless sleep, waking up around mid morning in an empty bed. He padded out of the bedroom and found Kibby dressed and reading a Sunday paper.

'Hello,' she said. 'What time did you make it home?'

'Late,' said Johnathan.

'What happened?'

'Well, he's fine, unfortunately. He'd gone clubbing.'

'Thoughtful of him.'

'He suddenly doesn't seem to be particularly concerned about his own safety, which is a view I am rapidly starting to have some sympathy with.'

'Poor you,' said Kibby. 'How's your head?'

'Fine,' said Johnathan guardedly.

'Oh good. You looked as if you might have a bit of a headache this morning.'

Johnathan said nothing.

'By the way,' said Kibby, 'what were you going to say to me yesterday before the phone rang? It seemed terribly important.'

'I don't remember.'

'Well, it looked important from the amount you were sweating.'

Bloody woman, thought Johnathan. She noticed everything.

That evening Johnathan introduced Kibby to Jake in the pub. He had been a little nervous, but needn't have been: Jake was not the sort of person to begrudge his friends their girlfriends. After ten minutes Kibby considerately went to the toilet to enable the initial judgement to be delivered.

'Mate,' said Jake. 'Nice one.' He raised his glass.

Johnathan beamed. 'She's great, isn't she?'

'Not bad.' Jake nodded in appreciation. Praise from Jake came no higher. 'Miles better than that other one. What was her name?'

'Chloe,' said Johnathan, marvelling at Jake's inability to retain information for which he did not have an immediate use.

'That's right,' said Jake, nodding. 'Chloe. She was nuts.'

'As nutty as a fruitcake,' confirmed Johnathan. 'A nutty fruitcake,' he elaborated.

Kibby returned, fully aware of what had been going on. When Jake went to the bar to get another round of drinks, she whispered, 'How did I do?' with a sardonic smile.

'You passed. Flying colours.'

'Glory be. First time for everything.'

When Jake returned, Johnathan was keen to discuss the problem of what to do about Gregory. 'I suppose it really depends when Spike realizes that I'm not who he thought I was,' said Johnathan. 'As soon as he does, he'll send someone round to Gregory's house straight away.'

'Wouldn't they break in and trash the place anyway?' asked Jake.

Johnathan shrugged. 'Maybe. But Spike wants his money,

rather than anything in the house, so they might just wait for him to return.'

'What, in an unmarked surveillance car drinking bad coffee from Styrofoam cups?' asked Kibby.

'I suppose so,' said Johnathan.

'Cool,' she said. 'Just like the movies.'

'I bet those scenes never make it to the trailers,' said Johnathan.

'Not unless the people in the car are having sex while they wait,' agreed Kibby.

'Complicated, this, isn't it?' said Johnathan after a while.

'I bet Scooby Doo never had these problems,' said Jake.

'But they had Thelma,' remarked Kibby.

'Who's Thelma?' asked Johnathan.

'Thelma was the uptight lesbian in the orange jumper and glasses who solved every case.'

Johnathan remembered. 'How do you know she was a lesbian?'

'It was obvious. The pretty one – was it Daphne? – was shagging the blond guy, who was a repressed homosexual.'

'He was?' said Johnathan and Jake together.

Kibby nodded. 'You could tell by that blue neck-scarf he used to wear all the time. Not very subtle in terms of homosexual iconography, but it *was* the seventies.'

Johnathan and Jake looked at Kibby in bewilderment. 'It's the classic stereotype of the genre,' she continued. 'The plain one in the glasses is the brainy one who solves the mystery while the other four members of the gang indulge in various sensual pursuits of one sort or another, whether it's bonking or making large sandwiches. And you could guarantee that every so often Thelma would lose her glasses, at which point she would of course be totally blind and helpless. The parallels with Piggy in *Lord of the Flies* are obvious.'

'But Piggy wasn't a lesbian, was he?' said Johnathan.

'Piggy was asexual,' said Kibby.

'For Christ's sake, Piggy was *ten*,' said Jake.

'Look,' explained Kibby, 'my point is that these intellectual iconoclasts rarely fit into the traditional, pre-ordained sexual roles expected of them.'

There was a bemused pause.

'Another drink?' asked Johnathan.

FIFTEEN

The rest of the evening had degenerated into a good natured discussion of various children's television programmes of their youth. No further progress was made as to what to do about Gregory.

Progress of another sort was made at the end of the evening, however. Kibby agreed to come back to Johnathan's flat again, and stayed the night.

The following morning Johnathan was intercepted by Sonya as he crept surreptitiously to his office, half an hour late.

'Johnathan, message for you,' she shouted.

Johnathan tiptoed into the reception area, making shushing motions with his finger. 'Yes?' he whispered.

'Mr Kyriakedes wants you to go and see him,' said Sonya.

'Thank you,' whispered Johnathan, and turned to leave.

'Why are you whispering?' asked Sonya pleasantly.

Johnathan smiled weakly and tapped the side of his head gently. 'Bit of a headache this morning,' he explained quietly, and tottered out. He was beginning to worry about the severity of his hangovers. He was concerned in particular about the increase in the amount of alien chemicals floating around his body on a more or less permanent basis: his intake of aspirin had multiplied hugely.

Johnathan made it to his office without seeing anyone. He sat down heavily and laid his head on the desk for a few moments. He enjoyed the small oasis of tranquillity and breathed a grateful sigh. He closed his eyes.

Ten seconds later the telephone exploded next to his ear. Johnathan sprang out of his chair in wide-eyed confusion. As he hit the ground he swiped the receiver angrily.

'What?' he demanded.

'Sorry,' said Sonya. 'I forgot to mention. He wants to see you right away.'

Johnathan sighed. 'Right,' he said, and slammed the receiver back into its cradle. He walked to Kyriakedes's office and pushed open the door. As usual, clouds of acrid smoke billowed towards him as he entered. As the smell hit his nostrils his hangover cranked itself up a gear or two.

'You wanted to see me,' he said.

'Yes, mate,' said Efthymios Kyriakedes. 'I just wanted to check you delivered that package on Friday.' He smiled pleasantly at Johnathan.

'Right. Yes. Well, I was going to talk to you about that, actually,' said Johnathan. 'Because in fact I didn't.'

'Oh?' said the Greek.

'Um, yes, I went to that address and knocked on the door and there was no reply. I waited around for a while to see if someone would turn up, but nobody did. And I thought I'd better keep it rather than stick it through the letter box if it's so important. You did say to deliver it personally.' He grinned his most apologetic grin. The effort almost took the top of his head off.

'Well, that's strange,' said Kyriakedes. 'There's always someone there. Perhaps they just didn't hear you knock.' He thought. 'Have you still got the package?' Johnathan nodded.

'All right. Look, it's no disaster. A few days' delay won't matter. Can you deliver it for me today? At lunchtime?' He named an address in Soho.

Johnathan's heart sank. 'Actually,' he began, 'I *am* a little tied up –'

'Well, I'm sure you'll manage,' interrupted Kyriakedes cheerfully. 'Thanks again. And just be sure to hand it to the guy personally. He cares about things like that. Cheerio.' And with the wave of a cigarette, Johnathan was dismissed.

Well, thought Johnathan as he slumped back to his office, that went as well as could be expected in the circumstances. He's only asked you to do the one thing that you really, *really* didn't want to do, which was to see Spike again. Johnathan's hangover had now established itself as a complex and unstructured beast, roaming across his cerebellum in a random way. Desperately Johnathan tried to think of ways he might avoid the confrontation. He decided that if he was going to have to give the package to Spike personally, he would just act innocently, and pretend he hadn't opened the other envelope with Gregory's name in it.

Johnathan pulled out the envelope Spike had given him and examined it carefully. Luckily he had pulled the flap open rather than ripping along the top of the envelope. He pressed the flap shut. There was still some residual adhesive on the flap, but not enough to keep it properly shut. Johnathan went to ask Sonya if she had any glue, and used that to stick the flap down properly. After he had finished, it looked more or less as it had done when he had been given it. He would have to risk it, he decided. The first plan would be to try and leave the package without actually seeing Spike. If that failed, the second plan would be to try to leave before Spike opened Kyriakedes's package and realized his mistake. If that also failed, the third plan was to hand back Spike's envelope, bluff with aplomb, and keep his fingers crossed.

That lunchtime Johnathan emerged from Leicester Square tube station, dodged the traffic hurtling up Charing Cross Road, and set off through the small streets lined with Chinese grocery stores and video shops towards Old Compton Street.

Soho had changed since Johnathan had last spent much time there. In those days there was still evidence of its earlier tawdriness if you knew where to look. Now the area seemed dry and characterless, the streets heaving with camera-touting tourists and second-rate buskers. Many of Johnathan's old haunts had metamorphosed into fashionable bars where you could go for a pre-theatre special menu with a free glass of Australian Chardonnay, provided you booked three weeks in advance, there were at least eighteen in your party, and you paid in cash.

Johnathan walked down Old Compton Street towards the junction of Wardour Street. He threaded through on to Brewer Street, where he could hear the gruff shouts of the vegetable sellers in the Berwick Street market. Eventually he turned off down a small side passage. Here at least there were still some shops with painted-out windows and long strips of coloured paper hanging over the door, fluttering in the breeze.

Johnathan consulted the piece of paper with Spike's address on it and finally found it. It was a shop. It didn't appear to have a name. In cut-out orange day-glo letters someone had stuck on the inside of the window:

VIDEO'S SOLD AND BROUGHT
MAGS
POPPERS
TOYS

Johnathan hesitated. He took a deep breath and went inside.

The shop was surprisingly busy. Beneath the artificial hue of a flickering strip light, fifteen or so men stood in line in front of a huge magazine rack, all facing the wall as if they were in a giant *pissoir*. Some were rapidly working their way through large numbers of magazines, picking them up, methodically flicking through, and replacing them. Others stood gazing impassively at one page, scarcely moving. Nobody talked. A radio hummed tinnily in the corner.

Johnathan went towards the 'PAY HERE' sign at the back of the shop. Behind a painted desk sat a fat, middle-aged woman smoking a cigarette. She wore a sequinned top several sizes too small. There was a considerable gap between the bottom of this and the top of her leopardskin leggings, from which her gravity-bound midriff tumbled in unstoppable rolls. Her badly dyed black hair fell messily around her shoulders.

The woman looked at Johnathan from behind her cigarette. She took a drag. When she did so she kept the hand holding the cigarette perfectly still and moved her mouth to the end of the cigarette, rather than the other way round. The action reminded Johnathan of someone taking a sip from a straw.

'Hello, love,' said the woman.

Johnathan wanted to run out back into the street. He glanced nervously around him. In front of the woman were stacked packs of playing cards. Each card was adorned with a high resolution colour photograph. Johnathan coughed and tried to look elsewhere. 'Yes, hello,' he began in a low voice. 'I wonder if you could help me.'

The woman's eyebrows rose. 'I dare say you do, love.' She leaned down to take another drag on her cigarette, looking Johnathan in the eye all the time. Johnathan felt ridiculous.

'I'm looking for Spike. I have something to deliver to him. He's probably not here today, is he?' he asked hopefully.

'Yes, love,' said the woman. 'He's here somewhere.' Johnathan's shoulders dropped. There goes Plan One. She ground her cigarette out. 'Hang on. I'll see if I can find him for you. Have a look around. I'll be back in a few minutes.'

'Right. Thanks.' Uncertainly Johnathan moved away from the counter as the woman disappeared behind a tatty curtain. He turned and faced the shop. Nobody paid him the slightest attention. The men were either engrossed in their magazines or were edging furtively around the rest of the shop, reading the backs of video boxes or examining the ranks of weirdly sculpted torpedoes of pink plastic which were displayed down one side of the shop, ends pointed heavenwards like some ghastly nuclear armoury.

Trying to look as inconspicuous as possible, Johnathan did a brief tour. As he was passing in front of a rack of magazines, to his horror he heard an unmistakable voice from the other side of the shop.

'Hey! Ahoy there! Corporal Burlip! Atten-*shun*! Hur hur hur!'

It was Derek.

Spinning deftly on his heel, Johnathan reached out and

grabbed the nearest available magazine. He opened it at random and thrust his face into it, desperately hoping Derek would either think he had been mistaken or would have the decency and sensitivity not to confront him publicly in this sort of place.

Derek bustled up, beaming in delight. 'Well! Hello there! What a surprise, I must say!'

'Hello Derek,' stammered Johnathan, lowering the magazine.

'Nice to see you again,' continued Derek, happily oblivious to Johnathan's crucifying embarrassment. 'You keeping well?'

'Er, OK, thanks.'

'Grand.' Derek paused. 'Didn't expect to see you in a place like this,' he said, looking around with satisfaction. 'Haven't seen you here before, have I?'

Johnathan coughed. 'I'm here for work, actually,' he said feebly.

Derek chortled. 'Har har. 'Course you are.' He winked his old wink. Johnathan was surprised at the ferocity of the waves of bilious hatred springing forth from his soul. 'Tell you what, mate,' said Derek, 'I never would've had you down as one of us.'

Johnathan waved his magazine in front of him. 'Really, Derek, you mustn't think –' He stopped, seeing Derek's face darken and turn into an ugly scowl. 'What is it?' he asked.

Derek pointed to the magazine in Johnathan's hand. 'I never would've had you down as one of *them*, either,' he muttered.

For the first time Johnathan looked at the magazine he was holding. On the front cover was a photograph of a naked man with a hairless chest, glistening from a recent application of baby oil. The man was grinning smugly. Above his head were the words: 'EURO PECKERS'. Johnathan recoiled in horror.

He looked up at Derek, who was now backing away with a look of scorn and suspicion etched large across his face. 'Look, Derek, really, you mustn't think for a moment –'

'Buying it for a *friend*, I suppose,' said Derek in disgust. 'Don't worry mate.' He spat out the last word. 'Spare me the excuses. Bloody pervert. *Disgusting*.' He shook his head in sorrow, turned on his heel and marched out of the shop.

Johnathan felt a hot flush of humiliation flood through his body and rise to his cheeks. 'Shit,' he said, with feeling.

Johnathan looked towards the back of the shop. The sequinned woman was back at her post behind the counter, smoking again. He approached. 'Any luck?' he enquired.

'Oh, hello, sweetheart,' said the woman. 'Thought you'd scarpered. Yeah, he's in. Up the stairs, on your right.' She gestured behind her towards the curtain.

'Right,' said Johnathan. 'Thanks ever so much.' On the other side was a narrow wooden staircase which was badly in need of a coat of paint. At the top was a door, which he cautiously pushed open. The door gave on to a poorly lit corridor. Johnathan stood for a while his eyes adjusting to the lack of light.

After a moment he sensed movement at the far end of the corridor. He looked to his right and could just make out in the half-light the enormous silhouetted bulk of a man. As the figure approached Johnathan saw that it was Terry, who had opened the door to him in Balham. He peered downwards at Johnathan.

'All right,' said Terry eventually, nodding curtly.

'Is Spike in?' asked Johnathan.

'Expecting you?'

'Oh. Yes. Sort of. Well. Not really. No.'

Terry seemed satisfied with this response. 'Hang on.' He turned around slowly and lumbered off down the corridor. After a few moments he reappeared. 'Come on, then,' he called.

Johnathan approached cautiously. Terry held the door open for Johnathan and ushered him in. He remained outside the room and shut the door firmly behind Johnathan.

'Have a seat,' said Spike from behind a large desk on the other side of the room.

Johnathan sat down on a chair in front of the desk. Spike said nothing, but instead lit a cigarette with a rather flashy gold lighter. He wore a pristine bright yellow shirt with two huge orange and white cockatoos embroidered on its front.

Johnathan watched Spike smoke the entire cigarette in six or seven enormous puffs. Quite what he was meant to say Johnathan didn't know. 'Wow, fantastic lungs,' perhaps. He decided to wait.

Spike finally ground the stub of the cigarette into an already over-flowing ashtray. 'Well,' he said. 'Our friend returns already. Excellent. Have you got something to report? Mission accomplished? Quick work, I must say. Very efficient. I can see that we may be using you again.' He beamed. Johnathan blinked in the glare of Spike's fluo-rescent teeth.

'Actually,' said Johnathan as casually as he could, 'I've got no news on that front. I'm here on a totally different matter. I've just been asked to deliver something to you.' He reached into his jacket and produced Kyriakedes's package, which he dropped on to the table. Timing was vital. He

173

stood up. 'So, anyway, there you go,' he said. 'Good to see you again. I'll let you know when I've got some news on the other thing.'

'Hold on,' said Spike. 'Sit down a moment. What is this?' He looked at the package suspiciously.

Johnathan shrugged nervously. 'No idea,' he said, truthfully for once. 'Anyway. Must dash.'

'I said, sit down.'

'No, look, it's OK, I've really got to make a move.'

Spike looked at Johnathan thoughtfully. 'Well you can try and leave if you want, but Terry is standing outside that door and won't let you go anywhere without my say-so, so you may as well sit down.'

Panic rose in Johnathan's throat as Plan Two flew out of the window. He sat down.

'Thank you,' said Spike. He addressed his attention to the package. 'Right,' he said. 'What have we here?'

He opened the envelope and pulled out the papers inside. He read them with a faint frown. After a minute or so he looked up at Johnathan. 'Just remind me,' he said. 'When you showed up on Friday, you said the Greek you sent you, right?'

Johnathan coughed uncomfortably. 'That's right.'

'Huh,' said Spike. 'Oh dear.'

There was a pause.

'Wrong Greek,' concluded Spike.

Johnathan shrugged, his intestines doing cartwheels of terror. 'I did wonder,' he admitted. 'But I didn't really have time to point out the mistake.'

'Hmm.' Spike watched Johnathan closely. 'You do leave me with something of a problem,' he said. 'You see, I don't know you at all. I gave you some confidential stuff the other day. And I wouldn't want it to fall into the wrong hands. Understand?'

'Oh absolutely,' said Johnathan. He pulled out the resealed letter. Here we go. Fingers crossed. 'I thought there might have been a mistake and so I didn't actually open the envelope at all. I suspected it might have something important in it I wasn't supposed to see. So you have nothing to worry about. I don't know anything.'

Spike looked at Johnathan. He took the envelope and examined it. Johnathan held his breath. Finally Spike grunted and opened the envelope to check its contents. He appeared satisfied.

'Sure you didn't open this?' he demanded.

Johnathan shook his head vehemently.

'Well,' said Spike. 'You obviously have some brains, which is good to know. For both our sakes. It means I can rely on you to keep your mouth shut and never to speak to anyone about Friday night and the conversation we had.'

'OK,' said Johnathan.

'It means that you have never seen me.'

'OK,' said Johnathan.

'And it means you've never visited that house in Balham.'

'OK,' said Johnathan.

'Good. Still, there are a few precautions I'm going to take just to make sure you understand how serious I am about this.'

'Er, OK,' said Johnathan.

Spike sat back in his chair and shouted, 'Terry? Couldn't come in here a moment, could you?' He turned to face Johnathan again. 'Right. Now listen, I hope you won't have any hard feelings about this, but I'm going to ask two of my colleagues to administer a small lesson so that we all understand each other and you're not tempted to open your mouth in the future. OK?'

Johnathan said nothing, now paralysed with fear.

The door swung open, and in shuffled Terry with an equally enormous companion.

'Boss?' enquired Terry.

'Terry, be so good as to escort this gentleman off the premises in the traditional manner,' said Spike. He stood up and walked out of the room, slamming the door behind him. Terry took his hand off Johnathan's shoulder. Johnathan stood up shakily.

'Right,' said Terry. 'Shall we go?'

SIXTEEN

Johnathan awoke to the sound of a nearby siren whooping. He opened his eyes and saw twin blue lights flashing on the top of the ambulance that had just arrived. He was vaguely aware of a sea of interested faces peering down at him. There was a bright pop as a flash gun went off.

Johnathan tried to move, and immediately wished that he hadn't. Blinding pain shot through his body in every direction. It flooded every nook and cranny of sensory vulnerability and exploded in a blaze of white light. He hurt.

Then he was being handled, in a sure, professional manner. Someone was talking to him gently. His body was prodded and pushed. And then some fine man pushed Johnathan's sleeve up, inserted a needle, and the pain rolled away into darkness as quickly as it had come.

When he next opened his eyes, the first thing Johnathan saw was the off-white ceiling of the hospital. He gazed at it with a detached curiosity as he tried to remember who he was, where he might be, and why.

He carefully moved his head to the right. A nurse in a dark blue uniform stood next to the bed. She smiled at him.

'Hello,' she said. 'Welcome back to the land of the living. Quite a nasty little fight you got into back there.'

Johnathan mumbled something. He wasn't quite sure what.

'We're going to keep you in here for a little while,' continued the nurse. 'Just for surveillance. It's quite routine. We always do when a patient's had concussion. Anyway, we need to check that those ribs set properly, don't we?'

Concussion? Ribs? Johnathan wanted to say. Instead he groaned quietly to himself.

'Your friend was here earlier,' said the nurse. 'I'll give her a ring now to tell her you're awake. Don't start getting any ideas about going anywhere. You're to stay exactly where you are. Understand?' Johnathan nodded. 'Anyway, you'll probably want to read about yourself in here.' The nurse threw a copy of the *Evening Standard* on to the bed, opened at page seven. Johnathan stared at the page for some time. Eventually the print came into some sort of focus. He read the piece in silence.

GAY BACKLASH CONTINUES – LATEST VICTIM FOUND

The increase in violence against members of the homosexual community in Soho manifested itself once more early this afternoon when a man was found suffering severe wounds to his head and upper body behind one of the quarter's best-known gay bars. The victim, Jonathan Burlip, a solicitor, was in possession of gay pornographic material, which police feel may have been the provoking factor in this attack.

This is the fifth attack on the homosexual community in Soho in recent weeks. So far police have failed to make any arrests and have not yet commented as to whether the attacks may be related. The investigation continues.

Johnathan's head slumped back on to the pillow in disbelief. He had forgotten about the magazine, which he must have stuffed into his pocket as he went up to see Spike. He shut his eyes for a few moments and then read the article again, noticing with irritation that his name had been spelled wrongly. He read it for a third time. He began to understand why journalists were so unpopular with the people they wrote about.

Some time later the nurse returned and gave him an injection. Later – how much later Johnathan was unable to tell – Kibby appeared by his bedside.

'What *happened*?' asked Kibby. 'Are you all right?'

'I suppose I'll live,' said Johnathan as pathetically as he thought he could get away with.

'You poor thing,' said Kibby sympathetically. 'Does it hurt?'

'Oh yes,' said Johnathan. 'Cracked a rib or two.'

'So. Go on. Tell me what happened.'

Johnathan explained as best he could about Spike's theory of the pre-emptive strike as an effective deterrent.

'God, how barbaric,' said Kibby. 'Is there anything you can do about it?'

'I don't suppose so. I could go to the police of course but I'm not sure what that would achieve other than putting myself back into hospital.' Johnathan winced.

'Probably the right decision, by the look of you,' said Kibby. 'Anyway, the most important thing is to get you better and out of here.' There was a small pause. 'Actually, I've got some news myself,' said Kibby.

'Oh?' said Johnathan.

Kibby looked awkward. 'Mmm. In fact it's good news and bad news.'

'Right.'

'Which do you want first?'

'Give me the good news,' said Johnathan.

There was a pause.

'Actually,' said Kibby, 'there isn't any good news. I made that up.'

'Oh.'

'Just bad news, actually.'

'Well, I suppose you'd better give me the bad news, then,' said Johnathan, suddenly feeling anxious.

'Right. Deep breath. Huh. Um.'

Johnathan had started to get agitated. 'Kibby,' he began, 'if you've got something to say then I'd rather you just came out and said it.' This was a complete fabrication, of course. He desperately didn't want to hear what was coming next. Not here, not now. Not ever, actually, if that was at all possible.

'I know, I know. Sorry. It's just – this is so difficult to say.'

Johnathan felt his world imploding inwards and collapsing like those slow-motion films of buildings being demolished by a few strategically placed explosives. This was it. He realized he was about to be unceremoniously dumped. He swallowed.

'Just say it,' he sighed. Make it quick and painless, he thought.

'Well, it's my parents,' said Kibby sheepishly. 'They want to meet you.'

'What?' Johnathan almost shouted.

'I know. I'm so embarrassed. Please don't be angry. I didn't know how to tell you. But they want to meet you. I suppose I must have mentioned you too many times and now they're curious. And I said yes. Do you mind?'

'Do I mind?' repeated Johnathan. He could feel his heart palpitating in a rush of elation. Fool, fool, he told himself. 'No, I suppose I don't mind,' he croaked.

'Oh good,' said Kibby, relieved. 'They're in Dorset. I said we'd go next Saturday.'

'OK,' said Johnathan. 'It'll be good to get out of London.'

'If you're sure.' Kibby sounded less than convinced.

'Of course I'm sure. It'll be lovely to meet them.'

'Hmm. We'll see.'

There was a pause. Kibby inspected her fingernails. Johnathan's heart was racing. It's meet the parents time, he thought. Woo-hoo. Things are looking up. The latest pain killers started to kick in. He grinned at Kibby in doped-up happiness.

Some time later Jake arrived.

'Bastard,' said Johnathan to Jake as he sat down on the end of the bed.

'What did I do?' asked Jake plaintively.

'Bastard journalist bastard,' explained Johnathan.

'Oh *that*,' said Jake. 'Shouldn't worry about that. I've seen worse.'

'Speaking of newspapers,' said Kibby, 'what on earth *were* you doing with that porn mag? Now everyone in London thinks my boyfriend is gay.'

Johnathan's eyes had shut and he lay back on his pillows. Perhaps if he closed his eyes the question would disappear. Jake and Kibby watched him impatiently.

'Well?' said Kibby.

'Hmm?' said Johnathan mistily. 'Well what?'

'The magazine,' said Jake and Kibby together.

'Oh.' Johnathan sighed. 'Do I have to explain now?'

'Yes,' said Kibby and Jake at once.

Johnathan explained about his encounter with Derek that afternoon. Suddenly he was struck by a thought. 'Where's Gregory?' he asked. 'He could have come to see me, couldn't he, since he's the reason I'm here in the first place?'

'Well,' said Jake awkwardly. 'He said he thought he'd better stay indoors from now on.'

'That's absolutely bloody charming,' said Johnathan. 'Although I suppose he has a point. Well, you'd better tell him to keep his head down for a while longer yet. Spike does still seem very keen on making his acquaintance. Oh Christ,' he groaned. 'Schroedinger. He's alone in the flat. He'll need feeding.'

'Have you got some keys?' asked Kibby. 'I'll go.'

Johnathan's ribs momentarily stopped aching so much. He smiled a fuzzy smile as his brain was lost in syrupy thought. He waved vaguely at the drawer where his belongings had been put.

Kibby retrieved the keys and put them in her pocket. 'Don't worry. He'll be safe with me.'

'Thanks,' mumbled Johnathan. He lay staring at the ceiling listening to Kibby and Jake chatting idly about nothing in particular. Finally his eyes fluttered shut. A series of images drifted through his mind. He thought of Terry's enormous hands on his shoulder, of the anodyne sterility of the hospital. He thought of Kibby giving Schroedinger his supper. Johnathan drifted off into a dreamless sleep.

That evening Johnathan's parents bustled into the ward, trying to hide their excitement beneath a thin veneer of concern for their son's health.

'Darling,' said his mother.

'Hello,' said Johnathan.

'Are you all right?' said his mother. 'Roger and I have been so *worried* about you. Imagine our surprise when we read that article in the *Standard*. First thing we knew about it was when Hermione telephoned to ask if you were feeling any better. So of course we had to rush out and buy a copy.' She paused for breath.

'I'm fine, really,' said Johnathan.

There was a pause. Johnathan's father inspected the clipboard hanging from the end of Johnathan's bed.

'So,' said his mother.

'So,' agreed Johnathan.

'Have the police been to see you yet?' she asked.

'Not yet.'

'It's awful, what's been going on. Quite dreadful. Such wanton discrimination. Shocking.'

Johnathan saw that his mother was looking down on him with a teary smile, prouder than she had ever looked before. Maternal, almost. Suddenly he understood.

'Mum,' said Johnathan. 'I'm not a homosexual.'

'Hush, now, you're tired,' said his mother. 'Probably still in shock, poor lamb,' she said to his father.

'I've got a girlfriend, actually,' said Johnathan. 'Her name's Kibby.'

Johnathan's mother nodded sympathetically, not listening to a word. 'We'll talk about this another time,' she said, looking at her watch. 'We're just off to a new gallery opening. Mud sculptures. Very proto-bohemian.' Johnathan looked back blankly. 'But we just wanted to see that you were feeling all right and to tell you that we're very, *very* proud of you.' Johnathan sank back into his pillows, defeated. His mother kissed him on the cheek. 'Can't *wait* to talk about it all when you're better,' she cooed. 'And I'm *desperate* to meet all

your friends. They're always so very handsome. Lucky boy.'
Johnathan's father beamed at him from the end of the bed.

Johnathan closed his eyes. 'Bye then,' he said.

'Let us know as soon as you get out, darling.'

'I will.'

'And don't let the buggers grind you down. If I can say bugger.'

Johnathan sighed. 'I won't.'

The next morning Johnathan was visited by a dour-looking policeman, who introduced himself as Detective Inspector Gold. He was accompanied by a serious young constable who remained silent throughout the interview.

'Nasty business, this, sir,' said Gold.

Johnathan nodded warily. He knew better than to tell the police anything which might be useful, as that would simply precipitate his return to intensive care.

'It's the fifth attack like this, you know,' said Gold.

'So I read. If it's the same people.'

'What makes you think it might not be?' asked Gold.

Because I know who beat me up, Johnathan wanted to shout. It was Terry and his mate. Instead he shrugged. 'Nothing. I don't know who did the others, do I?'

'Well, let's see what we can piece together, shall we?' said Gold. 'First of all, can you tell me where you were immediately prior to the attack?'

'In a shop,' said Johnathan.

'Where was the shop?'

'I don't know exactly. Down an alleyway. Off Brewer Street.'

Gold wrote something on his pad. 'What was the shop called?' he asked.

'I don't think it had a name, as such,' said Johnathan.

'Right. What sort of shop was it?' asked Gold without looking up from his pad.

There was a pause. 'You know,' said Johnathan.

Gold put his pen down, and looked at Johnathan. 'I'm sorry, sir, but I don't.' The two men stared at each other for a few seconds.

'It was a pornography shop,' said Johnathan.

Gold picked up his pen and wrote some more on his pad, and then ostentatiously underlined it three times. 'Go there regularly?' he asked.

'Certainly not,' said Johnathan indignantly.

The policeman eyed Johnathan with undisguised scepticism. 'Well, do you think you could identify the shop again?' he asked.

'Yes.'

'And was this the shop where you purchased the . . . literature that you were carrying when you were attacked?'

'Yes.' Johnathan didn't think it would be helpful to complicate matters by explaining that he hadn't actually paid for the magazine.

'So what happened when you left the shop?' asked Gold.

'Well, I don't really remember,' said Johnathan. 'I was just wandering along, you know, and suddenly the next thing I knew I woke up on the floor.' He paused. 'I didn't really see anything.'

'Nothing at all?' said Gold disbelievingly. Johnathan shook his head. 'How many men attacked you? More than one?'

Johnathan shrugged. 'Whoever it was came at me from behind. I didn't see a thing.'

Gold continued to quiz Johnathan in the same vein for another half hour, asking the same questions in different ways. Johnathan got the distinct impression that the policeman was doing his best to catch him out. He wondered whether Gold got out much.

Gold finally shook his head in defeat. 'I find this all rather hard to believe, sir.'

Johnathan shrugged. A pain shot across his chest. 'Me too,' he replied. 'It's not every day I get attacked in broad daylight.'

'Well,' said Gold, 'if you suddenly remember anything else which you think might be of interest, you must contact me at once. After all, sir, we're only trying to protect you people from any more attacks like this.'

'Actually,' said Johnathan, 'what they said in the paper about that wasn't quite —'

'Good day to you, sir,' said Gold, snapping his notebook shut and standing up in one movement. 'I hope you feel better soon.'

Could have fooled me, thought Johnathan.

SEVENTEEN

Soon after Detective Inspector Gold's departure, Johnathan's chest was X-rayed for a second time, and he was told he could leave the hospital and go home after lunch. He waited impatiently for the usual fare of tepid indefinables that passed as food to be trolleyed round and then got dressed, promising to return in a week's time for a further check-up.

At home, the answer machine was winking at him. Schroedinger got up from his bean bag to give him a welcoming sniff in the groin, but apart from that showed no signs of having missed him at all. Gee, thanks, thought Johnathan. Glad to see you too. He patted him distractedly and pressed the button on the machine.

'*Johnathan?*' Johnathan's heart sank. 'It's me. I've just seen the paper. I – I just don't know what to say. I suppose I'm happy for you, if you've finally been doing some real thinking about yourself and realized that this is your true self, your real sexual persona.' Johnathan sighed. 'I suppose what I'm wondering is whether this was always there, at the back of your mind, you know, when we, when we made love. Because if it was, well, I suppose that would explain a few things.'

Hang on. What few things? Chloe continued.

'I suppose I can't blame you and maybe I should even

admire you, as it can't have been easy. But you should know that I'm sad too, as I realize that this means that it's all over for us, romantically speaking. I just wish you could have felt able to tell me yourself.'

What few things?

'Anyway, give me a call. I want to help you through this difficult time. I wish you luck in your new adventure.' Oh, for Christ's sake. Johnathan pressed the button again angrily.

There were several other messages from people who had seen the report in the newspaper. Johnathan spent the rest of the afternoon issuing statements of denial. He failed to convince anyone that the story was wrong, because of a complete lack of alternative explanation as to what the magazine was doing in his pocket. He didn't call Chloe. At least this episode seemed to have convinced her that things really were over between them. He grunted. As linings went, that was of the cheap silver-plate variety.

He finally called Jake.

'He's still here,' said Jake as soon as Johnathan had identified himself.

'Thanks, mate,' said Johnathan.

'I didn't really have much of a choice, did I, what with you being in hospital,' answered Jake. 'But that's it. No more.' He paused. 'You didn't arrange to get beaten up to avoid having to take him in, did you?' he asked suspiciously.

'For God's sake,' said Johnathan.

'Believe me,' said Jake, 'that isn't quite as far-fetched as it may sound to you. Nothing would surprise me about the lengths people would go to to avoid your brother. Murder seems quite reasonable in the circumstances.'

Johnathan nodded. 'You'd have a good case to plead provocation.'

Jake snorted. 'You don't know the half of it,' he said. 'Anyway, now that you're back, the joy will be all yours. Congratulations, and if you *do* decide to inflict some sort of grotesque physical injury on him, will you please give me advance warning, because I'd like to come along and watch. Maybe even join in.'

'You couldn't just give me one more day to get things ready for him, could you?' asked Johnathan. 'Things are a bit of a mess here, obviously, what with my stay in hospital, and I'd like to get things sorted before he arrives.'

'Shouldn't bother,' said Jake. 'He'll hate it.'

'I know,' said Johnathan.

'He hates everything.'

'I know.'

'He's an arsehole.'

'I know.'

There was a pause. 'Shit,' said Jake. 'Go on then. One more night. But that's it. Tomorrow morning he's out on his arse and I sincerely hope that I never see him again.'

Johnathan breathed a large sigh of relief. 'Thanks a million.'

'Yeah. You owe me. Big time. Big, huge, enormous time.'

Johnathan put the telephone down and considered Gregory's imminent arrival. Having Gregory in his flat would provide all the incentive Johnathan needed to have the problem with Spike resolved as soon as possible. The flat was small, and the prospect of having a second person living there on a full-time basis was in itself unappealing. When the person in question happened to be Gregory the problem assumed acute brain-focusing proportions. Something would clearly have to be done, and the quicker the better.

That evening Kibby came round to see how he was.

'Hello, moron,' she said as he opened the door, thrusting a bottle of wine into his hand and kissing him gently on the lips. She dropped her shoulder bag on to the floor. 'I've brought my stuff, if that's OK. Thought I'd stay over. Easier to keep an eye on you that way. We could have a pyjama party. Or a non-pyjama party. Whichever you prefer.'

'Well, you needn't worry,' said Johnathan. 'As soon as I've got Gregory off my hands I fully intend to get back to my usual, dreary, hospital-free life.'

'That's good to hear,' said Kibby, bending down to scratch Schroedinger's head fondly. 'Less worry for me. I'm not sure I can cope with the excitement of never knowing if I should be calling the office or the emergency ward if I want to talk to you.'

'Believe me,' said Johnathan with feeling, 'those are sentiments I share entirely.'

A while later Johnathan and Kibby discussed their trip to Dorset the following weekend to visit Kibby's parents. Kibby was cautious about the whole enterprise.

'You don't understand,' she said. 'You haven't met my parents. They're . . . I suppose I'm just worried.'

Johnathan stared silently at his wine glass. He knew that he would still be potty about her even if her parents were awful. Dorset was far enough away for it not to matter too much, after all. What struck him most, though, was that he had discovered the weak link in Kibby's emotional armour. This was something she was actually worried about. That should have been the cue for Johnathan to reassure Kibby magnanimously that there was no cause for concern. Actually what he wanted to do was strut cockily around the flat beating his chest in mean-hearted triumph in celebration of the fact that he was not the only one who suffered the occasional crisis of self-confidence.

'It'll be fine,' he said. 'I'm sure they're lovely.'

'No, you misunderstand,' said Kibby. 'I'm not worried about what you think of them. I'm concerned about what they're going to think of you.'

Johnathan's spirits deflated. 'Oh,' he said.

'It's just that both my parents are a bit mad. And they do have some rather fixed views about the sort of people I should be liaising with, and you, my duck, don't really fit in with their ideas. And they're both very forthright people,' she continued, sipping her wine. 'Neither was ever destined for a career in the diplomatic service. They probably only want to meet you so they can tut disapprovingly down the phone at me afterwards and point out all your shortcomings. I don't want to put you through that sort of ordeal if I can help it.'

'I see,' said Johnathan. And what exactly, he wanted to ask, do you think they might have to say about me which you're so worried about? Tell me about all my shortcomings. His brain obligingly began to churn out possible complaints, reservations, and put-downs. He closed his eyes in misery. Latest score from the London Confidence Crisis League: Kibby 0, Johnathan 103 (all own goals).

'Let me tell you what I think they might have to say about you which I'm so worried about,' said Kibby after a few moments.

Johnathan put up his hands. 'Really,' he said, 'no need.'

The next day Johnathan went back to work. To his surprise, when he opened the door to his office he saw Efthymios

Kyriakedes sitting on the desk, which was creaking dangerously beneath his weight. As usual one of his powerful cigarettes was hanging from one side of his mouth, filling the room with acrid smoke.

'Hello, pal,' said Efthymios Kyriakedes.

'Hello,' said Johnathan. 'Bit early for you, isn't it?'

Kyriakedes pointed a fat finger at him. 'Less of that tone, thanks very much. I'm here to talk about you.'

'About me?'

'Your little adventure in Soho. The hospital.'

'Oh, *that*,' said Johnathan. 'No need to worry about that. Just a bit of a misunderstanding.'

Kyriakedes looked at Johnathan sharply. 'Yeah, well. I just heard things. You know.' He sniffed.

'Oh, listen,' said Johnathan, 'if you're wondering about that report in the paper then I can explain that all very easily –'

'Don't worry, no need,' interrupted Kyriakedes, waving his cigarette. 'Your personal life is your own. Live and let live, I say. I've got nothing against you lot personally. I'm very liberal-minded. As a matter of fact, some of my best friends know people who are queer.' The Greek's nose wrinkled in distaste. 'Just as long as it doesn't affect your work.'

Johnathan nodded. 'Don't worry. It won't happen again.'

'Good. I should hope not.' He paused. 'I take it you managed to deliver that letter before you had your little accident?'

Johnathan sighed. 'Yes I did.'

'Well, that's something,' said Kyriakedes. 'I think I'd prefer it if you kept your other interests to outside office hours. Best not to mix business and, er, pleasure.' He eased himself gingerly off the desk. 'Just try and stay out of trouble,' he advised. 'You look relatively sensible. But it always seems to be the quiet ones who attract the trouble. Like flies to shit.'

Wow, thanks a million, thought Johnathan. 'I'll do my best,' he said.

'Good boy,' said Kyriakedes, and disappeared through the door. Johnathan opened the window in an attempt to clear the room of smoke. He sat down behind his desk, trying not to breathe in too deeply.

Johnathan spent the rest of the day catching up on the mountain of correspondence that had amassed on his desk during his brief stay in hospital. It was extraordinary how much paper lawyers produced: letters, memoranda, contracts, notes, bills – swathes of rain forest were sacrificed every day to provide justification for their continued existence and their ever-increasing stranglehold over the lives of ordinary people.

At six o'clock, as Johnathan was thinking about going home, the telephone rang. It was Sonia. 'Couple of people here to see you,' she said. She sounded put out. They had probably interrupted her at a crucial stage of nail buffing.

'Who is it?' asked Johnathan, frowning. He had no appointments in his diary.

'Didn't say. Actually they're already on their way up.'

As Sonia was speaking, the door to Johnathan's office opened and Spike walked in, followed by Terry, who turned and shut the door carefully behind him. A screaming sound shot through Johnathan's head. He realized that he was clutching the receiver in white-knuckled terror. He opened his mouth and then shut it again.

Spike waved casually to Johnathan. Johnathan was too

petrified to move. He stared blindly at Spike and Terry. Terry gazed at Johnathan implacably. Spike smiled affably.

'Mr Burlip?' said Sonia. 'Are you there?'

'Yes,' croaked Johnathan eventually. 'I'm here.'

'Have your clients arrived?'

'Oh yes,' said Johnathan.

'So they're there.'

'They're here. We're all here.'

'All right then.'

'All right.'

'Bye.'

'Bye.' Johnathan carefully put the phone down. He shut his eyes and said a brief prayer of vague but intense supplication.

'Hello again,' said Spike.

'Hello.'

'How are you feeling?'

Considerably worse than I did a few minutes ago, thought Johnathan. His ribs had started to throb. 'Rather sore, actually,' he stammered.

'Yeah well,' said Spike. 'I did explain. Need to make sure you keep your word, and all that.' Spike winked.

'Oh, absolutely,' said Johnathan. 'Quite understand.' He nervously watched as Terry wandered around the perimeter of the room, cracking his knuckles as he examined the walls. Johnathan wondered whether he was calculating whether or not they were thick enough to muffle the sound of screams to people outside.

'Yeah. Well. I didn't actually come to ask about your health. Thing is, you see, I've got a bit of a problem,' confessed Spike.

'Really?'

194

'Yeah. You see, I always read the *Evening Standard*, and I saw that you got a little mention in it.'

Johnathan grimaced. 'Ah yes. Fame at last.'

'Right. Anyway, one thing in particular struck me about that newspaper article,' said Spike.

'Oh, look,' said Johnathan, 'if you were wondering about that magazine they mentioned then I can explain exactly –'

Spike looked at Johnathan with contempt. 'I don't care about the bloody magazine,' he said. 'What you choose to read in the privacy of your own home is your business.'

'No, exactly,' said Johnathan. 'That was my point. You see, I wouldn't want you to think –'

'Anyway,' interrupted Spike. 'That wasn't the thing that interested me.'

Johnathan paused. 'No?'

'No. What I found far more interesting was something else about you.'

'Oh really?'

'Yeah, really.' Spike paused. 'Your name.'

There was a long pause as Johnathan and Spike looked at each other over the desk. The only noise was the castanet-like sound of Terry's knuckles punctuating the silence like a small jazz rhythm section. Johnathan swallowed.

'What about my name?' he asked.

'Well,' said Spike. 'It might just be a huge coincidence and nothing to worry about, but I've never really been one for taking risks about things like that.'

'Go on,' said Johnathan, as innocently as he could.

'The thing is this. D'you remember that envelope I gave you?'

'Of course I do,' replied Johnathan. 'I thought that was the reason you asked Terry to, um, you know.'

'Yeah. Quite right. Well, you won't believe this, but it transpires that the guy whose name was in the envelope I gave you has the same surname as you.'

'*No.*' Johnathan blinked in astonishment.

'True. I swear.'

'How extraordinary. What a coincidence.'

'Yeah. And I did a little bit of checking and you'll never guess what I found out.'

Oh dear. 'What?'

Spike thrust his hands deep into his pockets. 'You two are brothers.'

Johnathan did his best to look astonished whilst at the same time trying not to panic. 'Are you telling me,' he said, 'that my brother Gregory was the guy in that envelope?'

Spike nodded, his smile now gone. 'Amazing, isn't it?'

'That *is* amazing,' said Johnathan. 'But why are you telling me this? I thought the idea was that I should just go away and pretend that the whole thing had never happened.'

'Well, that is what I said at the time, granted,' said Spike. 'But this does change things a bit. Because now I'm asking myself, what if you did actually open the envelope? What if you lied to me and warned your brother about me?'

'But I didn't open the envelope,' squeaked Johnathan.

Spike shrugged. 'Look. Maybe you did, maybe you didn't. But I'll tell you one thing. Your brother isn't at home any more.'

Johnathan did his best to look perplexed. 'He's not?'

'No. It's suspicious, you have to admit. It's as if someone had warned him to lie low for a while.'

Johnathan looked at Spike miserably. 'It wasn't me,' he whispered. He so much wanted it to be true that he almost had started to believe it.

Spike considered Johnathan for a few moments. 'Hmm. Of course, if I found out that it was you and that you'd lied to me then I would need to take some sort of action. Redress the balance. Teach you another lesson.'

Johnathan's stomach went into free-fall. 'Right,' he stammered.

'It's bad enough being lied to and cheated on by one guy without having his brother doing it to you as well. That really would upset me. A lot.'

'Noted,' said Johnathan, eyeing Terry cautiously.

'Anyway,' said Spike more cheerfully. 'My mother always said that you should turn your problems into your advantages. Make things work for you rather than against you. So I've been thinking how we can use this situation to its best advantage.'

Johnathan nodded mutely.

'So you'll be glad to know that I'm not going to have Terry put you back in hospital. Not yet, anyway.'

'OK,' said Johnathan, who did not exactly feel waves of relief flood through his body.

'Instead,' continued Spike, 'I'm going to give you the benefit of the doubt, and I'm going to ask you a small favour.'

Johnathan stared at the two men. 'Uh-huh,' he said eventually.

'It's quite easy,' said Spike. 'I want you to persuade your shit of a brother to pay me the money he owes me.'

'How am I supposed to do that?' asked Johnathan.

Spike shrugged. 'I don't know. But you're brothers. You must have some influence.'

Johnathan saw that now was not the time to explain to Spike that he and Gregory were not close. 'Well,' he said lamely, 'I can certainly do my best.'

'Here's what I suggest,' said Spike. 'Tell him that if he doesn't pay within a week then I'll make sure that he won't be walking anywhere for a very long time. That ought to do the trick.'

'OK,' said Johnathan, suspecting that it wouldn't.

'And of course you could always appeal to his sense of brotherly love.'

Johnathan frowned. 'Why?' he asked.

'Because, old son,' replied Spike, 'if he doesn't pay up, I won't just go after him. It'll be you, too. Just think, you'll be able to share neighbouring beds in the intensive care ward. Won't that be cosy?'

Johnathan went white. 'Oh God,' he said.

'So there you go,' said Spike. 'I'll give you a week to get me my cash. Until then I'll leave you both alone. And if I haven't got the money by six o'clock next Wednesday, then I should start practising using a wheelchair if I were you.'

Johnathan gulped. 'Right,' he said.

Spike stretched out his hand. 'Good to see you again, mate,' he said. 'No hard feelings, eh? It's just business.'

Johnathan shook Spike's hand. 'Just business,' he repeated dully.

'We'll see ourselves out,' continued Spike. 'See you in a week, yeah?' He walked towards the door. Terry opened it and nodded towards Johnathan before following his boss into the corridor and closing the door behind him.

Johnathan flopped down into his chair and buried his head in his hands. Perfect, he thought. Just perfect.

The telephone rang. It was Jake, telephoning to arrange what time Gregory was to arrive at Johnathan's flat that evening, and doing a poor job of hiding the glee in his voice. Johnathan explained what Spike had just proposed.

'So what you're saying is that basically this money has sort of become your responsibility,' said Jake.

'I suppose so. He's relying on me to persuade Gregory to pay it back.'

'Huh. Good luck.'

'Quite,' said Johnathan bitterly. There was a pause.

'So where does that leave you?' asked Jake.

'Not best placed, actually,' said Johnathan.

'Up shit creek without a paddle?'

'God no. I'm at the bottom of shit creek with slabs of concrete tied to my legs and a swarm of hungry piranha fish heading my way downstream.'

'Do piranhas swim in shit?'

'No, they hate swimming in shit. So they're really pissed off piranhas, too.'

Jake whistled. 'Wow.'

'As you say,' said Johnathan. 'Wow.'

EIGHTEEN

As Johnathan stood on the tube that evening as it rushed beneath the heart of the city he considered Spike's proposal with a heavy heart. Gregory was the most stubborn and selfish person he knew. Persuading him to pay the money to Spike either for his own safety or for Johnathan's was not going to be easy. Johnathan resolved to keep his conversation with Spike to himself. Gregory was too contrary a character to confront him with anything as potentially dangerous as the truth. And whilst Gregory could have gone back to his house in safety for a week, Johnathan realized that his chances of persuading him to pay Spike the money were better if Gregory stayed on his sofa, however unpleasant that might be for both of them.

Back at the flat Johnathan prepared a small space in the sitting room for Gregory to leave his things. He lay on the sofa and found to his satisfaction that it wasn't quite long enough to relax on properly.

Two hours after he was due to arrive, Gregory turned up at Johnathan's front door.

'Here I am,' he said unenthusiastically.

'I suppose you'd better come in,' said Johnathan. He led Gregory into the sitting room. 'There you go,' said Johnathan. 'This is where you're staying.'

Gregory looked at the sofa, appalled. 'On *that*?'

'Absolutely. It's very comfortable.' If you're a dwarf, thought Johnathan gleefully.

'Christ. How ghastly,' said Gregory. He put down his bag, switched the television on, and flopped on to the sofa. 'It'll have to do, I suppose. Have you got a drink?'

A little while later Johnathan and Gregory were watching television.

'I gather you got into a spot of trouble,' said Gregory as a commercial break arrived. 'What happened?'

Hooray, thought Johnathan. Finally. Here we go. 'I met Spike again. He still wants to use you as his own personal punch bag.'

'Oh,' said Gregory.

'And,' continued Johnathan, 'if I were you, I would stop playing games and pay the man what you owe him. He means business.'

Gregory sniffed. 'I don't *owe* him anything. That's the point. He cheated. If anything, *he* should pay *me* for all the bets we had had up to that point.'

Johnathan closed his eyes. 'But look at you,' he said, a hint of desperation creeping into his voice. 'You have this nice pad in Chelsea and here you are staying with me in Tooting. I mean, something isn't quite right, is it? How long are you going to go on running like this?'

Gregory sipped his glass of wine thoughtfully. 'How long? Don't know. Not very. I'll give it a week or so, then go back to the house and carry on as before. He will have forgotten all about by then. He's pretty stupid, this Spike. Nothing holds his attention for very long.'

'You don't think a hundred and twenty thousand quid is

likely to hold his interest for longer than a week?' asked Johnathan.

'Well, perhaps a bit longer than that, but not much. He'll get distracted.' Gregory settled back into the sofa and changed channels without consulting Johnathan, who did his best to hide his irritation.

'I just get this feeling that you're underestimating him, you know,' said Johnathan. 'Look what he did to me, after all. And I'm just your brother.'

'Half brother.'

'Half brother. So don't you think that was supposed to give you some sort of message?'

'What *did* happen to you, anyway?' asked Gregory. 'What did they do?'

'They cracked a few selected ribs, and generally livened up my skin's colour scheme with a choice selection of purples, blacks, and greeny-yellows.'

'Oh *well*,' said Gregory. 'If that's all, I may as well go back tomorrow. That's nothing.'

'But Gregory, I'm not the guy who owes all the money. You are. I think you can expect slightly different treatment.'

Gregory looked unimpressed. 'We'll see,' he said.

'And yes, it does still hurt, thanks very much for asking,' said Johnathan bitterly.

'What?' said Gregory, whose attention had turned back to a wildlife programme about rutting wildebeest.

'Don't worry,' muttered Johnathan. 'Wasn't important.'

'What's for supper?' said Gregory.

The next few days passed slowly. Johnathan worked as late as he could at the office. Spending time in the flat meant he had to talk to Gregory, who lazed about the house all day eating Johnathan's food and watching television. Work was infinitely preferable.

On a number of occasions Johnathan tried to broach the subject of Spike and the repayment of the debt, conscious that Spike's deadline was approaching, but every time, Gregory dismissed the subject with a bored sniff and refused to discuss it. Gregory's sense of moral self-righteousness about the whole matter made things even worse. He seemed to be under the impression that what he was doing was somehow heroic. As each day passed, Johnathan was running out of both options and patience.

Finally the weekend came, and Johnathan was relieved to be able to leave Gregory to his own slobbiness as he and Kibby drove to Dorset on the Saturday morning to have lunch with Kibby's parents.

Kibby's mood worsened the further they got away from London. She had descended into a state of broody intro-spection soon after they had set off, and had spent the journey staring out of the window at the passing countryside, occasionally emitting a long and serious sigh. Had he not been driving, Johnathan would have chewed his nails right off his fingers. He was preparing himself for a prolonged and painful humiliation. By the time they arrived in the village where Kibby's parents lived, they were both feeling edgy. They had barely spoken a word to each other during the entire journey.

The house was set back a good quarter of a mile from the road. To reach it they had to negotiate a long and winding drive. As they turned the last corner an enormous mansion materialized out of the surrounding greenery. 'Good grief,' said Johnathan.

Kibby coughed. 'It's a bit big for them now,' she conceded. 'They live here on their own.'

'You could house half the population of Tooting in there,' said Johnathan, whose nerves had started to jangle almost audibly by now.

'Just remember,' said Kibby, turning to Johnathan, 'try and not take anything they say too seriously. They're harmless really.'

Johnathan parked in front of the impressive steps which led to the front door. They sat in the car in silence for a few moments. Johnathan was about to suggest that they leave again before anyone noticed they had arrived when the front door of the house opened and seven or eight black Labradors flew out of it, barking enthusiastically.

Kibby sighed. 'Rumbled,' she said.

The dogs were followed out by a tall woman in a heavy-knit sweater and a sweeping tartan skirt. Her iron grey hair spilled out in all directions. She trudged towards the car, shouting obscenities at the Labradors.

'My mother,' explained Kibby.

Johnathan smiled bravely. Kibby opened the car door.

As they got out of the car they were immediately surrounded by yapping dogs. 'Don't worry,' called Kibby's mother, 'they're quite harmless. Stupid buggers. Hello.'

'Mother, this is Johnathan,' said Kibby.

Kibby's mother looked Johnathan up and down appraisingly. She frowned. 'He's not very tall, is he?' she said.

'Oh mother. Don't start.'

Kibby's mother considered Johnathan a moment longer, and then extended her hand towards him. 'Well, never mind,' she said. 'Felicity.'

'Johnathan Burlip,' said Johnathan. 'Very nice to meet you.'

'Yes, well, let's not count our chickens,' said Felicity. 'Awful business, this meeting the parents affair. Everyone hates it. Well, we do. And I'm sure you aren't exactly relishing the prospect either. But we'll muddle through, for Kibby's sake.'

Johnathan stared back. Kibby wore a look of weary resignation.

'Anyway, come on in, both of you,' continued Felicity. She turned to Kibby. 'Your father's had a bit of an accident. He fell off the gun turret.'

'God. Is he all right?' asked Kibby.

'Well. You know your father. You'd never know one way or the other anyway. He's hobbling a bit, though. Come on, you useless animals.'

Inside, the house was cheerfully chaotic. The entrance hall, which was dominated by an imposing staircase which swept majestically up one side, was littered with various items of outdoor shoe-wear, dog-walking accoutrements, and a vast array of jackets and coats, some of which were hung up on pegs, others cast messily over the floor. As the herd of Labradors passed through at speed, much of the tableau was slightly rearranged by flying paws and errant tails.

'Well, here we are,' said Felicity. 'Let's go through to the sitting room, shall we?' Without another word she strode to the far end of the hall and pushed open a large door.

The house seemed to sprawl in every direction. There was a faint layer of dust everywhere. After a few minutes' walk they arrived in the sitting room, which in contrast to the rest of the house, was spotless. It was cluttered full of mahogany antiques, which Johnathan supposed must be very expensive. The room overlooked the garden. Kibby wordlessly linked her arm through Johnathan's, and led him to admire the view.

The garden was certainly impressive. Flowers of every hue and description erupted colourfully from numerous flower beds. A wall of blazing rhododendron bushes stretched down one side of the garden. Stretching off into the middle distance was an immaculately tended lawn, as perfect as any putting green.

'Wow,' said Johnathan. He was not commenting on the garden. The remark was prompted rather by the incongruous presence in the middle of the lawn of a large military tank, resplendently bedecked with camouflage materials and military insignia, whose vast gun was pointing directly at the house.

'My father's hobby,' whispered Kibby. 'Some people rebuild classic racing cars. My father has always wanted to do a Sherman tank.'

'OK,' said Johnathan uncertainly. As he spoke a man appeared from behind the tank's enormous crawlers, and waved at them. In his other hand he held a walking stick which he leaned on.

'And there he is,' said Kibby, brightening slightly. She waved back. The man began to hobble towards the house.

'Sherry?' asked Felicity, bearing down on them with a silver tray with four glasses already poured.

Johnathan had always hated sherry. He smiled broadly and accepted the proffered glass. 'How lovely. Thank you.'

'Kibby tells me you're a lawyer,' said her mother.

'Yes, I am,' Johnathan said.

There was a pause. 'We knew a solicitor a long time ago when we first lived in London,' said Felicity. 'Fantastically tedious man. Self-obsessed beyond belief. And he only had one testicle.' She calmly raised her sherry glass to her lips and took a delicate sip.

'Well,' said Johnathan, 'not all solicitors only have one testicle.' He blinked, astonished by his own nerve.

'No,' agreed Kibby's mother, unflappable, looking out now towards the tank. 'But most of them are fantastically tedious, you must admit.'

Before the ensuing silence could develop into an irretrievable one, the door opened and Kibby's father hobbled across the carpet.

'Hello. You must be.' He shook Johnathan's hand limply.

'Johnathan Burlip, hello,' said Johnathan.

'Avery,' said Kibby's father. He kissed his daughter's cheek in a perfunctory manner and picked up the remaining sherry glass. He raised it towards Johnathan, and then swallowed the contents in one swig. 'God,' he said. 'Needed that. Been struggling with the second machine gunner's cross-wires all morning. Absolute bugger. Fiddly work.'

'Must be,' said Johnathan politely.

'D'you like tanks?' asked Avery.

'Tanks? I don't know, really,' said Johnathan. 'Never thought about it. I'm sure they're fascinating.'

'I've always been interested since I was a boy during the war,' said Avery. 'Big buggers. Powerful. I like that.'

'Have you been working on it long?' asked Johnathan.

'Not really. Well. Eight years.'

'*Eight* years,' repeated his wife with feeling.

'And has it always been, er —?'

'Stuck in the middle of my beautiful lawn?' asked Felicity. 'Oh yes. We own several acres of the surrounding countryside but rather than put Herman out of sight in a field somewhere we have to have it there, slap bang in the middle of the croquet lawn.'

'But we don't *play* croquet,' protested Avery.

'Well that's hardly surprising, is it?' snapped Felicity with some venom. Johnathan began to see some hereditary traits showing through.

'Anyway,' said Avery, 'you know I hate it when you use that name.'

'Oh come on. It's got to be called Herman.' Kibby's mother turned to Kibby and Johnathan appealingly. 'Herman the Sherman,' she said, quite without humour.

Johnathan tittered dutifully until he saw Avery glaring at him. Kibby sighed.

'And another thing,' said Avery. 'She's a she, not an it, as you very well know.'

'Oh please. It's a bloody tank, not some swish sports car or yacht. A *tank*.'

There was a moment's silence.

'It's certainly a talking point,' observed Johnathan.

Kibby sighed again.

'Quite a conversation piece,' tried Johnathan.

'Not really,' replied Kibby's mother, pouring herself another glass of sherry. 'Conversations by definition require at least two people to participate. Which I don't as I have absolutely no interest in the thing at all. So, quite a dreary monologue piece, perhaps.' She sniffed.

'Dad, Johnathan's a lawyer,' said Kibby.

'Oh.' Avery looked unimpressed. 'So when are we eating, then?' he demanded.

Felicity looked at her watch. 'In about five minutes, I should think. I'll go and see how it's getting on.' She put her sherry glass down on the tray and swept out of the room with a parting scowl at her husband.

Avery seemed to brighten visibly as his wife left. He turned to Kibby. 'So, apple of my eye, what have you been up to? Tell all.'

As Kibby started to talk, Johnathan could not help feeling slightly aggrieved. Kibby's parents had displayed so little interest in him that his primary reaction of relief was in danger of being trumped by wounded pride. Did he really merit no more than a disparaging comment about his height and an anecdote about a testically-challenged solicitor? It looked as if all his worrying was going to have been for no purpose. He was an irrelevance. Kibby's parents were far too preoccupied fighting with each other to bother fighting with him.

Moments later Felicity appeared at the door. 'Luncheon,' she said gravely, 'is served.'

'Great,' said Avery. 'I'm starving. Come on, let's go.' He set off, leaning heavily on his stick. Kibby looked worriedly at Johnathan. She reached out and took his hand.

'You OK?' she whispered.

'I suppose,' replied Johnathan. 'How am I doing?'

Kibby shrugged. 'It's difficult to say. They seem a bit preoccupied.' She squeezed Johnathan's hand gently. 'But it's not you I'm so worried about. It's them.'

'Are you two coming or not?' echoed Avery's voice from down the hall. 'It'll get cold if we wait any longer. Perhaps we should start without you.'

'Coming,' called Kibby. She released Johnathan's hand and set off down the corridor.

The meal itself was moderately disastrous. The roast beef

was so overcooked that conversation was kept to a minimum, as everyone chewed furiously in attempt to break the meat down into manageable pieces for swallowing. In addition to having the consistency of a brand-new Chelsea boot, the meat tasted, miraculously, of absolutely nothing at all. The overdone Yorkshire puddings flopped on to the cold plates like sodden brown powder puffs. The vegetables, in contrast, had been on no more than nodding terms with boiling water. The meal was conducted over the impressive sonic backdrop of four sets of jaws crunching away on raw carrot. Everything was covered in a congealing and tepid gravy, in which swam a flotilla of small croutons. At least Johnathan thought they were croutons until he tried to pierce one on his fork, at which point it crumbled and dissolved into the surrounding gunk.

In comparison to the conversation, however, the food would have qualified for three Michelin stars. Every effort to start a conversation by Kibby or Johnathan was deftly side-stepped or ignored by Kibby's parents, who sat chewing sullenly on their food and not looking at each other. In desperation Johnathan tried to tell of his adventures with Spike, but this elicited no more than a bored, 'Oh really?' from Felicity before she returned to attacking her beef energetically with a blunt knife.

As Johnathan chewed on a particularly leathery bit of meat he racked his brains for another topic of conversation. As the beef was eventually dispatched with a painful swallow, he had an idea: 'Kibby tells me you both like to travel.' Avery was taking a swig of wine, and so obviously didn't have his mouth full. Johnathan turned towards him expectantly.

Caught, Avery had little option but to respond. 'That's right,' he admitted sulkily.

'Where have you been recently?' asked Johnathan.

'Let me think. In February we spent two weeks in Koblenz, and then in June we were in Volokolamsk.'

'Where?'

'Volokolamsk. In Russia.'

'Goodness. That sounds interesting. They're not your usual holiday destinations, are they?'

'And why do you think that is?' demanded Felicity. 'Do you have any idea what both god-forsaken places have in common? Apart from the fact that they're cold, boring, and full of ghastly foreigners?'

Johnathan shook his head, his heart sinking.

'Tanks,' she spat. 'Bloody, bloody tanks. Museums about tanks. Libraries about tanks. Crowds of tank bores. My utter worst nightmare.'

'Oh come on,' complained Avery. 'You're going to give him the wrong impression. Don't be so unfair about it, just for once in your life.'

Johnathan thought he should plough on. 'There must be lots of other things to see in places like that, I'm sure,' he said.

Kibby's mother snorted a magnificently derisory snort. 'No. Just tanks. Just huge bits of fortified metal slapped together into killing machines. It's morbid. I don't know which unnerves me more. The question of how many people that pile of junk in the middle of my lawn has killed, or the whole concept of sad, sad people like – *him*, quietly obsessing about these grotesque machines. It's sick. I think these tanks have become some sort of lust objects. Because you know what rhymes with 'tank'.'

'*Mother*,' said Kibby in an exasperated tone.

'Well, you must admit it's all very suspicious. These

211

people traipse all over the place worshipping these awful heaps of junk. There's got to be a reason for it. And it's bound to be something to do with sex.'

'Why, for Heaven's sake?' demanded Avery.

'Because you're all *men*,' said Felicity.

'Which means?' said Avery, a trifle more defensively.

'I don't know. You probably all suffer from some sort of Freudian penis fixation with those enormous guns.'

There was a polite silence around the table as everyone waited for Felicity to expand on her theme.

'Perhaps you all feel inferior and so worship these machines because they've got massive substitute phalluses. And guess what? The massive phalluses actually explode, blaze with fire, and kill people. Fantastic.'

'So, what basically you are saying, is that I am a sad, power-crazed necrophiliac with a fixation about my small penis,' said Avery acidly.

'I suppose that's right, yes,' replied his wife. 'Would you pass the salt, please?'

Johnathan numbly handed her the salt cellar.

After a singed apple pie, they moved back to the drawing room. There was a nervy silence as everyone sipped their coffee. Johnathan tried to finish his as quickly as he could without slurping or burning his tongue. He wanted to escape. Kibby's parents clearly had little or no interest in him, and the last thing he wanted was to hang around to be caught in the cross-fire of marital acrimony.

Just as he was about to whisper to Kibby that they should perhaps think about leaving, Avery put down his coffee cup and stood up.

'Right, then,' he said. 'I think you and I need to have a little chat.'

'Me?' stammered Johnathan.

'Yes, you. Come on. Let's go outside. Let me show you the tank.'

Felicity sighed. Johnathan hesitated, and glanced towards her. 'Oh don't worry about *her*,' said Avery. Johnathan waited.

'Oh, go on, then,' said Felicity. 'Go and get it over with.'

Johnathan followed Avery into the garden. They went around to the far side of the tank. There was a ladder planted in the ground. Avery hung his stick on a rung of the ladder. 'I'll go first,' he said, and made his way up the ladder. At the top he swung open the hatch and disappeared inside without another word.

Johnathan stood at the bottom of the ladder, pondering this turn of events. So they *had* registered his presence, he thought. Now he was due for the 'what exactly are your intentions towards my daughter?' conversation. Well, all right, he said to himself. I'm ready for this. They would discuss his prospects, his hopes, his aspirations. He just hoped they wouldn't discuss his salary. He climbed the ladder.

When he arrived at the top of the tank, he couldn't help feeling a certain boyish excitement. He peered down through the hatch. Avery was squatting beneath him, surrounded by flashing green lights. He looked happier than he had been all day. 'What are you waiting for?' he demanded. 'Come down.'

Johnathan climbed down into the cramped cockpit. He manoeuvred himself around so that he was facing Avery. The older man stood up and slammed the hatch shut. Without sunlight, the space was illuminated only by the glow from the dials. Avery sat down again and looked at Johnathan. A thought struck him. 'Hang on,' he said, scrabbling around behind him. 'I've got something here. Where – ah.' He turned around, brandishing two green camouflage helmets. They were covered in netting and were speckled with variegated leaves. Johnathan took the proffered helmet dumbly.

'Well, come on,' said Avery. 'Put the thing on. It's not for putting cocktail dips in.' As he spoke he pulled his own helmet firmly on to his head.

'Right,' said Johnathan, and put the helmet gingerly on top of his head. It didn't fit. 'I think it's a bit small,' he reported.

'Don't be daft,' said Avery, and reached across and slammed his palm hard down on the top of the helmet. With a discreet plop, it somehow squashed down past Johnathan's ears and settled snugly around his head.

'We're in the turret of the tank,' said Avery. 'Usually there was just one machine gunner in here, which is why it's a bit cramped with two of us. This bit would ordinarily rotate, but it'll be a while before I sort that out.'

'What?' said Johnathan.

'These tanks started to be built by the Americans in 1942,' continued Avery. 'Originally they were called the M4. There was also the M4A1, M4A2, M4A3, and M4A4. This one was used by the British. It's an M4A4. Otherwise known as the Firefly. The British upgraded their Shermans to incorporate 76mm guns rather than the original 75mm ones. The old ones couldn't penetrate the front of the German tanks. One of the cleverest things about this design is the gyro-stabiliser. It enabled the gunners to keep the gun aimed at a specific target, even when the tanks went over bumps.'

'What?' said Johnathan.

'There are also two .30 cal Browning machine guns,' continued Avery.

Johnathan removed his helmet. 'I'm sorry,' he said, 'I can't hear a word you're saying.'

'What?' said Avery.

Johnathan motioned to Avery to remove his own helmet. Reluctantly Avery did so.

'Sorry,' said Johnathan again. 'Those helmets make it rather hard to hear.'

'Quite right,' said Avery. 'There was a communications system built into the original leather helmets which enabled the operators to talk to each other. I'm still searching for some of those. In the meantime I have to make do with these.'

It seemed prudent to move things along a little and get down to business before Kibby's father bored him to death. 'You wanted to talk to me,' said Johnathan.

'Yes,' said Avery. 'Yes, I did.'

There was a pause.

'I imagine it's about Kibby,' said Johnathan.

Avery frowned. 'Kibby?'

'Your daughter.'

'I know who Kibby is. What did you think I wanted to talk about her for?'

'Well, I suppose you might have wanted to discuss what plans we had.' Johnathan shifted uncomfortably in his seat.

'Good heavens, no,' exclaimed Avery. 'Kibby's more than capable of looking after herself. You seem all right. Better than some of the louses she's brought home in the past. Far be it for me to interfere.'

Johnathan hesitated. 'So what was it you wanted to talk about?'

'Well, this, obviously,' said Avery, gesturing as best he could in the confined space. 'I thought you might be interested in how it all works. I particularly wanted to show you this Indirect Sighting Device. Very clever.' Avery turned away and began to fiddle somewhere behind him.

Johnathan saw if he did not act now he would be in serious trouble. 'Actually,' he said, 'we should be getting back soon. Traffic. On a Saturday afternoon. You know. Dreadful.' He put his helmet down beside him and tried to stand up. His head connected solidly with the roof of the tank. He sat down again. Avery looked at him, disappointed.

'Well, I suppose if you must, you must,' he said. 'Shame, though. It's terribly interesting. Lots to learn.'

'Yes, I can see that,' said Johnathan obsequiously as he began to stand up again, this time with more caution. 'It's fascinating.'

'Perhaps next time,' said Avery, a little forlornly.

'Absolutely,' replied Johnathan, as he tried desperately to open the hatch. Finally there was a click and he managed to swing it open. Sunlight flooded into the confined space. Johnathan gasped gratefully as fresh air swept into his lungs. Without risking another look down, he hauled himself up and escaped back into the house.

'Well,' said Kibby a while later. 'I think that went pretty well, all things considering.'

'You did?' asked Johnathan. They were stuck in a traffic jam on the London-bound carriageway of the motorway.

'Mother said you didn't talk much.'

'Good grief. I did try. Either they refused to talk to me or I couldn't get a word in.'

'I suppose they were squabbling a bit,' conceded Kibby.

'A bit? Jesus.'

'Anyway, she thought you were all right.'

'I thought she was all right.'

'Liar.'

'Really. A bit odd, but all right.'

'Hmm. Well I think you did very well.'

Johnathan grinned. 'Thank you.'

'As a reward, you can come and stay at mine tonight.'

'Oh, go on then. Twist my arm.'

NINETEEN

As he lay in bed that evening after what he modestly considered to be a relatively successful frolic with Kibby, Johnathan listened to her steady breathing as she slept and pondered the problem of what to do about his brother and his stubborn refusal to pay Spike the money he was owed.

It seemed clear that no amount of reasoned argument was going to work. Johnathan couldn't really appeal to Gregory's better nature either, as he didn't appear to possess one. He stared at the ceiling and did a quick calculation. He had three days to persuade Gregory to come up with the hundred and twenty thousand pounds or they could both expect a personal display of Terry's extraordinary upper body strength and accurate kicking ability. Johnathan realized that he couldn't just hope that he would wear Gregory down. Time was running short. What was needed was a new plan, something radical which would shake his brother up and make him see sense. Johnathan continued to stare at the ceiling until he finally drifted into an uneasy sleep.

Sunday morning arrived with no answers. Kibby had arranged to meet some of her female friends for brunch. Johnathan had learned very early on that that was one coterie which he would never be invited to join, and suspected that he probably wouldn't want to either. He had read about the sort of things that women talked about when they got together with no males within earshot, and on that basis he wanted to be as far away as possible to avoid hearing the gales of ribald laughter which would undoubtedly follow Kibby's turn at telling a lurid tale of sexual inadequacy. Kissing goodbye at the bottom of the tube station escalator, Johnathan and Kibby each took a train in a different direction.

When Johnathan got home, the flat was in chaos. Gregory sat on the sofa in Johnathan's dressing gown next to Schroedinger, watching a crowd of school children belt out 'All Things Bright and Beautiful' as if their lives depended on it. On the table sat a pile of four unreturned videos from the local store and a pyramid of silver oblong boxes from which wafted the unmistakable smell of cold curry.

'Wow,' said Johnathan as he pulled off his coat, 'you really didn't need to go to all the effort.'

'Hello,' said Gregory, barely moving. 'Good evening, was it?' The question was so loaded with leery, hob-nailed innuendo that Johnathan was momentarily pole-axed into silence at its unashamed vulgarity. Even for Gregory, it was something rather special.

'Yes, thanks,' muttered Johnathan. He looked around his sitting room with a growing sense of distress. Gregory's debris was everywhere. It had managed to spread itself over every available square inch of floor. Since Gregory's arrival, Johnathan had become self-conscious about going in there. Gregory had made the sitting room unmistakably, unquestionably his. He might as well have just wandered around pissing on the furniture. The territory was as clearly marked.

'So,' said Johnathan, 'had much more of a chance to think about saving your skin and paying off the money?'

Gregory scratched his crotch through Johnathan's dressing gown. 'Christ. I've told you. I'm not paying the guy. I don't *owe* him any money.' He inspected the contents of the nearest foil container.

Johnathan watched his brother in amazement. He could not understand how he could be so reckless. Gregory suddenly seemed so convinced of his own invulnerability that even Johnathan's recent injuries didn't cause him the slightest concern. Something radical was needed to get through to him. Extreme measures were needed. He telephoned Jake, and arranged to meet him in their usual pub. Inspiration was needed. That or alcoholic oblivion. He also needed an excuse to get out of the house.

'Right,' said Johnathan, coming back into the sitting room. 'I'm taking Schroedinger for a walk.'

'Good,' said Gregory ungraciously.

'Come on, then,' said Johnathan to Schroedinger.

Schroedinger regarded Johnathan with a curious frown, uncertain as to what he was supposed to do.

'We're going for a *walk*,' explained Johnathan. Schroedinger's head cocked to one side, marvelling at this unfamiliar word. Johnathan sighed. He went over to the sofa and pulled a surprised and rather aggrieved Schroedinger by the collar out of the door.

At the pub Johnathan explained the problem to Jake. 'I have no idea what to do. I've run out of options,' he complained. 'He just won't listen to reason. Well, he just won't listen, full stop.'

Jake looked unsympathetic. 'What did you expect?' he asked. 'That's a pretty standard reaction when you have shit for brains.'

'Thank you very much,' said Johnathan. 'That's terribly helpful.' He paused. 'Anyway. On the assumption that I'll never be able to persuade him by talking to him, I think I need to adopt a different approach.'

'Like what?' asked Jake.

'I don't quite know. He needs a large kick up the bum. Do you think we could *scare* him into paying the money?'

Jake nodded thoughtfully. 'That's more likely to work than trying to convince him any other way. After all, he seemed fairly wound up when we first went to see him, didn't he?'

'True. He was frightened enough back then,' agreed Johnathan. 'He reckons that just because they haven't caught him yet they never will now. So we need to do something to make him realize Spike is still on to him, and that he means business.'

'What though?'

Johnathan laughed without much humour. 'I could just tell him about the conversation I had with Spike last week. Let him know that the clock's ticking. Three days to go before we're scheduled to be making our appearance in the Accident and Emergency Department.'

'Why don't you?'

'Wouldn't work. He'd just assume I was making it up in an attempt to make him change his mind.'

Jake nodded. 'You're right. It is pretty unbelievable. Too much like the bloody Kray twins.'

Johnathan looked at him. 'Jake,' he said, 'the Kray twins were real.'

'Yeah, whatever,' said Jake.

'Anyway, whatever we do needs to look as if it's been done by Spike himself, rather than anyone else,' said Johnathan.

221

Both men lapsed into thoughtful silence. 'Could we arrange for him to get beaten up ourselves?' asked Jake.

'How?'

'I could organize it,' said Jake. 'Shit, I could *do* it. It would be a pleasure. We could wear masks.'

Johnathan had to admit that the scheme did have its attractions. 'I'm not sure,' he said. 'Tempting though it is, I think we'd just be bringing ourselves down to Spike's level, which wouldn't achieve anything.'

'It bloody would,' retorted Jake. 'He'd pay the money, you'd be safe, and I'd be happy.'

'Hold on,' said Johnathan, as an idea popped into his head. 'You know how people always say that being burgled is one of the most unpleasant experiences?'

Jake nodded. 'Something to do with having your privacy invaded.'

'Well, what if we were to break into Gregory's house and leave some sort of message for him, threatening him if he doesn't pay?'

'Johnathan, Gregory is living at your place.'

'I know,' said Johnathan pointedly.

'So how is he going to see it?'

'Oh I don't know. We can find some sort of excuse for him to go back. After all, we know for a fact that Spike's lot won't be there for a few more days yet. And anyway, the fact that Gregory himself won't actually be there should make the job easier rather than harder. There'll be nobody to disturb.'

Jake nodded. 'Good point.'

'So how about it?'

'Do you want my honest opinion?' asked Jake.

'Of course.'

'Personally, I think your idea is a load of old bollocks,

222

but in the absence of any decent alternative I say we should try it.'

Johnathan looked pleased.

'What are you going to do to scare him, though?' asked Jake. 'I would think we would need to leave some fairly specific signals. Nothing too subtle. Otherwise there's a danger Gregory will miss the point.'

'We could paint a message on the walls,' suggested Johnathan. 'Something along the lines of, what, "Pay up or die", that sort of thing.'

Jake frowned. 'That's good for addressing the specific point. I just think you might need something to pull him up short, something to show him that whoever left the message means business.'

'What did you have in mind?'

'I don't know. Some sort of gruesome calling card, almost. A human heart, a severed ear, that sort of thing.'

There was a pause. Schroedinger let out a long and pleasurable yawn from underneath the table. 'Jake,' said Johnathan, 'you've been watching too many movies.'

'Actually, it's my natural flair for melodrama, which you need in a job like mine, given how much of what I write I make up. Hang on,' said Jake. 'I've just had an idea. Do you remember that story about vampires near the M25 I was doing a few weeks ago?'

'What about it?'

'Well, we managed to get some dead bats with their necks cut open which we used for some of the photographs.'

Johnathan looked appalled. 'Dead bats?'

'Not real dead bats, obviously. Fake ones. They're made of rubber, I think. We got them from a toy shop. They were early stocks for Halloween. All we did was give them a lick of red paint around the neck and Bob's your uncle. They looked pretty good in the photos.'

Johnathan rolled his eyes back in his head. 'And you're suggesting that, what, we leave one of these dead rubber bats in Gregory's flat to put the wind up him?'

'That's right.'

'Christ. And you thought *my* plan was a load of old bollocks.'

Jake looked affronted. 'Got any better ideas?' he demanded.

'No,' admitted Johnathan. There was a pause. 'Bats it is, then.'

Jake and Johnathan left the pub a while later and returned to Jake's flat, where Jake rooted around in search of the rubber bats in question. Jake kept a large trunk full of bizarre items that he had used in various journalistic endeavours. As Jake searched, Johnathan caught a glimpse of handcuffs, a snorkel, a dog lead, and various plastic vegetables. He thought it best not to ask what they had been for. Possibly all part of the same story.

'Here we are,' said Jake finally. He stood up brandishing what looked like a handful of unrolled black condoms which hung limply from his fist.

Johnathan looked at the condoms thoughtfully.

'What do you think?' asked Jake.

'Well, it's not awfully bat-like, really, is it?'

Jake looked at the thing in his hand. 'Oh. Don't you think so?'

'Not really.'

Jake considered. 'I suppose it may have more symbolic value rather than being a literal representation,' he conceded.

'I think the significance might be lost on Gregory if we

had to put a little note by it explaining what it was supposed to be,' said Johnathan. 'He needs a more direct approach.'

'What you're saying,' said Jake, 'is that we need a real live dead animal.'

'I think so. Anything else just won't be effective.'

'What do you have in mind?'

'I don't know,' admitted Johnathan. 'As long as it's dead, I think the message will be fairly clear.'

'Where on earth do we get dead animals from?' asked Jake.

'Dead animal shop?' suggested Johnathan.

'Seriously,' said Jake.

'Well, we could raid an incompetent vet. Or go grave robbing in the nearest animal graveyard.'

'All right,' said Jake, 'Forget the dead animal idea. Think about live ones.'

'What, get an animal and then kill it? Are you serious?'

Jake shrugged. 'What else do you suggest? It's our only option.'

'All right, I see your point,' said Johnathan.

'So, what sort of animal do you want to leave?'

Johnathan considered. 'Something dramatic. What about a severed horse's head?'

'Yeah, that's easy enough. I think I've got Shergar in here somewhere.' Jake paused. 'I think you need to be a more realistic.'

'OK. What about a small sheep?'

Jake looked at Johnathan. 'Johnathan, we're in South London, not the bloody Yorkshire Dales. Where can we get a sheep from? Let's at least be practical. It's got to be a pet of some sort.'

Johnathan thought of Troilus lying in Chloe's vegetable

garden. He'd done it once. He could probably do it again. 'What about a cat?' he asked.

'No way,' said Jake.

'Why not?'

'Jesus. Cats have personalities. They're like little people. I can't kill a cat.'

Johnathan bit his tongue. Don't go there, he told himself. He needed Jake's help.

'Anyway,' continued Jake, 'cats have nine lives. It would take ages to kill one.'

'Rabbit?' tried Johnathan.

'Not bad. But too much like *Fatal Attraction*. Gregory's so arrogant he'll probably think some beautiful but unbalanced woman has a crush on him.'

'Budgie?'

Jack pulled a face. 'Dead budgies don't really do it for me,' he said.

'What about a mouse?'

Jake sighed. 'It can't be a mouse. He'll just think it crept out from the skirting board. It's got to be something at least a bit weird so he'll get the message.'

'OK, seeing as it's Gregory, how about a rat?'

'Better, and admittedly appropriate, but I think the irony would be lost on him and he would probably just think it was a large mouse anyway.'

'Haven't you got any ideas of your own?'

'What about a hamster?' said Jake.

Johnathan considered. 'Well, it's small enough. It's cute enough. It's cheap enough.' He nodded. 'We could try a hamster.'

Jake stood up. 'There's a pet shop on Balham High Road,' he said.

'Will it be open on a Sunday?'

Jake spread his arms wide. 'Especially on a Sunday. It's their busiest day of the week. People buy pets when they're bored.'

Leaving Schroedinger asleep in Jake's kitchen, half an hour later Johnathan and Jake were wandering through a chaotic and bewildering menagerie of domestic pets. There was a pervasive odour of stale hay. As they inspected the cages, an ever-moving sea of excited children shifted past them, screaming at their long-suffering parents to come and look. Weary grown ups would follow, refusals already forming on their lips as they approached the cages.

Having gone up and down the length of the shop twice, Johnathan found a cage with three still balls of fur lying in one corner. On the chicken wire was a small plastic sticker which said, 'Hamster. £7.50'.

'Bingo,' said Johnathan.

'Right,' said Jake, 'let's find some help.'

This proved more difficult than they had anticipated. Finally they managed to attract the attention of a spotty teenager wearing a dirty T-shirt beneath an equally dirty green uniform.

'Help you?' she asked unenthusiastically.

'Yes, we'd like to buy a hamster, please,' said Johnathan.

The assistant considered this. 'Hamster. Right. Know where they are?'

Johnathan pointed. 'Over there.'

When they had battled their way back to it, the girl looked at the three balls in the cage. 'Which one d'you want?' she asked.

Johnathan shrugged. They all looked the same to him. He pointed randomly at the nearest bundle. 'That one.'

'Cage?'

'What?'

'Have you got a cage?'

'Oh.' Johnathan thought. He didn't want to buy a cage for a hamster who wasn't going to get the chance to make himself very at home in it. 'No,' he improvised. 'I've got one at home and I'll just put him straight in that with my other hamsters.'

'Well how are you going to carry him home?' demanded the girl. 'Haven't you got a carrying cage?'

'No. I mean, I had one, obviously, but it broke.' Johnathan paused. 'Would we absolutely need a cage to buy the hamster?' he asked.

'Too right,' answered the girl. 'How else would you get him home? In your pocket?' She grinned at this apparently ridiculous suggestion.

Johnathan hadn't really thought about it. 'So how much are these carrying cages, then?' he asked.

The girl named a price. 'Isn't there one we could perhaps borrow?' asked Johnathan.

'Sorry. Strict policy not to lend cages. Shop rules.'

Johnathan took a deep breath. 'All right, then. Give me that hamster there and your smallest, cheapest cage.'

The girl nodded in a bored way and shuffled off towards the back of the shop. Ten minutes later she reappeared with a cage the size of an old-fashioned television set. 'This is the smallest we've got at the moment,' she said. 'That do?'

Johnathan shrugged helplessly. 'I suppose it'll have to,' he replied. The girl went to retrieve the chosen hamster and shoved it into the cage, where it sat back, looking at its new surroundings in a bewildered way, still groggy from its rudely interrupted sleep. Johnathan looked at it with despair. As its beady black eyes darted about, Johnathan knew trouble lay ahead. Its little snout twitched nervously. Hamsters were quite a different proposition to cats, he realized. This was going to be difficult.

'This one is called Morty,' said the girl, examining a sheet of paper. 'Obviously you can call him what you like, but that's his name at the moment.'

'Morty. Right. Thanks,' said Johnathan, his spirits spiralling downwards. Morty.

The shop assistant named a price. Johnathan morosely handed over his credit card. Alas, poor Morty. Rarely had he felt quite so wretched. He walked out of the shop in a daze, followed by Jake, who had begun to enjoy himself.

'Excellent,' said Jake, as they walked back to his flat. 'Stage one successfully accomplished. Well done. Now all we need to do is kill it.'

'Him,' said Johnathan, watching Morty scrabble around in the corners of his new cage.

'What?'

'Kill *him*. He's a him, not an it. And he has a name. Morty.'

'Oh dear,' said Jake. 'You're not going to make this easy, are you?'

Some time later Johnathan and Jake sat at Jake's kitchen table. On the table sat the cage. In the cage sat Morty. Who was still very much alive.

'Look,' said Johnathan. 'Can't we just think of something else?'

'Like what?' asked Jake.

There was a pause. 'I don't know,' said Johnathan. Their first attempt at killing the hamster had been unsuccessful. Having ruled out some of the obvious but more violent methods of execution such as smothering, squashing or a blast of pulsing in the food processor, they had finally decided to try and poison Morty. They had concocted what would, from a technical culinary perspective, be called a *roux* of ant-poison and butter, which was rather heavy on the ant-poison, and had watched with satisfaction (tinged with sadness on Johnathan's part) as Morty had heartily scoffed the lot in thirty seconds flat. To their dismay, however, it had no effect at all: thirty minutes later Morty was still sniffing inquisitively around his cage as if nothing had happened.

'We just have to work out the best way of doing this,' said Jake. The two men looked at the hamster, who was nibbling a lettuce leaf, quite unconcerned. 'With minimum fuss.'

'And with minimum gore,' said Johnathan. He had an idea. 'Isn't drowning supposed to be a nice way to die?' he asked. 'You lose consciousness before you actually die.'

'How on earth does anybody actually know that?' asked Jake.

'I don't know. Maybe from someone who's had a near-death experience.'

'Do you think hamsters have near-death experiences in quite the same way?' asked Jake.

'Look, I'm not saying it's perfect.'

'OK,' said Jake. 'Fair enough. Drowning it is.'

'I suppose the loo is the obvious place,' said Johnathan. Morty had stopped eating lettuce and was now investigating what lay beneath the layer of old newspaper that lined the bottom of his cage, his fur bristling with excitement and vitality at this exciting new turn his life had taken. He looked genuinely happy to be alive.

'Come on then,' said Jake, and strode off towards the bathroom. Johnathan reluctantly reached inside the cage and extracted Morty with both hands, and followed Jake.

Jake lifted the toilet lid, and they stared into the toilet as if they had never seen one before. Their reflections in the calm oasis at the bottom of the bowl stared back up at them.

'You haven't put anything nasty in it like bleach, have you?' asked Johnathan. 'That would be horrible.'

'Johnathan, you're forgetting what it is that we're actually trying to do here,' said Jake mildly. 'Morty is going to die.'

Johnathan stood unhappily in front of the toilet bowl.

'Go on, then,' said Jake impatiently. 'What are you waiting for? Get it over with.'

Johnathan crouched down by the rim of the bowl, holding Morty out in front of him. After a few moments he shut his eyes and dropped Morty in. There was a discreet plop as he landed. Johnathan immediately shut the lid.

'What are you doing?' demanded Jake.

'At least let him die in peace,' said Johnathan. 'Spare him that final indignity.'

'For Christ's sake,' muttered Jake. The two lapsed into an edgy silence.

After about a minute Johnathan looked at Jake. 'What do you reckon?' he asked. 'Is that enough time?'

Jake shrugged. 'Have a look.'

With a heavy heart Johnathan lifted the toilet lid and

peered in. At the bottom of the bowl Morty was doing tiny clockwise laps, paddling with his little legs for all he was worth.

'Fantastic,' said Jake. 'The world's first swimming hamster. Just our luck.'

Johnathan looked stricken. 'Now what?' he asked.

'Just leave him for a while longer,' said Jake. 'He's got to tire eventually. He can't go on for ever, can he?'

'You're right,' said Johnathan. He shut the toilet lid and they returned to the kitchen.

'Coffee while you wait, sir?' asked Jake, switching on the kettle.

'Instant?'

'Afraid so.'

Johnathan sighed. 'Go on, then. I can't feel any worse than I already do.' He looked at his watch. 'I'll give him another five minutes. That should do it.'

A few minutes later Johnathan sat at the kitchen table, looking at the empty cage. 'This had better all be worth it,' he said to Jake accusingly. 'This dead animal thing was all your idea.'

Jake put his hands up. 'It was only a suggestion,' he said. 'I never said it was the only answer.'

'We could have done it without, I suppose,' said Johnathan.

'Not as effective, but yes, the dead animal option was only really a finesse,' said Jake.

A finesse? We killed Morty for a *finesse*? 'Well, it's too late now,' said Johnathan sadly. 'If I could turn back the clock I wouldn't have done it. It seems a terrible waste of a life.'

When Johnathan returned to the bathroom, he went alone. He took a plastic bag with him to put Morty's body in so as not to drip on the carpet. Bloody Gregory, he thought. Bloody, bloody Gregory.

He lifted up the toilet seat and almost dropped it again. Morty was still paddling gallantly, although this time he was going in the opposite direction. 'He's alive!' he shouted to Jake.

Jake arrived at speed. 'I don't believe it,' he said. 'Your hamster's bionic.'

Johnathan reached into the bowl and pulled Morty out. The hamster looked at him and began to shiver uncontrollably.

'Sorry about that,' said Johnathan to Morty, barely able to suppress his excitement. 'Anyway, you needn't worry any more. We've decided that we can do this thing with Gregory without your help.' Morty's nose twitched.

Johnathan headed happily back to the kitchen. Good thing he had bought the cage after all, he thought.

Once Morty had been dried and returned to his cage with a compensatory piece of carrot, Jake and Johnathan settled down in front of the television to watch an old black and white film with people who wore hats and spoke in unintelligibly posh accents. Finally Johnathan got up.

'I suppose I should go home and see what my brother has been up to,' he said. 'Much as I would prefer to stay here.'

'And tomorrow is the big day?' asked Jake.

Johnathan nodded. 'We'll meet up at about ten o'clock tomorrow evening. Sound all right?'

'Fine. I'll buy some paint for the message on the wall.'

Johnathan put on his coat. 'Right,' he said. 'Let me go and collect my old pet and my brand new pet and take them both home with me.'

'Are you really going to keep him?' asked Jake.

Johnathan nodded. 'I rather like him. And that whole thing with the swimming. That was a sign. It obviously wasn't meant to be.'

'Hamster karma. That's a new one.'

They walked into the kitchen. The cage sat on the kitchen table, as before. The door, though, had swung open on its hinges. The cage was empty.

Johnathan let out a gasp. '*Shit*,' he said. 'He's escaped. That's all we need.' He crouched down and scanned the floor. There was no sign of Morty. Johnathan sighed. 'Great. He could be anywhere by now.'

'Where should we start?' asked Jake, looking around him.

'Jesus. No idea.' He squatted down and peered underneath the fridge and the oven. 'Not here.'

They systematically went through the flat, looking under every item of furniture. Morty was nowhere to be found. After an hour's increasingly frustrated searching, they returned to the kitchen and slumped into their chairs.

'This is typical,' observed Johnathan bitterly. 'No sooner do I decide to keep him than he disappears. So it's a complete waste of bloody time and everything else.'

'He'll turn up,' said Jake. 'He can't have gone very far. All the outside doors are shut, after all. He'll be in here somewhere.'

'Well I hope so,' muttered Johnathan. He stood up. 'Right. I'll leave you to it. If you find him then just stick him back in the cage and I'll come and collect him tomorrow. Just give him another lettuce leaf and make sure you shut the door properly this time. Come on, Schroedinger.'

Schroedinger stirred in the corner and raised a weary head off the floor. Johnathan froze. 'What's that?' he said.

'What's what?' asked Jake.

Johnathan pointed at Schroedinger. 'What's that thing in his mouth?'

Jake bent over to look at Schroedinger. 'Oh. Oh dear.'

'Is that what I think it is?' said Johnathan, barely audibly.

Schroedinger obligingly sat up and displayed a mouthful of familiar brown and white mottled fur. The fur did not appear to be moving. Schroedinger looked at Johnathan and Jake enquiringly. Johnathan sat down again, aghast.

'Yup,' confirmed Jake.

Johnathan approached Schroedinger slowly and bent down to open his jaws. The dog opened his mouth and Morty tumbled on to the kitchen floor, horribly inert. Schroedinger looked where Morty had fallen and licked his lips. Johnathan gingerly picked up the hamster and examined him.

'He's dead.'

Jake came up and inspected the soggy ball of fluff. He raised his eyebrows. 'Seems so,' he agreed.

'Schroedinger, how *could* you?' asked Johnathan. Schroedinger stared happily up at Johnathan, wagging his stump.

'Looks like all those latent hunter-predator instincts finally came good,' observed Jake.

'Shit,' said Johnathan. 'Great timing.'

'Well, look on the bright side,' said Jake. 'At least you can use him for what you originally intended. You can leave him in Gregory's house now. He can fulfil his destiny.'

Johnathan stared miserably at Morty.

'Look at it this way,' said Jake. 'He's doing his bit towards preventing you getting beaten up. He's protecting his master. Died in the course of duty.'

'Jake.'
'Yes, mate.'
'Shut up.'
Johnathan walked home.

TWENTY

The next day Johnathan called Jake again.

'There's one thing we haven't really thought about,' he said. 'And that's the technical side of actually getting into the house.'

'Yes,' said Jake.

'Well. I thought it might be an area you had experience in,' said Johnathan carefully.

There was a short silence on the other end of the telephone. 'For why?' asked Jake finally.

'Oh, I don't know, I just wondered whether you'd ever had the need to, you know, gain access to private areas as part of your job.'

'God. Certainly not.' Jake's distaste was audible.

'What, never?' asked Johnathan.

'It's interesting, isn't it,' observed Jake wryly, 'the mutually low regard in which we each seem to hold each other's profession. You may find this hard to believe, but most journalists operate under a strict ethical and moral code.'

'You do?' said Johnathan.

'Yes, we do. But thanks for the huge vote in my moral standing.'

'I'm sorry. I just thought you would be the most likely person to be able to help.'

Johnathan could almost hear Jake's nose wrinkling. 'Nope.' He paused. 'If we need anything to be stolen from private property we wouldn't dream of doing it ourselves. That would be lunacy. Instead we out-source all of that sort of work to a small independent unit which can't be linked or traced back to the newspaper. Professional crooks, in other words.'

Johnathan brightened. 'So you *do* know someone who could help.'

'Well, not really. We don't get too involved with the whole process. Obviously the journalist's integrity mustn't be compromised. If, on the other hand, a package should coincidentally arrive on his desk full of stuff which just happened to be exactly what he needed for a particular story, but he had no idea or involvement as to where that information came from, then he would be quite entitled to use it. In our view.'

Johnathan frowned, trying to piece this together. 'Right,' he said.

'It's a bit like Father Christmas,' continued Jake. 'Every Christmas Day your stocking gets filled with presents, and whilst you don't perhaps believe in Father Christmas yourself, you aren't particularly worried how the presents arrive as long as they keep on coming each year.'

'I see,' said Johnathan doubtfully.

'So I'm afraid I know nothing about that sort of thing.'

'Oh. So now what?'

'We could always just make it up as we go along,' suggested Jake.

'I don't think it quite works like that,' said Johnathan, despondent. 'This sort of thing you need experienced help for.'

'What about your clients?' asked Jake. 'Some of them must have first hand experience in this sort of thing.'

Johnathan considered. 'Good idea. Let me have a think.' He hung up. There was a cough from the door. Johnathan looked up. Clark was standing by the door.

Johnathan went white. 'How long, er, hello, well, how long have you been there for?' he spluttered.

Clark smiled. 'I just heard your conversation.'

'All of it?'

Clark nodded.

Johnathan nodded too. 'Obviously just a bit of a joke. Old friend. University mates. Winding each other up, you know.' He winked with as much enthusiasm as he could muster, which wasn't much.

Clark nodded again. 'I heard,' he repeated.

'Listen, Clark,' said Johnathan. 'You mustn't worry about all that nonsense. No need to tell anyone. It's just a joke. Ha ha.' He rubbed his belly in simulated mirth. 'All right?' He beamed. 'What can I do for you, anyway?' he asked, changing tack desperately to avoid further embarrassment.

'What you said about locks and stuff,' said Clark. 'I'm your man.'

Johnathan stopped rubbing his belly. 'You what?' he said.

That lunchtime, Clark told Johnathan his story, aided by three pints of beer dispensed by the vinegar-faced barmaid of the local pub. It had taken a supreme effort on Johnathan's part to remain patient, on account of the extraordinarily slow speed at which Clark spoke; he would periodically drift off into a thoughtless reverie, staring at the whirring one-armed bandit which clicked and beeped on the other side of the pub.

Clark, it transpired, had enjoyed a certain success during his school days in Bow by breaking into the teachers' common room after school hours to copy test papers a day or two before exams and then selling them to his schoolmates. After school, he moved on and branched out. He became an expert house-breaker, working on commission, offering what he called a bespoke burglary service – if you wanted something particular stolen, Clark was your man.

His little operation had been doing well for a couple of years when a professional rival called him anonymously and asked for a painting to be removed from a particular house. When Clark arrived the police were waiting for him.

'So what happened?' asked Johnathan.

'Arrested. Charged. You know.' Clark took a large swig of lager.

'Does Kyriakedes know about all this?' asked Johnathan.

'Of course,' said Clark. 'He was my solicitor. It was his idea. He suggested I try the law as an alternative career. Thought I'd be good at it.' He yawned.

Johnathan sighed in disbelief.

'So what is it you're up to, then?' asked Clark.

Johnathan outlined his plan, hoping that Clark would not be interested in the reasons behind what he wanted to do. He wasn't.

Clark nodded slowly. 'I get it,' he said. 'Nice one.'

'So really it's quite simple,' said Johnathan breezily. 'I just want to break into his house, leave my little present for him, make it look as though there's been a forced entry, and leave again.'

'A piece,' said Clark, 'of piss.'

That evening Johnathan, Jake and Clark met up in an oak

panelled pub in Chelsea, about five minutes away from Gregory's house. When Johnathan arrived, Jake was sitting at a table, contemplating his glass of beer, dressed in black jeans, black polo-neck jumper, and black leather jacket. At the next table sat Clark, reading a soiled tabloid, and dressed in a garish Hawaiian shirt. Both men waved a greeting to Johnathan and, seeing the other do so, looked at each other suspiciously.

'Hi,' said Johnathan. 'Jake, this is Clark, Clark, this is Jake.'

Jake and Clark looked at each other, and after a moment's hesitation shook hands.

'Interesting stuff you're wearing,' observed Clark. 'Have you got a mask to put on and a bag with "swag" on the side too?'

'I thought you were supposed to wear black to make it harder to be seen,' said Jake mildly.

Johnathan coughed supportively. He had gone for the same colour scheme as Jake.

Clark sniffed. 'You might as well have a badge with "Burglar" on it pinned to your chest,' he said. He leant forward conspiratorially. 'Misdirection, that's the thing,' he whispered. 'Put them off the scent.' He pulled at his shirt. 'Nobody in their right mind would go burgling in a shirt like this, would they?'

'No,' agreed Jake and Johnathan together.

Clark sat back. 'Well then,' he said, satisfied.

For the first time it occurred to Johnathan that perhaps enlisting Clark's help in this endeavour might not have been quite as prudent as it had at first appeared. 'I'll get a round in, then,' he said, and left his two accomplices eyeing each other cautiously.

He returned a few minutes later. 'So,' he said to Clark. 'You've got, er, all the stuff?'

Clark patted a chunky bag which nestled between his feet. 'All in there. Everything you need for a decent bit of house-breaking.' He looked radiant. 'This is great. Just like old times,' he said nostalgically, taking a large swig of his beer.

'Well, that's nice,' said Johnathan unenthusiastically. He looked at Jake. 'Got the paint?'

Jake nodded. 'Got Morty?'

Johnathan nodded and patted his jacket pocket where Morty lay, bundled up in a small plastic bag. Since the accident the previous evening he had tried not to think about Morty too much, but still he was consumed by guilt. He stared miserably at his beer, unable to raise his eyes to meet Jake's.

'It's what he would have wanted, Johnathan,' said Jake seriously.

After a few minutes' silent drinking, they finished their beers. Clark looked at Johnathan eagerly like a young puppy waiting for its owner to throw a stick for it to chase. Johnathan saw a small blob of spittle form at the corner of Clark's mouth and considered abandoning the whole thing. Then he thought of Terry and Spike.

'Let's go,' he said.

A few minutes later the three men stood outside the front door of Gregory's house in silence. There didn't appear to be anyone about. The only sound was Clark's excited breathing and a muffled oomph-oomph from a neighbour's stereo system. Johnathan couldn't help noticing how Clark's Hawaiian shirt had a certain florescent nature which made it glow in the dark. He tried not to think about it.

'Now what?' he asked.

'We should go round the back,' said Jake. 'We'll be more out of sight.'

'Good idea,' said Johnathan, remembering the locks and other fortifications on the inside of the front door. He and Clark followed Jake through a large wooden gate at the side of the house. Jake led them to a back door. Clark stood in front of it and twisted the door handle.

'Well,' he reported, 'the door is locked.'

'No kidding,' said Jake.

'So,' said Johnathan. 'Do we pick the lock with a bit of wire or something? Cut a hole in the window by the latch?'

'Could do,' said Clark. 'But all that sort of stuff takes ages.'

So saying he put down his bag and unzipped it. Johnathan peered downwards into the darkness but could see nothing. After a quick rummage Clark stood up brandishing the largest torch Johnathan had seen. It was at least two feet long.

'Are you going to examine the lock mechanism?' asked Johnathan, impressed.

'God no,' said Clark, and smashed the window next to Gregory's back door with the end of the torch.

The noise was terrible. It must have been audible from several streets away. Johnathan stared at Clark in horror.

'Wow,' said Jake sardonically. 'This guy is *good*.'

Johnathan was too petrified to move or speak. He stood, frozen, waiting for enquiring doors to be opened, lights to be switched on, and for the searing wail of a police siren to break the calm.

Nothing happened. After about a minute Johnathan started to relax a little. Clark and Jake were peering into Gregory's house through the broken window.

'How do we actually get in, now that everyone knows we're here?' hissed Johnathan.

'Through the window, obviously,' said Clark. 'Hang on a sec.' He then knocked out all of the remaining glass in the window with his torch, cheerily ignoring Johnathan's anguished hopping up and down beside him. 'There you go,' he said when he had finished. 'Easy.' He gestured towards the open window.

'Couldn't you have just reached in and opened it from the latch?' asked Johnathan.

Clark considered. 'Yeah,' he said. He put the torch back into his bag. 'Come on, then.' He climbed up on to the window sill and threw his bag into the house, where it landed with a resounding thump, and then slipped inside. Johnathan and Jake looked at each other.

'After you,' said Johnathan politely.

'After *you*,' said Jake.

Reluctantly Johnathan hoisted himself through the window and gingerly climbed down on to the bed of broken glass which lay on the floor inside. It was very dark. Jake arrived behind him and clapped him on the shoulder.

'All right?' he whispered.

Johnathan shrugged helplessly.

All Johnathan could see was Clark's Hawaiian shirt moving around at the other end of the room. 'Where's the torch?' he whispered. 'I can't see anything.'

'Hold your horses,' said Clark in his normal speaking voice. 'I'm just looking for – ah, there you go.' He switched the overhead light on.

Johnathan and Jake stood transfixed as the sudden glare blinded them. Clark started to hum, and began examining the contents of the room with interest.

'Are you completely insane?' whispered Johnathan as thunderously as he could. 'You can't just turn the light on like that. People will see us.'

'What's wrong with using the torch?' asked Jake, who by now was rattled too.

'The torch doesn't actually work,' explained Clark. 'Not, you know, as a torch. No batteries.'

'Jesus bloody Christ,' said Johnathan with feeling.

'You could always close the curtains if you wanted,' said Clark, opening a drawer and inspecting its contents with a practised eye.

'Curtains. Right,' said Johnathan, and went to close them. There was a pause as the three men looked at their new surroundings. They had broken into the kitchen where Johnathan and Jake had spoken with Gregory a few nights earlier.

Clark looked around. 'Nice,' he said. 'Bit poncy, but generally nice.' He walked over to a shelf and picked up a carriage clock. He examined it critically.

'What do we do now?' asked Jake.

'I suppose we need to think where to put Morty.'

Clark put the carriage clock into his bag.

'What are you doing?' asked Johnathan.

'Well look, we want this to look like a proper burglary, don't we? Otherwise it's going to look very suspicious if people break in and don't actually steal anything. The police will smell a rat right away. So we'd better take something to put them off the scent. Anyway, that's a lovely clock.'

Johnathan closed his eyes, took a deep breath, and thought. He shrugged. 'OK. Do what you want.' He went into the hall, leaving Clark to pilfer what he could from his brother's possessions.

He tried the door immediately on his right. It was a sitting room. Jake followed him in. They examined the room in silence. It was fairly sparsely furnished, with one large sofa dominating the middle of the room, which sat directly in front of the largest television set Johnathan had ever seen. In between the sofa and the television was a low table which was stacked with old copies of the Radio Times and a remote control with more buttons on it than a small computer. Crisp packets and empty biscuit wrappers lay in small piles on the floor.

'Doesn't look as if he got out much,' observed Jake.

'That's my brother,' said Johnathan. 'Always expected the world to come to him.' He put down the bag. 'What do you reckon?' he asked, pointing at the wall, which was bare of any pictures. 'Nice friendly message on there?'

'Smashing,' said Jake. 'Make things a bit more homely.' He bent down and pulled a can of paint and screwdriver out of his bag, and levered the top off the can. 'Right,' he said. 'I got red paint. More effective, I thought. Overtones of blood, that sort of thing.'

Johnathan nodded approvingly. 'What did we decide on again?'

'Pay up or die,' said Jake.

'I like it,' said Johnathan. 'Short, to the point, eloquent in its own way.'

He set to work.

When he had finished, he took Morty out of the plastic bag in his pocket and left him on the carpet immediately in front of the message. Thankfully Schroedinger had been too lazy to bother chewing very hard and so Morty was more or less in one piece.

'Hang on,' said Jake, once Johnathan had artfully arranged

Morty in an appropriately macabre position. He dipped the paintbrush into the pot of paint and applied a spattering of red to Morty's neck. 'What do you think?' he asked, stepping back to admire his handiwork.

'Not bad,' admitted Johnathan. 'He looks pretty awful.'

'Excellent. Then he shall not have died in vain.'

Clark came into the room eating a piece of toast. 'All right,' he said with his mouth full.

Johnathan looked at Clark with despair. 'Jesus, make yourself at home, why don't you? Are we doing a burglary or enjoying a cheese and wine party?'

'Tell you what,' said Clark. 'There's some nice stuff here. He's doing all right for himself.'

'What have you found?' asked Johnathan. 'Anything interesting?'

'Sure. A Rolex watch. Real one. Some very fancy cufflinks. And guess what?'

'What?' said Johnathan wearily.

'We share the same shoe size.' Clark opened his bag to show four or five pairs of expensive shoes. He was beaming.

'Right,' said Johnathan. 'I reckon we're about done.' He looked at Clark. 'Got everything you want?'

Clark nodded happily. 'I've done very well, thank you.'

'Good. Let's go.'

They walked back to the kitchen and climbed back through the broken window. Clark stood with his bag, now considerably heavier, hanging from his right shoulder. His Hawaiian shirt was still glowing in the dark. 'Right, well, thanks for everything, Clark,' said Johnathan. 'It's been an education. See you tomorrow.'

'No worries,' replied Clark cheerily. 'Thanks for letting me come along. If you ever need my help again, just ask.'

Johnathan smiled weakly. 'Thanks.'

Clark walked off whistling. Jake and Johnathan turned to go back towards the King's Road.

'Now what?' asked Jake.

'Now we wait,' said Johnathan.

TWENTY-ONE

There were a number of issues that Johnathan now had to address, which could be summarized as follows:

1. Gregory obviously needed to see what Johnathan and Jake had done to his house to make the psychological warfare work. The problem therefore was to concoct a suitably compelling reason to persuade someone as innately slothful as Gregory to travel half way across London to his old house.

2. Inspired by the relative success of their trip to Kibby's parents the previous weekend, Johnathan had decided, against his better instincts, that he should introduce Kibby to his parents. That way he would reinforce the whole parent-meeting-as-an-indication-of-seriousness issue.

3. Gregory's continuing presence in his flat was making Johnathan's life utterly miserable. Although Johnathan had never really considered himself to be a particularly house-proud person, being forced to share his living space with someone of Gregory's pre-historic hygienic and social habits was gradually changing him into a ferocious anal retentive, which he found rather unnerving.

249

No inspiration arrived as to how to get Gregory to go back to his own house – he was so well settled on Johnathan's sofa that Johnathan was beginning to wonder if he ever got off it at all. However, he saw an opportunity to kill the remaining two birds with one proverbial stone. The following day he telephoned his father and mentioned as casually as he could that Gregory might need some temporary accommodation.

'So, hang on, what are you suggesting?' his father said. 'That he comes to stay with us?'

'Just for a short while,' said Johnathan. 'You've got a lot more room than I have.'

'Absolutely not,' said his father. 'Out of the question.'

'Why not?'

'I hardly know him.'

'I realize that,' said Johnathan. 'I thought it would be a good chance to rebuild those bridges.' Johnathan, to his credit, blushed as he said this.

'Well, I'm not really sure,' replied his father.

'At least think about it,' said Johnathan.

'What's he like now, anyway? Last time I saw him he was a spoiled little brat.'

'Oh, he's absolutely fine now. Perfectly fine. Fine. All right. Ordinary. You know.'

Johnathan's father sounded doubtful. 'I'll have to think about it.'

'Wouldn't you at least like to meet him?' tried Johnathan. He realized that once his parents actually met Gregory they would never even contemplate taking him in, but he was running out of options.

His father sighed. 'Go on, then. I suppose so. Come for dinner tonight.'

'Can I bring Kibby?'

'Bring who you like.' The lack of enthusiasm was audible.

That evening, therefore, Johnathan drove Kibby and Gregory to his parents' house in North London. The mood in the car was tense. Kibby was worried about meeting Johnathan's parents, and Gregory sat in the back of the car chewing his fingernails at the prospect of meeting his father for the first time in years. He had descended into a quivering wreck of histrionics as soon as the prospect of a reunion with his father had been suggested and this showed no signs of abating.

Johnathan was also worried. He had not explained to Kibby about his parents' aspirations and, since the appearance of the newspaper article, their belief, about his homosexuality. He didn't know quite how his parents would react when they realized that he and Kibby were having sex together.

'Here we are,' said Johnathan as they pulled up in front of his parents' house in a leafy Hampstead street. Kibby whistled appreciatively. Gregory merely looked a little green. They got out of the car and trooped up in single file to the front door, Johnathan leading the way and Gregory bringing up the rear, looking furtively around him as he went as if he might make a run for it at any moment.

Johnathan rang the bell and moments later the door was thrown open by his mother, who stood framed in the doorway for a few seconds without moving, her arms outstretched towards her visitors, giving them the opportunity to appreciate the aesthetic and dramatic tableau she had created for their benefit.

'*Darlings*.'

Johnathan sighed inwardly. He stepped forward and offered

his mother a cheek. 'Mum, can I introduce Kibby and of course Gregory.' Kibby stepped forward and thrust her hand out.

'Pleased to meet you, Mrs Burlip,' she said.

Johnathan's mother's face clouded over momentarily. 'Please, call me Penny,' she said, obviously not entirely sure whom she was talking to.

'Pleased to meet you, Penny,' said Kibby obediently.

Penny turned her attention to Gregory, who was skulking behind the other two. She gazed at him without much enthusiasm. 'Hello Gregory,' she said, advancing towards him and kissing him firmly on both cheeks. She took a step backwards and looked him up and down. 'When was the last time I saw you?' she asked.

'Years ago,' replied Gregory pointedly.

'Haven't you grown, though.'

'Well I would have hoped so.' Uh-oh, thought Johnathan. Here we go.

'Anyway,' said Penny, unflappably serene in the face of such aggression, 'do come in, all of you. This is really very nice. Come and meet Roger.' She turned and retreated into the house. Johnathan's father was in the kitchen drizzling balsamic vinegar over sun-dried tomatoes and roasted vegetables. He greeted Kibby in the same, slightly baffled manner as had his wife, and then reluctantly shook hands with Gregory. Gregory meanwhile had gone as white as a sheet and seemed to be hyperventilating.

'When was the last time I saw you?' asked Roger.

'Years ago,' gasped Gregory, who was staring at his father as if he were a ghost.

'Haven't you grown, though.'

Oh God, thought Johnathan. This time, however, Gregory

merely nodded mutely, acknowledging that yes, he had indeed grown.

A few minutes later everyone was sitting with a much-needed drink in the conservatory, which was filled with rattan furniture and colourful ethnic cushions. Conversation was stilted. Gregory gawked in a mesmerized way. Kibby was ignored. Johnathan had the distinct impression that everyone, himself included, would rather be somewhere else.

'So what is it exactly that you do?' Penny asked Gregory.

'This and that,' stuttered Gregory.

Penny's nose wrinkled. 'What does this and that entail?'

'Whatever comes along. Bits and pieces. Odds and sods.' Gregory paused miserably. 'This and that,' he said again.

Johnathan decided to pep things up a little, and help Gregory's cause at the same time. He went straight for his parents' weak spot. 'I suppose you might say that you're a kind of New Age portfolio-managing performance artist,' he said to his brother.

Gregory's face clouded over. 'I suppose so,' he agreed doubtfully.

Johnathan saw his parents' interest perk up immediately.

'A performance artist? How so?' asked Roger.

Seeing his brother's mouth open and shut in silent bafflement, Johnathan jumped in again.

'Gregory performs a satirical indictment of the evils of amassed wealth and the capitalist ethos,' he explained. 'It's very clever. He displays the pervasive corrupting influence of vast and unearned riches with a fine eye for detail.'

Gregory looked down, completely lost. 'Yeah, well,' he said awkwardly. 'You have to do something in this life, don't you?'

There was a pause. Kibby was looking at Johnathan

disapprovingly. Roger and Penny were exchanging glances with each other. Gregory was concentrating hard on his shoes.

Eventually Penny checked her watch. 'Well,' she said brightly, 'it's just about time for supper. Shall we go through?' She stood up with a broad smile. Everybody got to their feet and followed her through to the dining room.

Penny turned towards Kibby after everyone had been served their ferociously trendy food. 'How long have you and Gregory known each other?' she asked.

Kibby frowned. 'Not long at all. I've only met him a couple of times.'

Roger laughed ill-naturedly. 'Good heavens, Gregory. And already you're introducing her to the parents. Well, one of the parents.'

'Sorry,' said Kibby, shooting a glance at Johnathan. 'I don't quite –'

'Haven't we been having wonderful weather?' asked Johnathan.

'She's not *my* girlfriend,' said Gregory.

'She's not?' said Penny.

'God, no,' replied Gregory rather rudely.

'Johnathan?' said Kibby questioningly.

'Sunny without being too humid,' elaborated Johnathan.

Roger frowned. 'I must be missing something here,' he said.

'Me too,' agreed Kibby darkly.

Johnathan took a deep breath. 'Kibby is *my* girlfriend,' he admitted.

Roger and Penny looked at Johnathan in amazement. 'What?' they both said.

'Kibby is *my* girlfriend,' repeated Johnathan.

'But I thought —'

'I know what you *thought*,' said Johnathan. 'But you didn't listen. I did tell you in the hospital, but you ignored me.' He turned to Kibby in the hope that this would explain matters. By the look on her face, it didn't.

'So you're not —' said Penny querulously.

'No,' agreed Johnathan. 'I'm not. Never have been. Never will be.'

'Not what?' asked Kibby.

Penny looked at Johnathan and then at Kibby, crestfallen. 'But I thought —' she began, before trailing off into an unhappy silence.

'No,' said Johnathan. 'Sorry.'

'Not what?' asked Kibby.

'Mum,' said Johnathan, 'this is not exactly news.'

'But what about the newspaper report?'

'Oh, I can explain that.'

'I wish you would, then.'

'Not what?' asked Kibby.

Johnathan turned to Kibby. 'Um, look, do you mind if I explain later?'

'Yes,' said Kibby. 'I mind a lot.'

'Oh. Right.' Johnathan cursed himself for not explaining this earlier. 'It's just that Mum and Dad were under the impression, after that article in the newspaper, that I was gay.'

Kibby looked long and hard at Johnathan. 'Go on,' she said eventually.

Johnathan shrugged. 'And I'm not.'

'I know,' said Kibby. Penny let out a small whimper of distress.

'And that's all there is to it,' said Johnathan.

255

There was a pause.

'Right,' said Kibby.

An awkward silence descended over the table, which was eventually broken by Penny explaining in unnecessary length the convoluted plot of a Bulgarian film they had been to see at the Barbican a week earlier. Gregory sat quietly eating his food without saying a word. Roger and Penny said as little as they could to Kibby, seemingly affronted by her presence. Johnathan battled gamely on, trying to ignore Kibby's dark brooding next to him.

At the end of the meal Penny directed Johnathan and Kibby into the sitting room and enlisted Gregory's help in clearing the table and preparing coffee. Kibby grabbed Johnathan's arm as they stood up from the table. 'Right, you. I want a word,' she whispered.

'Sure,' said Johnathan unhappily.

'What was all that about?' she demanded as they entered the sitting room.

'My parents. What can I say?'

'Well, you could explain why you've never even *mentioned* me to them before, for starters,' replied Kibby angrily. 'That was seriously awful.'

Johnathan nodded. 'I know. I'm sorry.'

'They thought I was *Gregory's* girlfriend,' said Kibby. 'Do you have any idea how that makes me feel?'

'I can imagine,' said Johnathan.

'What is it? Are you ashamed of me?'

'God, of course not. That's absurd.'

'Worried they'll disapprove?'

Johnathan took a deep breath. 'Well,' he said. 'Frankly, yes.' He explained about his parents' aspirations for his sexuality. Kibby's face clouded over in disbelief.

'That,' she said, 'is not normal.'

Johnathan put his hands up. 'Believe me, I know. I *did* try and tell them about you. Honestly. When they came to see me in the hospital.'

'You don't seem to have made a very good job of it.'

'No. Well, that's my mother. She makes denial an art form. If she doesn't want to hear it, she won't.'

Roger, Penny and Gregory came into the room bearing coffee and cups. They sat down awkwardly. Gregory still seemed in a trance-like state. Roger eyed proceedings in stony-faced silence. Penny smiled bravely as she poured the coffee. Oh dear, thought Johnathan. The family reunion was not going too well, then.

Once the coffee had been distributed another uneasy silence descended. Johnathan was now regretting his grand plan to reunite the family. All that he had managed to achieve was to widen the already gaping chasm between him and his parents, to upset Kibby, and to turn his brother into monosyllabic vegetable. Whilst the last result was something to be welcomed, Johnathan knew that it was probably only a matter of time before Gregory became his old charmless self again. And of course, he had completely failed to persuade his parents to take Gregory in. He suddenly felt very tired. He thought of Morty lying on Gregory's carpet, waiting to be discovered, and his spirits sank still lower.

'Tell me, Johnathan,' said Penny, 'how's the new job going?'

Johnathan shrugged. 'Not badly, I suppose. There's a lot to learn, obviously. It's a whole new area of law for me.'

'So much more interesting than working in the City, I should imagine,' said Roger, alighting on the subject as will a hungry vulture on a rotting carcass.

'It's certainly different,' conceded Johnathan.

'You must get a much greater satisfaction, don't you, working with ordinary people?' persisted Roger.

'Like I say, it's different. Each job has its attractions, and each has its problems.'

Roger replaced his coffee cup on the table, which was thoughtfully strewn with catalogues from recent art exhibitions. 'I must say, I'm surprised,' he said.

Johnathan sighed. His father was an architect, and as such was speaking from a position of profound ignorance. He designed grotesque post-post-modern, post-good-taste office complexes which looked like bad jokes. They punctuated the London skyline with increasingly self-important exclamation marks of urban madness. Roger rarely met any of the people who had to live and work inside them. And he was never exposed to what he referred to as ordinary people. Ordinary people built his buildings, of course, but that was hardly his concern. The only thing his father was really qualified to build, thought Johnathan, was an ivory tower.

'All I'm saying,' replied Johnathan, 'is that it's still early days.'

'But you're not thinking of going back to the City, are you darling?' asked Penny anxiously. 'We were so proud when we heard you were moving to Finsbury Park. Everyone was most impressed.'

Oh I see, thought Johnathan. Hence the reason for the concern. They've been playing their dinner party games again.

'*I'm* gay,' said Gregory.

'Well, I do hope you'll at least give this new job a chance,' said Roger. 'It's a marvellous opportunity to put something back into the community.'

Oh, for God's sake, thought Johnathan. Hypocritical old

git. 'What,' he asked, 'did you ever put back into the community?'

Roger shifted uncomfortably in his seat. 'Well, you know, I pay my taxes.'

Johnathan looked unimpressed. 'As do we all.'

'What did you say?' Kibby asked Gregory.

'And I always buy a copy of the Big Issue,' said Roger.

Johnathan's eyebrows went up in mock surprise.

'We always give our old clothes to Oxfam, too,' said Penny.

'And I think we sponsor a boy in West Africa, don't we?' Roger asked his wife.

Penny nodded. 'Indeed we do,' she said.

'That's good. What's his name?' asked Johnathan.

Roger and Penny looked at each other blankly.

'Can't remember just now,' said Penny uncertainly. 'Something strange. African. Ekwo or Esho. Something like that.'

'I'm gay,' said Gregory to Kibby.

'Well I'm impressed by how much interest you take in this child,' said Johnathan. 'Lucky him.'

'Good grief, the boy's in Africa. What else can we do?' said Roger.

'That's very interesting,' said Kibby to Gregory. 'Are you sure?'

'Oh yes, quite sure,' replied Gregory. 'Always have been.'

'Have you told, er, Roger?' asked Kibby.

Gregory shook his head. 'Not yet. Do you think I should?'

Kibby nodded. 'Definitely.'

For the first time Johnathan and his parents turned their attention to Kibby and Gregory.

'Definitely what?' asked Johnathan, keen now to change the subject before his parents began asking what *he* did for charity.

'I think Gregory may have something of interest to say to your parents,' said Kibby, nudging Gregory gently.

'Really?' said Roger, not sounding convinced.

There was a pause as everyone looked at Gregory. Kibby nudged him again. 'Go on, then,' she said. 'Out with it.'

Gregory started. 'Oh. Well. It's just that, if you're interested in that sort of thing, then I'm gay.'

There was silence for several moments. Roger and Penny looked at each other and then both turned slowly towards Gregory.

'*Really*,' said Penny. 'That *is* interesting.'

'Are you sure?' asked Roger.

Gregory nodded, obviously rather nonplussed. 'Quite sure.'

'Well,' said his father warmly. 'I said to Penny just before you arrived how much I was looking forward to seeing you again after all these years. We really have left it too long. There's an awful lot to catch up on.'

'Absolutely,' purred Penny. 'We're both looking forward to getting to know you *much* better.'

'More coffee?' suggested Roger smoothly.

Hello, *hello*, Johnathan wanted to shout. It was as if he and Kibby had suddenly become invisible. He looked at Kibby, who was watching his parents' change in attitude with amusement. Gregory now commanded Roger and Penny's full attention.

'So tell me,' said Penny, eyelids fluttering in excitement, 'do you have a boyfriend?'

'Not at the moment,' replied Gregory, confused.

'Oh.' Penny sat back, a little put out.

'I have had them in the past, though,' said Gregory quickly, glancing nervously between Penny and his father.

Jonathan remembered the orange top Gregory had worn to go clubbing. A small penny dropped at the back of his brain.

'Well,' said Roger, 'this is *splendid* news.'

Gregory looked back at his father blankly.

'You must come and stay with us, of course,' continued Roger.

'Oh yes,' murmured Penny, visions of presenting Gregory to all their friends doubtless already drifting through her head.

Oh, perfect, thought Jonathan bitterly. Just perfect. He comes in after twenty years and with two words manages to eclipse me *completely*. The fact that Gregory's admission had actually secured exactly the result Johnathan had been hoping for was momentarily obscured by a fit of intense fraternal jealousy. *I'm still here*, he wanted to shout. I'm still your son. I may be straight, but I'm still your son. Look at me.

'Something very interesting happened at work last week, actually,' he said.

'We've got any number of bedrooms for you to choose from,' said Roger. 'This will be a lot of fun.'

Penny squealed with excitement. 'Do you think we'll be able to get an extra ticket for that Austrian erotic minimalist exhibition?'

'I should have thought so,' said Roger.

'It involved an ordinary person,' said Johnathan hollowly. Kibby squeezed his hand gently on the sofa.

'Do you have many other clothes?' asked Penny, inspecting

Gregory critically. 'I imagine you do. You're all wonderful clothes horses, aren't you?'

'I have other stuff,' said Gregory, who was beginning to rally a little. 'But not that much. Nothing special.'

'Nothing more . . . flamboyant?'

Gregory shook his head. 'Oh no,' he replied. 'I'm not really into all that.'

'Well, never mind,' said Penny in a determined way. 'We really ought to go shopping together. Find you some new outfits.'

Gregory coughed doubtfully. 'To be honest, I'm not sure —'

'Oh, absolutely,' interrupted Penny. 'Of course we must. Find you something special to wear for big nights out.'

Johnathan looked at his brother, and could not help feeling a little sorry for him. Gregory would not know what had hit him. When Roger and Penny's self-promotion machine cranked itself up to full throttle there was little he would be able to do to stop it. He would be totemized, celebrated and ruthlessly used by Johnathan's parents to drive up their stock on the North London Stock Exchange of Bullshit. He would be paraded around exhibitions, introduced at dinner parties, and fêted in the bar at the Royal Opera House, all the while probably dressed in some ridiculous outfit chosen by Penny which was designed to ram his homosexuality down everyone's throat, so to speak, with the subtlety of a Polaris missile.

'OK,' said Gregory to Penny, unaware what he was letting himself in for.

'Oh *good*,' said Penny, patting her knees in excitement.

'Kibby works in films,' said Johnathan.

Penny and Roger both turned to him with a slightly

surprised look, as if they had forgotten that he and Kibby were still there. Roger looked at his watch. 'Good heavens,' he said. 'Look at the time.'

Johnathan looked at his watch. It was ten o'clock. He looked at his father enquiringly.

'Must be time for you to get home, I would have thought,' continued Roger.

Johnathan blinked in disbelief. They were being dismissed.

'Er, right,' he said numbly. He looked at Gregory. 'What are you doing?' he asked.

Before Gregory could reply Penny interjected, 'Gregory can stay with us from now on. No trouble. Really.'

'What about his stuff?' asked Johnathan. 'It's all at my flat.'

'It's probably easiest if we could come round tomorrow to pick it up, if that's no trouble,' answered Penny.

No trouble? It's shed loads of bloody trouble, fumed Johnathan. 'All right,' he said lamely. He suddenly had an idea. He turned to Gregory. 'You'll probably want to go back to your own house, won't you, to pick up a few more things, now that you'll have more space.'

Gregory thought about this. 'Yeah,' he said eventually. 'Think that'll be all right?'

Johnathan nodded. At least some good had come from this. Gregory would now get to enjoy the small display Johnathan and Jake had prepared for him. 'You'll be fine. I'd go first thing tomorrow, if I were you, just to be safe.'

Gregory nodded. 'Right,' he said. 'I'll do that.'

'Good.' Roger stood up with a finality that made Johnathan's heart lurch a little. This was brutal. 'Well, thanks for coming,' he said to Johnathan.

263

Johnathan and Kibby stood up as well. 'Thank *you*,' said Johnathan. 'For a lovely evening. Super food.' Fantastic display of familial ex-communication. Very touching banishing from the family fold. Nice.

Kibby shook Johnathan's parents' hands. 'Nice to meet you,' she said. 'Very interesting. Explains a lot.'

Roger and Penny shook her hand with auto-pilot smiles firmly in place, herding them both to the door as they did so. From the sofa Gregory watched them go with a look of edgy desperation in his eye.

Johnathan maintained as much dignity as he could as they were bundled out on to the pavement. 'Thanks again,' he said bitterly.

'See you tomorrow, darling,' said Penny.

Oh Christ. 'Yup, see you then,' he replied. Johnathan took Kibby's hand in some ill-defined gesture of defiance and turned to walk towards the car. He unlocked the doors in silence and they climbed in. As he turned the ignition key and revved the engine with more force than was strictly necessary, Kibby leaned across and kissed him gently on the cheek.

Johnathan drove off, staring ahead of him. They travelled in silence for several minutes. Eventually they stopped at a set of traffic lights. Johnathan exhaled deeply, and turned to look at Kibby. Kibby touched his arm softly.

'Are you all right?' she asked.

'I suppose so. Wounded pride, though.'

'I thought you were very brave.'

'Really?'

'Really. I thought *my* parents were odd. But they can't compete with that.'

Johnathan shrugged. 'That was weird, even for them.'

'Still,' said Kibby brightly, 'you got what you wanted. We're driving home alone. Gregory's out of your life.'

Johnathan reflected. 'You're right,' he conceded, as he eased away from the lights. But at what cost? he wondered to himself. He had surprised himself at the intensity of the jealousy he had felt at his parents' breathtakingly fatuous change in allegiance to Gregory. He would have to wait and see whether they would get bored with him once they had shown him off to all their friends.

'Where are we going?' asked Johnathan.

'Actually? Metaphysically? Or metaphorically? In the short term? In the long term? You must learn to be more specific,' said Kibby.

'Actually I meant where am I driving to.'

'Oh, right. That's easy. Your place.'

Johnathan perked up a little.

TWENTY-TWO

Johnathan was cutting it very fine.

He tapped his biro against his legal pad, deep in thought. Things were out of his hands now. All he could do was sit and wait for the telephone to ring. He glanced at his watch. It was mid-morning on Wednesday, the day after his parents' dinner party, and the last day of the week that Spike had given him to recover the money. Gregory was probably just about out of bed. He would get to Chelsea by about lunchtime, Johnathan estimated, at which point it would become clear whether or not Johnathan and Jake's efforts with Morty and the red paint would have the desired effect. If nothing happened, Spike would be in touch later on, once the six o'clock deadline had expired. Johnathan tried not to think too much about that. Once thing at a time, he reasoned.

Johnathan scanned the letter in front of him, but failed to assimilate any of its contents. He looked at the telephone distractedly. This waiting really wasn't good for his nerves. He spent the morning doing no work whatsoever. At one point Clark tentatively pushed the door open and proudly showed off a pair of Gregory's shoes which he was wearing for the first time.

'Very nice,' said Johnathan.

'Aren't they?' agreed Clark. 'Fit like a glove.'

At lunchtime Johnathan went out for a few minutes to soak up a little bit of carbon-monoxide drenched sunshine and to buy a tuna and mayonnaise sandwich. He ate it at his desk, not wanting to miss Gregory when he called. Just as he was finishing, the telephone rang. He picked up the receiver.

'Herro?' he mumbled through a mouthful of bread.

'Aaagggghh.'

It was Gregory. Johnathan swallowed quickly.

'Hello?'

'I'm at my house. God. God.'

Johnathan waited.

'They've been here. They mean business.'

Johnathan felt relief flooding through his body. 'What's happened, exactly?' he asked.

'There's, there's, there's. Blood. On the walls. Threatening message. They've broken in. Mess everywhere. Horrible,' Gregory gibbered.

Johnathan closed his eyes in delight. Only Gregory would assume that the message was actually painted in blood. Unexpected bonus. As for the mess – they had done nothing; that was how Gregory had left the place.

'Hold on. Calm down. What does the message say?'

'Christ. "Pay up or else you die", something like that.'

'Crumbs,' said Johnathan. 'Sounds serious. What are you going to do?'

'I'm going to pay the bastard. I think I underestimated him. The guy's a fucking psycho. You should see what he's done here.'

Johnathan suppressed the urge to holler in triumph. Something had finally gone right.

'What's he done?'

'There's just this blood everywhere. All over the walls. And he stole some stuff, too.'

Johnathan thought of Clark proudly walking around in his brother's shoes. 'Anything else?'

'Jesus, that's enough, isn't it? No, nothing else.'

Johnathan frowned. 'Are you sure?'

'Well, a mouse crept out from the skirting board and died on the carpet. So I'll have to get the exterminators in. But apart from that, no, nothing else.'

Johnathan's grip tightened around the telephone. A *mouse*? That was a hamster, you witless cretin, he wanted to shout. That was Morty. Courageous, heroic, tragic Morty.

Putting his regrets behind him, he asked, 'So what are you going to do now?'

'Call the bastard, I suppose,' said Gregory. 'I'll get the money right away and arrange to meet him this afternoon.'

'Good idea.'

'I need to pick up my things from your flat, so I'll meet him there, if that's all right.'

'Sure.'

'Johnathan?'

'Yes?'

'You wouldn't mind coming along, too, would you?' Gregory sounded sheepish. 'The guy's clearly slightly deranged, so I'd just feel a bit safer if there was someone else there when he turns up, so that he doesn't decide to slap me about a bit on a whim.'

Johnathan's afternoon was looking fairly empty. He could spare a few hours. 'Why not?' he said. 'I'd like to make sure you actually pay the guy anyway.'

'Oh, don't worry, I'll pay him,' said Gregory. 'It'll be a

relief, to be honest. I'm missing my own house. Being in Hampstead is a bit weird.' Gregory paused. 'Your mother is very odd,' he said.

'I know,' said Johnathan.

'Sort of, intense.'

'I know,' said Johnathan.

'They seem excited about having me to stay but I think I'd rather not. It's scary.'

'I know,' said Johnathan.

'Yeah,' said Gregory. 'So I'll pay the money and go back to Chelsea.'

'You do realize, don't you, that you won't escape now?'

'Escape? From Spike?'

'No, from my parents. Now they've got their claws into you, they won't let you go. Live where you like, but they'll still find you and drag you out to be admired by their friends. You're their property now. Your life is no longer your own.'

Johnathan could almost hear Gregory shrug on the other end of the telephone. 'Whatever,' he said. 'It's good to see Dad again.'

Oh, just you wait, thought Johnathan.

A few hours later Johnathan arrived back at his flat, where Gregory was packing his things into a small bag.

'Did you call him?' asked Johnathan.

Gregory looked at his watch. 'Yup. He should be here soon.'

'Have you got the money?'

Gregory nodded. 'In the bag in the hall.'

'You got *cash*?'

'Well he's hardly going to want a cheque, is he?' said Gregory.

'No, I suppose not,' said Johnathan. He wandered into the hall. 'Mind if I take a look?' he asked. 'I've never seen a hundred and twenty thousand quid in cash before.'

'Be my guest,' shrugged Gregory.

Johnathan opened the bag and peered inside. It was full of thick bundles of fifty pound notes. Johnathan took a deep breath. He closed the bag quickly. He didn't really want to think about such a large amount of money sitting in his flat. All he wanted was for Gregory to go and for his life to get back to normal as soon as possible.

The doorbell went. Both Gregory and Johnathan straightened up, and looked at each other. 'That'll be him,' said Gregory.

'I'll go, shall I?' offered Johnathan.

Johnathan went to the front door and opened it. There was Spike, dressed in a lurid gold lamé shell suit. He wore a pair of gleaming white trainers which increased his height by at least three inches. He had on a pair of wrap-around sunglasses, which made him look like an extra from a low-budget science fiction film. He held up his hand in greeting and flashed his teeth.

'So, we meet again,' he said. 'You managed to make him see sense. Just in time. Well done.'

'Think nothing of it,' muttered Johnathan, standing aside to allow him in, relieved that Terry had not joined them as well.

Spike strolled into the flat. 'This your place?' he asked.
'Yes.'

Spike nodded. 'Hmm.'

'Thank you,' said Johnathan meekly, unsure if this was the correct response.

'Right, then,' said Spike, suddenly clapping his hands

together and rubbing them vigorously, 'where is the little bastard?'

'The little bastard is in the sitting room,' said Johnathan. 'He's expecting you.'

'Excellent.' Spike walked to the living room. Gregory was waiting for them.

'All right,' he said to Spike.

'Hello, Greg,' said Spike.

'I got your money,' said Gregory, indicating the bag.

'Good. About bloody time, if you don't mind my saying.'

Gregory looked sheepish. 'Yeah, sorry about that.'

'You're a very lucky boy,' said Spike. 'Lucky for you that I've been in a good mood. Lucky for you that I met your little brother.'

'Yeah.' Gregory looked at Johnathan sourly.

Gee, that's OK, thought Johnathan. Don't mention it.

Spike took the bag. 'I won't count it now. Just rest assured that if I find this is a penny short you'll be receiving a visit, and then paying one. To hospital.' Johnathan thought Spike looked slightly silly, issuing such threats while dressed like a camp Martian.

'Don't worry, it's all there,' said Gregory. 'Tell me one thing, though.'

'What?' said Spike.

'Why did you take all my shoes?'

Spike's forehead creased into a frown. 'Your shoes? What are you talking about?'

'Coffee, anyone?' blurted Johnathan.

'My shoes,' said Gregory. 'You nicked them. They'd all be too big for you. Everything else I sort of understand, but that I just don't get. What's the point?'

'Hold on, tiger,' said Spike. 'What the fuck are you on about?'

'Milk? Sugar?'

Gregory looked at Spike. 'Oh, come on. Who are you trying to kid?'

The doorbell went. Johnathan almost jumped out of his skin.

The two other men looked at him. Johnathan stared back, desperate. He didn't really want to leave them to carry on their conversation in case either or both worked out exactly what had been going on.

'Well?' said Spike with the authority of someone used to having his orders obeyed. 'Aren't you going to open it?'

Johnathan hesitated. 'Right,' he said. He turned and went to the front door, wondering who it might be. Was it Terry, coming as the late cavalry to support Spike? He opened the door.

'Hello, darling. How's things?'

Johnathan walked back to the sitting room, wondering what sort of spectacle would greet him. Gregory and Spike were standing where he had left them. Spike was still clutching the bag of money. Both men turned towards him. He saw Gregory's shoulders slump.

'Oh,' said Gregory. 'Hi, Penny.'

'Hello, *darling*,' oozed Johnathan's mother, who rushed forward and grabbed Gregory by the shoulders and administered three awesomely loud kisses in the general area of his face. 'All set?' she asked when she had finished. She looked radiant.

'More or less,' said Gregory uncertainly. 'Actually, Penny,

I was thinking that it might be a better idea if I went back to –'

'And who is this?' asked Penny, looking Spike up and down.

'Mum, this is Spike,' said Johnathan.

Penny extended a well manicured hand. 'Hello, Spike. Delighted to meet you.'

Spike extended an equally well manicured hand. 'Hello,' he said awkwardly.

'So,' said Penny, wrinkling her nose slightly as a whiff of Spike's poisonous aftershave sneaked up her nostrils, 'are you a friend of Gregory's?'

Oh dear, thought Johnathan, who suddenly saw what was about to happen. Not perhaps an unreasonable assumption in view of the gold shell suit.

'I, uh, yes,' said Spike. He shot a questioning glance at Johnathan. Johnathan smiled back affably, wondering how to avert the cataclysmic misunderstanding towards which his mother was hurtling.

'Well, how lovely,' cooed Penny. 'I'm delighted. I'm so looking forward to meeting a lot more of you people.'

'Of us people?' said Spike.

'Absolutely,' said Penny. 'Tell me,' she said, leaning conspiratorially towards Spike. 'Gregory's awfully shy. Are you his *special* friend?' She winked.

Spike's face was clouded in confusion. 'Special friend?' he repeated, quite lost.

The doorbell went again. Johnathan froze. 'Hang on,' he said. 'Nobody move.'

He tore back to the front door and threw it open, ready to repel whoever was there. 'Sorry –' he began.

'Oh God. Oh God. Oh thank Christ. You're safe.'

273

Johnathan stopped in disbelief.

'I was so worried. You haven't returned my calls. And so I assumed the worst. You were talking about ending it all.'

Johnathan staggered backwards.

'And after what I read in the paper about you. About that magazine. People have trouble adjusting to change. I was worried.'

Johnathan finally managed to get his mouth to work. 'What are you doing here?' he hissed.

Chloe spread her arms wide. 'I'm here to see you. I'm here to help you.'

'Thanks very much,' replied Johnathan, 'but you needn't bother.'

'Listen, your recent, ah, *conversion* doesn't mean we can't still be friends,' said Chloe sincerely.

'Uh, sorry, yes it does, I'm afraid,' said Johnathan, who was desperate to get back into the flat. 'Look, sorry, but I really *have* to go.'

'And who is this?' said Penny, appearing at Johnathan's shoulder.

'Nobody,' said Johnathan hastily.

'*Johnathan,*' screeched Chloe.

Johnathan stopped. 'Sorry. Mum, Chloe, Chloe, Mum. Chloe's an old friend. OK. See you.' He waved at Chloe, using his other hand to steer his curious mother back into the flat.

'Peculiar girl,' mused Penny as Johnathan slammed the door shut.

'She is a bit,' agreed Johnathan. He led his mother back down the corridor.

'Gregory, are you ready to go?' asked Johnathan eagerly as he walked back into the sitting room.

Gregory paused. 'Yeah, well. I wanted to talk to Penny about that, actually.'

'Don't you think you'd better discuss that on the way home?' asked Johnathan.

'Well, the point is –'

'Sure. I understand. Anyway, listen, I really think you should talk about that between yourselves.'

Gregory frowned. 'Yeah, but –'

'Mum? Ready to go?'

Penny looked around. 'What? Oh yes, I suppose so.'

'Good. Excellent. Spike? You happy?'

Spike still looked rather baffled. 'Er, yeah. Subject to counting this lot.'

'So, as long as you're happy with that, we're all OK? We can forget about all of this?'

'I suppose so,' said Spike.

'All of what?' asked Penny.

'Nothing,' said Johnathan, Gregory and Spike together.

'Right, then. Off we go.' Johnathan clapped his hands and pointed at the door. 'Bye,' he said.

'Goodbye, dear,' said Penny. She turned to Spike. 'Goodbye Spike. Look forward to seeing you again *very* soon.' She nudged Gregory. 'Aren't you going to say goodbye to Spike?' she asked.

'Er, bye, Spike,' said Gregory awkwardly.

'Yeah. Whatever,' muttered Spike.

Penny cocked her head to one side. 'That's so sweet. You're both so shy.'

'Right,' said Johnathan again. 'That's about it, I think.' He led his three guests to the front door. 'Thanks for coming, everyone. Have a safe journey home.'

Johnathan opened the front door.

'Who's that?' said Gregory.

'Oh bollocks,' said Johnathan under his breath.

'We need to talk,' said Chloe. She was still standing where he had left her, an all-too-familiar look of unshakeable determination on her face.

Spike looked at Chloe with interest. 'All right,' he said, looking her up and down.

Chloe looked at Spike's shell suit and wrinkled her nose. 'Hello,' she said shortly.

Spike turned to Johnathan. 'Aren't you going to introduce us?' he asked.

'No,' replied Johnathan. 'For both of your sakes.'

Chloe nodded towards Spike. 'I suppose this is the sort of person you see nowadays,' she said to Johnathan acidly.

'"See"?' said Spike, who was finally becoming suspicious. 'What's she mean?'

'Nothing, nothing,' trilled Johnathan.

'Well, it was terribly nice to meet you all,' said Penny. She turned to Gregory. 'Come on, darling. The car's over here.' She led Gregory to the car. Johnathan saw that he was steeling himself to tell Penny that he didn't want to move in with them. He looked terrified. Johnathan didn't rate his chances much.

Spike and Johnathan watched the car drive off. Spike turned to Johnathan. 'Your mother,' he said, 'is fucking weird.'

Johnathan nodded. 'She has her moments.'

'Anyway, thanks for all your help in getting this little lot back for me.' Spike patted the bag.

'Think nothing of it,' said Johnathan, suddenly very tired.

Spike gave Chloe a last approving look, and turned and strolled off whistling down the street, the shiny gold of his shell suit glinting in the late afternoon sun, with a hundred and twenty thousand pounds in cash tucked under his arm. Johnathan watched him go and let out a long sigh. Suddenly he had an idea.

'Right,' he said, turning back towards Chloe once Spike had turned the corner of the road. 'Time for some explanations.'

Chloe looked at him appraisingly.

'Coffee?' said Johnathan.

TWENTY-THREE

Later that evening Johnathan went round to Kibby's flat for supper.

'Come in,' said Kibby. She walked back to the kitchen. A large pot was gurgling on top of the cooker in a comforting way, smelling wonderful. She lit a cigarette.

'We're coming up the back straight,' she reported. 'Can you open the wine and get some knives and forks out?'

Johnathan busied himself with the corkscrew as Kibby carried the pot to the kitchen table. 'Stroganoff,' she announced. 'With extra Strog.' She whipped off the lid with a flourish and inhaled deeply. 'Fanbloodytastic, even if I do say so myself.' She reached for the ladle and stirred the contents of the pot with relish.

Johnathan watched her fondly as he extracted the cork from the bottle. He joined her at the table. It had been a long day, but Kibby's powers of reinvigoration were working wonders.

After Spike had left with his money, Johnathan had taken Chloe into the flat, and lied at her relentlessly for well over an hour. He spoke of his newly-discovered sexual orientation, and his new life. He told her that he was discovering fulfilment, that he was finally happy. He expressed the fervent wish that one day they might become friends again, but explained that at the moment, what he needed, more than anything, was space.

It was quite a performance. Chloe had lapped it up, professed heartfelt joy that Johnathan's soul was finally receiving the spiritual nourishment that it had been lacking for so long, and, with only the briefest of theatrical sniffs, had left.

'Guess what happened today,' he said as he poured wine into Kibby's glass.

'Oh, goody, I love these games,' said Kibby, clapping her hands together in mock delight. She began to dollop enormous helpings of food on to two plates. 'I don't know,' she said. 'Tell me what happened today.'

'Gregory paid the money he owes. I watched a man in a truly disgusting shell suit walk off down the road with more cash than I've ever dreamed of. I am now officially safe from any further risk of meeting Terry and his friend in a dark alleyway one night.'

'Thank heavens for that.'

'As, rather unfortunately, is my brother.'

'Oh well. You can't have everything.'

'I guess not. This is delicious, by the way. I am enjoying some element of revenge for everything Gregory's put me through, though.'

'Which is?'

'I think my parents are gearing up to make his life absolute hell for at least the next few months. He's already getting a bit twitchy about it, but they haven't even begun yet. He really won't know what's hit him.' Johnathan stuck a forkful of stroganoff into his mouth with glee.

Kibby regarded Johnathan with amusement. 'You're all heart.'

Johnathan nodded happily. 'Let me tell you,' he said, his

mouth still full, 'in this job, in this town, in this century, it's the only way.'

'There are times,' said Kibby, 'when you talk an awful lot of crap.'

Johnathan nodded. 'You're right. And I usually charge for it by the hour. But you, lucky, lucky you, are getting it all for free.'

'Hallelujah,' said Kibby. 'Ain't life grand?'

Johnathan smiled. 'Could be worse,' he agreed.